CRAZY FOR HER

CRAZY FOR HER

A K2 Team Novel

Sandra Owens

This is a work of fiction. Names, characters, organizations, places, events, and incidents are either products of the author's imagination or are used fictitiously.

Published by Montlake Romance, Seattle

www.apub.com

ISBN-13: 9781477824788
ISBN-10: 1477824782

Cover design by Eileen Carey

Library of Congress Control Number: 2014904441

Printed in the United States of America

This book is dedicated to my very own hero, my husband, Jim.

In case you've not figured it out yet, babe, I'm keeping you.

CHAPTER ONE

June 2011

Afghanistan

"Ambush!"

Hissed with urgency, the word crackled in the SEAL team's headsets. At the front of the adobe house, Lieutenant Commander Logan Kincaid faded into the shadows along with two of his men. The other three members of his small band of brothers were hopefully slipping unnoticed into the back of the building made of mud bricks and timber. Supposedly abandoned, Intel had received information that the missing army captain was being held inside by the Taliban.

Peering through night-vision goggles, Logan saw no movement in the watery green scene in front of him. "Dog, report in," he whispered into his mouthpiece. Roberts didn't answer.

The distinctive rat-a-tat-tat of Russian-made machine guns filled the air. The sudden three-round bursts of Roberts's M4 were quickly followed by the rapid firing of O'Connor's and Prescott's assault rifles.

"Shit," Romeo hissed from Logan's left side. "Thought they didn't know we were coming."

Logan glanced at Buchanan. "Fucking Intel."

Saint, pressed against Logan's other side, crossed himself. "All aboard. Next stop, hell."

Logan agreed with Turner's assessment. They had trained and trained and then trained again for this night. A piece of cake, the

Intel officer had claimed. Slip in unnoticed, get the hostage, and be gone before even the dogs knew they were there. Logan had never been fond of cake, and judging by the furious barking, the fucking dogs definitely knew they were here. "Let's go rescue our guys." Logan pushed away from the wall.

"Lead the way, Iceman," Buchanan said.

The more dangerous the situation, the calmer Logan became, his mind able to see and process everything around him at once, the reason his teammates called him Iceman. He didn't know why it happened. It just did.

Before they left the cover of the building's shadowed doorway, six Tangos, AK-47s slung carelessly across their shoulders, turned the corner, coming straight at them.

Stupid fools. If they were going to play with guns, they should learn how to hold them. Logan held up one finger, then two, then three. He and his two teammates stepped out of the doorway. Controlled fire from their M4s terminated the threat.

Fierce gunfire continued from the back of the building. Logan raced down the alley, followed closely by Buchanan and Turner. At the end of the alley, he stopped and peered around the corner where he saw Roberts and O'Connor crouched in front of Prescott.

Christ. Evan's down.

The second half of his team was trapped behind an ancient, rusted-out truck while the bad guys shot at them from two windows located at the first level of the building.

Logan turned to Buchanan. "I'll take the far window, Romeo, you take the other. Saint, you cover us." He pulled out two fragmentation grenades and waited until Buchanan did the same. "Dog," he whispered into the radio to Roberts. "We're coming in. Keep firing, but aim high."

Hugging the side of the building, Logan made his way to the window and turned to make sure Buchanan was in place. Bullets whistled above his head as chunks of the mud wall bounced off his helmet. At his nod, he and Buchanan pulled the rings from their grenades and tossed them into the windows. Logan hurled himself facedown, Buchanan following suit—both hugging the filthy street.

Panicked yelling in Farsi sounded from above in the seconds before the explosion. After the dust settled, Logan listened for any sound of life inside the building, and hearing none, he pushed to his feet. Within ten minutes, they had the building secured and had rescued Army Captain Bryce Davis.

"They were expecting us," Logan said.

Davis nodded. "They were. They leaked word to known informants that they had me in this location. From what I could gather, they wanted to kill some SEALs in revenge for us killing bin Laden. Sorry about your man there."

Logan knelt and met the eyes of Doc, kneeling on the other side of Prescott. He didn't like the message he saw in O'Connor's eyes. "Call in and change our pickup to the rooftop ASAP," he said to Buchanan. Every minute counted. Their scheduled pickup was three miles to the south. No fucking way he was waiting another two hours for the bird while watching Cowboy bleed to death. With O'Connor's help, he picked up Prescott and hoisted him over his shoulder, Cowboy's weight nothing compared to the heaviness in his heart.

On top of the building, Logan lowered Prescott onto the timber rooftop, leaning back as Doc pulled gauze packs out of his medic's bag. Although not a man who knew how to pray, he found himself pleading with God to save his friend.

"You got an extra gun on you?" Davis asked.

Doc handed the captain his gun, then ripped Prescott's shirt open.

Logan sucked in air when he saw the blood pouring from three bullet holes in Prescott's chest. For the first time since becoming a SEAL commander, he questioned his orders. What had they accomplished on the mission but to possibly trade a life for a life? He didn't know Davis, didn't know if he was a good man, married, had children, and went to church every Sunday or if he worshiped the devil, but Evan was the most honorable and loyal man he knew. Evan had a wife who loved him. How could Logan face her if he failed to bring Evan safely home to her?

The thump, thump of rotor blades in the distance gave him hope they might get Evan to triage in time. "Cowboy, hang on, man. Don't you dare die."

Evan focused pain-filled eyes on Logan. "Take care of her, Kincaid." He took a rasping breath as a trickle of blood rolled from his mouth and down his chin. "Promise." He gulped for air, and the sound every battle-weary soldier recognized and dreaded resonated in the air. The sucking noise coming from Evan's chest declared there was no hope for the man who was closer to Logan than any brother could have been.

"Damn you, Evan. If you won't live for me, then do it for Dani."

A gurgle sounded in Evan's throat. He grabbed Logan's arm, his strength surprising. "Didn't tell you. Dani's pregnant. Take care of them. Promise."

Unshed tears burned Logan's eyes. He put his hand over Evan's and squeezed. "I promise."

The Black Hawk came in and hovered a few feet above the rooftop.

"Go!" he yelled to his team. He and O'Connor picked up Evan and followed the others as they ran for the open door. After pushing Evan and O'Connor inside, Logan reached for the hand waiting to pull him in when pain exploded in the back of his head and everything went black.

CHAPTER TWO

August 2012

South Carolina

Logan twisted the throttle of the Harley-Davidson V-Rod to full open and raced recklessly up I-95. It was four in the morning, so the chances were slim a state trooper hid behind a tree pointing a radar gun at him. His speed was a dare to the gods, a challenge he'd made often since walking out of Bethesda Naval Hospital fourteen months earlier.

He was on his way to keep a promise made to a dying friend and SEAL brother. He'd started on this journey more times than he cared to count but had never made it to his destination. The Harley's headlights illuminated the road sign announcing I-26 two miles ahead. As he had each time before, he pulled onto the shoulder.

He'd never taken the exit that would lead him to her, had come this far and each time turned around and gone home. Now she'd asked him to come. Stepping off the bike, he removed his helmet and walked the cramps out of his muscles. He stopped in front of the sign and stared hard at it. He was a coward who couldn't face the woman he'd been in love with since he and Evan first met her in a bar near their home base of Little Creek, Virginia.

They'd been enjoying a few beers at Sinner's when the heated conversation at the next table intruded on their last few hours in the States. Logan tried to shut out the argument between the couple, but their voices grew louder. The asshole was pressuring the girl to go home with him.

"For the last time, no," she insisted.

The man ran his fingers over her arm. Logan shared a look with Evan. If the dude didn't back off, he would soon realize his bad luck that two SEALs had chosen that night to have a beer at Sinner's.

"I didn't take you for a tease, babe."

Logan glanced at the girl to see her reaction to the man's words. The air left his lungs. She was gorgeous. The auburn-haired beauty met his gaze, embarrassment in her eyes. She reached into her purse and fished out a cell phone.

"Who're you calling, babe?" the man asked.

"A cab, and I'm not your *babe*."

Logan smothered a grin. If she'd looked at him like that, he would've called the cab for her. The jerk snatched the phone out of her hand.

"You came with me, *babe*. You leave with me." He wrapped his hand around her upper arm, his fingers digging deep.

Logan rose from his seat, but before he could do more than that, Evan pushed away from the table, swiveled his chair around, and grabbed the man's hand. Snatching the phone from the man's grip, he handed it back to her.

"Take a hike, dude," Evan ordered. "My friend and I will see the lady safely home."

Logan eased back into his seat.

The man narrowed his eyes. "Get lost, douche bag."

Evan flashed Logan a shit-eating grin. "Did you hear that, Kincaid? This piece of dog doo just called a SEAL a douche bag."

"I heard."

The girl's eyes were wide and uncertain. She likely wished she could close those beautiful eyes and blink herself home.

The man's Adam's apple bobbed as he swallowed hard. Logan gave him an I'm-going-to-kill-you stare.

"SEALs?" the dude squeaked.

Logan sent him an evil smile and one slow nod. Being this close to Little Creek, and from the cut of his hair, Logan could tell he was navy, but the lack of muscle said he spent most of his time behind a desk. Even a desk jockey knew it was wise to fear a SEAL. Or two.

Dickweed scurried off like a cockroach, and Evan took less than a second to slide into his seat, claiming the girl for his own.

She peeked at Logan from under her lashes, her lips curving in a shy smile. That was the moment he lost his heart to a green-eyed stranger. That he had fallen for Dani MacKenna, now Dani Prescott, was a deep secret he held close.

Shaking off the memory, Logan returned to his bike. He started the V-Rod, and for the first time turned onto I-26, the road that would take him to North Carolina, to her home in Asheville. He had no choice. She'd sent him a message asking for help. He should have called on her after he left the hospital, but he hadn't been able to face her. She'd asked him to keep Evan safe, and he had failed her.

But he had watched over her from afar.

A low rumble announced the approach of a motorcycle. Dani stood and put Regan in her crib. She picked up the gun from the dresser and went to the front window. Lifting the blinds only enough to peek out, she watched the biker approach. He wore a full-faced helmet with a tinted shield so she couldn't see his features, but it was him. Of that, she had no doubt.

Logan Kincaid, the man Evan told her to turn to if something ever happened to him and she needed help. Knowing Logan had gone through a difficult time after being shot, she hadn't wanted to ask him to come. Other than send her a text with his address and phone number, he hadn't made any effort to keep in touch. That had hurt. A lot.

He'd been Evan's best friend. Her friend, too, or so she'd thought. She'd expected him to visit after he left the hospital, had imagined they would go out for a beer and share memories of Evan. Maybe even have a few laughs over their Evan stories. God, she'd needed that. But he'd stayed away.

She'd hesitated to call him, partly from not wanting to burden him with her problem—whatever that was, exactly. The other part hated needing the help of a man who apparently didn't give a damn about Evan's wife and child.

To keep Regan safe, however, she'd swallowed her pride and sent for the most dangerous man she knew. Sticking the gun into the waistband at the back of her jeans, she waited as he turned off the bike and put the kickstand down. The biker removed his helmet and glanced toward the cabin. Once she was sure it was Logan, she dropped the blinds and walked outside.

Suddenly nervous about seeing him, she stayed on the porch. A slight lift of his chin acknowledged her presence; then he busied himself with removing a tote bag held down by bungee cords.

While his attention was elsewhere, she studied him. His dark brown hair—now cut close in the military style—suited him. In their SEAL days, he and her husband had worn their hair longer to help them blend in with the Afghan people. His black leather jacket stretched over broad shoulders; his jeans encased long legs she was certain were rippled with muscles.

Logan was still eye candy. That sure hadn't changed. A little sigh escaped her lips. He must have heard because his dark brown eyes turned her way and he raised a questioning brow.

Strangely, the arrogant gesture put her at ease. He was still the Logan she'd once known and liked. She walked down the steps. "Nice bike. What is it?"

He moved next to her and eyed the motorcycle with a fond smile. "A Harley-Davidson V-Rod Muscle." His gaze captured hers, and he grinned. "It's very fast."

And dangerous. Like him. She remembered he'd always been like this. *Intense and focused.* When they'd met at Sinner's, she'd been disappointed that his friend had been the one to make a move on her. At first. Until she fell for Evan.

Standing close enough to feel the heat from Logan's body, Dani fought the crazy urge to lean into his protective warmth. Moving to put more space between them, she faced him.

"Hello, Logan. Thanks for coming." Once Evan had been their link—the friendship among the three of them had been easy and fun. Now that it was just the two of them, it was awkward. Eyes she'd always thought never missed a thing raked her from head to toe.

"You're not sleeping," he said, proving her right.

She laughed. "As usual, straight and to the point. I'm relieved to know you haven't changed. I'm fine, thank you, and you?" she said, more to tease him than to remind him of social niceties.

Her reward was a slight twitch of his lips. "Forgive me. How are you, Dani?"

"I've been better. Come inside. Have you had lunch?"

"Yeah, I didn't want to inconvenience you."

Inconvenience her? She'd waited for him to get in touch with her after Evan's death. One lousy phone call, was that asking too much? "Hi, Dani, you doing okay?" or "Hi, Dani, I miss my friend and I knew you'd understand." But nothing. No call, no visit, no hint he cared.

"Bloody hell, Logan. If you're gonna treat me like a stranger, then you can get back on your bike and go find someone else to annoy."

"Bloody hell? Still writing those bodice rippers, are you?"

"They're Regency romances. And no, I'm writing children's books now."

"I hope you've resisted inserting a 'bloody hell' here and there."

Dani punched him on the arm, and he poked her back, his eyes turning soft as he looked down at her. Her resentment faded as fast as it had arrived because . . . because? She gave a little shake of her head. There'd been something in his expression—sadness, maybe?—but it'd disappeared before she could be sure.

"Come inside." She climbed the steps ahead of him.

"What's this?" He grabbed the gun resting at the small of her back.

She tossed him a look of mock astonishment. "Why, Logan, I would have thought you of all people would know that's a gun."

"Smart-ass woman." He held it up for inspection. "Why's a snub-nose special tucked into your waistband?"

"The answer to that is the reason I asked you here." She opened the screen door and when he was inside, closed the heavy wood door, sliding both deadbolts into place. When she caught his eyes following her actions, she shrugged. "You'll understand soon enough."

Going to the kitchen, she turned on the burner under the teakettle. Logan followed her and propped his shoulder against the doorway. It was both comforting and strange having him in her home. "Still a coffee drinker?"

"I am."

Having already put coffee beans in the grinder, she pushed the ON button and then took two mugs out of the cabinet. "Where'd you spend the night?"

"I rode straight through."

"Seriously? That's what, ten hours from Pensacola to here?" Her butt constricted at the thought of tolerating ten straight hours on a motorcycle seat.

"About that. I got in this morning around seven and checked into a motel room so I could shower and grab a few hours of sleep."

"You're made of sterner stuff than me."

"Why am I here, Dani?"

She picked up the coffeepot, poured him a cup, and dropped a green tea bag into hers. Handing him the mug, she squeezed by him, resisting the impulse to rest her head on his broad shoulder, where she was certain she would feel safe.

"Come into the living room. I have something to show you."

Logan tensed when she brushed past him. She smelled like spring—like lavender, maybe—and he wanted to bury his face against the soft skin of her neck and inhale her fresh scent. She was more beautiful than ever, but her eyes didn't sparkle like they used to and the skin underneath them was shadowed. He growled his displeasure at the mug in his hand and then followed her to the other room.

Curled up on the sofa with her bare feet tucked under her, she appeared vulnerable and alone. The thought that often came to him in the darkest part of the night slammed into his gut. Why had he lived and Evan died when he had a wife and a child on the way? Guilt was a parasite with nasty teeth, slowly devouring his ability to find any kind of peace.

Taking a seat in a comfortable, oversized leather chair, Logan let his gaze wander over the room, settling on the large stone fireplace. "This is a nice place."

She chuckled softly, drawing his attention back to her. "You should've seen it when Evan and I bought it. It was going to be our home after he got out of the navy." Her voice trailed off and she blinked against the tears pooling in her eyes. Her gaze lifted to his. "Sorry, didn't mean to get weepy." She fanned her face with a hand. "Anyway, the cabin was a wreck, but remodeling kept my mind from dwelling on everything while I waited for Regan to be born."

The parasite saw her sorrow and its bite grew sharper. "I'm sorry, Dani. I wish it had been me instead."

"Don't. Don't say it. Don't think it. It was just his time, that's all." She brought her mug to her lips.

Not saying it again, he could control. Not thinking it was another matter. A companionable silence fell as they drank their tea and coffee, and Logan had the passing thought he might be able to find some kind of peace in this cabin. With her.

But she was not for the likes of him.

Setting his empty mug on the table, he rested his head on the back of the chair and closed his eyes. What if he had been just a bit faster and slid into that chair next to her at Sinner's before Evan had? Would he belong with her now? Would he be able to lay claim to that elusive word *happiness*? There was no way to know if a relationship with her would have progressed that far, and he had to stop wanting something that wasn't meant to be.

He opened his eyes. "Why did you send for me, Dani?"

She uncurled one leg and with her toes, pushed a shoebox sitting on the coffee table closer to him. He hadn't noticed the box before, but he had noticed her toenails were painted a pale pink, though he'd tried hard not to.

Taking a hint from the way she barely touched the box, Logan gave it a wary stare. With his index finger, he lifted the lid just as a baby started to cry. He dropped the lid, he and Dani exhaling in sync. Without a word, she stood and disappeared down the hallway.

Logan considered the shoebox and decided to wait for her to return before opening it. He removed his heavy motorcycle boots, poured another cup of coffee, and checked the locks on the doors and windows. At least she had a first-rate alarm system. Whatever was going on had her spooked, and the Dani he knew didn't scare easily.

Growing curious, he walked down the hallway and stopped at the door of a nursery. Multicolored butterfly cutouts adorned the walls of the bright-yellow room where Dani sat in a rocking chair, nursing a baby.

The air swished out of his lungs. Not even on his most dangerous missions had he feared his legs would fail to hold him up, but the picture before him threatened to bring him to his knees.

Christ, Evan, how could you go and miss seeing this?

She glanced over her shoulder and smiled. "You can come in." The smile morphed into a frown. "Unless you're the kind of man who thinks seeing a mother nurse her child is vulgar. If you are, then get lost."

He should get lost. He should get on his bike and ride as fast and as far away from her as he could. Instead, he walked into the room, leaned against the wall near the window, and peered out. Behind the house, the yard sloped down to a briskly running creek. Beyond the creek, mountains dressed in lush green trees rose in the distance.

"Beautiful," he whispered.

"You should see it in the winter after a snowstorm."

"I would like to," he said softly, allowing her to believe he'd been speaking of the view.

Dani slid a pink blanket over the baby's head and then lifted her up. Logan silently thanked her for inviting him into the room.

He'd never seen a mother nurse her child. It was a sacred thing, something he would never forget.

She bounced her daughter on her knee and patted her back. Logan laughed when a loud burp echoed through the room. The baby grinned at him, showing off two tiny teeth.

"Gawh." She waved a fist in the air.

Logan was charmed. "She has Evan's eyes."

"My Regan has her daddy's hazel eyes, yes, she does," Dani cooed, and tapped Regan on the nose, causing the baby to squeal and bounce harder.

He could spend a lifetime watching them play. Another squeal, louder than he would've believed a baby could make, issued from Regan's mouth. She looked up at him with another grin, clearly very proud of herself.

Dani's shirt was unbuttoned, the pink blanket still over her shoulder, concealing her breast. Figuring she would probably appreciate a few minutes of privacy to get herself in order, he told her he would wait for her in the living room. He commanded his unwilling feet to carry him out of the nursery.

Restless, Logan treated himself to a tour of the cabin. Beyond the kitchen was a mudroom with a door leading to the backyard. He opened three deadbolts and stepped out onto the deck. Glancing back at the house, he frowned at the French doors. All that glass was impossible to secure. From the outside, the cabin was cleverly designed to look like a two-story structure.

At the deck railing, he took in the amazing view. Seven horses of various colors grazed in a meadow beyond the creek, the mountains he'd admired earlier in the background. On his right was a vegetable garden and behind it, a garage and storage shed. On his left, beyond the recently mowed yard, was a wooded area.

Just as he started to turn to go back inside, a movement caught his gaze. *Probably some kind of animal.* Still, the hair on the back of his neck stood up, and his instincts screamed at him to beware. He had learned long ago to trust that reaction.

Was Dani in danger? Was that why she'd asked him to come? He should never have stepped outside without his SIG and shoes. "Stupid move, Kincaid," he muttered, debating whether to run inside and get his gun. But even without a weapon, he was lethal. He started down the steps.

"There you are."

Dani stood in the doorway holding Regan. He blanked his expression but apparently not fast enough. Her eyes searched his and then shifted to the woods.

"Is he here?" she asked before she and her daughter disappeared from sight.

Is who here? Sweeping his gaze across the wooded area one last time, he followed her inside and slid the deadbolts closed. Two on the front door and three on the back meant that whoever he was, Dani was afraid of him.

Logan went straight to the tote he'd dropped on the foyer table, took out his SIG Sauer, and stuck it at his back in the waistband of his jeans. Until he found out what was going on and put an end to the threat to Dani and Regan, he wouldn't be caught without it again.

His plan had been to keep his room at the motel for sleeping, but if there was someone lurking about, he wasn't going anywhere. Hopefully there was a guest bedroom. If not, he'd slept on worse things than a couch. He had promised Evan he would take care of Dani, and a SEAL didn't break his word to a brother. Even without the pledge, he would have considered Dani and Regan to be under his protection.

In the living room, he sat down and stared at the box. Regan babbled at him from inside a playpen. "Where's your mama?"

"Right here." Dani walked in carrying two bottles of beer and handed him one before curling up on the couch.

"You can drink beer when you're nursing?"

"As long as it's a few hours before. I only allow myself one beer or one glass of wine a day."

He took a long drink of the cold brew. "This is good."

"It's a local beer. Asheville's well known for its microbreweries."

He knew that. When Evan died, Logan downloaded facts and maps, studying everything he could find about the town. It was his job to watch over her and Evan's child, a promise made and kept. Finishing the beer, he set the bottle on a coaster. It was time to get the answers to his questions.

"You asked me if he was here. Who is 'he,' Dani?"

"He says he's Evan."

CHAPTER THREE

Disbelief followed by anger crossed Logan's face. Dani understood. The one time she'd talked to the man claiming to be Evan, rage had pounded through her bloodstream.

"You've spoken to him?"

She nodded. "Once, on the phone. The strange thing . . . he sounded like Evan, but the accent was different. He didn't speak with Evan's Texas drawl. It was more like a deep-South good-ol'-boy accent."

"When did you speak to him and exactly what did he say?"

Logan's voice was deceptively calm, but she heard the underlying steel in it. His jaws were rigid, his eyes cold and focused on her. Not a man she would ever want for an enemy, but she was damned glad to have him for a friend.

"The first phone call was two weeks ago. When I answered, he said, 'I've missed you, Danielle, and I want to come home.' I asked who was speaking, and that's when he said he was Evan."

"Did he say anything else?"

"No, I slammed the phone down. I realize now I should've tried to find out more, but at the time, I was just so angry someone would play that kind of joke on me."

"Are you sure that wasn't all it was, someone's sick idea of a joke?"

"I'm very sure because he's been in the house." The mere idea of a stranger coming into her and Regan's home made her stomach churn. She pulled her knees up to her chest and wrapped her arms around her legs. "Look in the box."

His gaze shifted to the shoebox. He lifted the lid, revealing the teddy bear inside. Picking it up with the caution he might use when handling a grenade, he read aloud the note pinned to the bear. "For Regan. Daddy's little girl."

"That was in her crib when we returned from the grocery store last Tuesday. He was in my home, Logan."

Just like that, he changed. His eyes slitted, viperlike, and the muscles in his jaws flexed, forming hard lines below his cheeks. The mouth she'd earlier thought might feel soft to the touch thinned into a harsh slash of lips. The team had called him Iceman, and now she understood why. A shiver raced up her spine at seeing this side of him. This man was a warrior, a lethal one.

"He's a dead man. Did you touch the note?"

Startled out of her musings about him, she tried to remember. When she'd first seen it, she hadn't wanted to handle it at all. "I'm sure I didn't touch the paper. I think just an arm of the bear, only long enough to put it in the box."

His gaze lifted to hers and she sucked in a breath at the savagery in his eyes. Her stalker didn't have a clue who he was messing with. As Logan continued to regard her, his expression turned soft and warm. The little flutter in her stomach took her by surprise. As slowly as possible so he wouldn't hear, she let out her breath.

"Is the phone call and the bear the only contact you've had with him?"

Jerked back to their conversation, she nodded. "He calls, but I don't answer the phone now unless it's a number I recognize. He doesn't speak, just breathes into the phone for a minute or two before hanging up. I've not erased the recordings, but I don't know what you can learn from them."

"Have you called the police?"

"Of course, but other than writing up a report, they said there wasn't much they could do. I don't think they took the gift of a teddy bear all that serious."

Logan stood and walked to the window, lifted the blinds, and peered out. The gun tucked against his back was bigger than hers, and she wanted it.

He dropped the blinds back into place and faced her. "We can't discount he's someone you know, although—"

"Believe me, I'd remember anyone who sounded like Evan."

"Although, that's why I think he's a stranger, someone you've never had contact with."

His presence in her home gave her a feeling of safety, and with him by her side, she knew she could get to the bottom of this. "So, where do we go from here?"

"I don't go anywhere, but I want you and Regan to go stay at my house. Buchanan and Turner work for me now, and they'll keep you safe while I run this asshole to the ground."

Jumping up from the couch, she shook her head. "No, I'm not going to let some psycho run me out of my home. Besides, if he knows I'm gone, he'll just disappear and wait for me to come back."

"I can get you to Pensacola without him ever knowing you've left, and trust me, I will find him."

She didn't like the determined expression on his face, didn't want to leave her home, hated feeling afraid, and didn't want to leave him. The last thought came out of nowhere, adding confusion to the anger and fear she'd been living with the last two weeks. God, she hated feeling helpless. Stupid tears welled up and rolled down her cheeks, and the next thing she knew, his arms were around her.

"Hush," he whispered. "I'll keep you safe."

Sniffling against a chest as hard as a wall of steel, she nodded and closed her eyes. He would protect her and Regan—all the more reason not to run away like a terrified mouse. Heat from his body seeped into her, warming her. Was it a betrayal to Evan to like being held in Logan's embrace? No, it was only a friend comforting her, and her husband would have understood.

Logan put his hands on her shoulders and gently pushed her away. "Better?"

There was some emotion in his eyes, but it disappeared before she could decipher it. "I'm okay, but I'll be better when all this is over. Thank you."

"For what?"

"For coming here when I asked. It was probably an inconvenience to drop everything at a moment's notice."

Again, something flittered in his eyes, and he glanced away. When his gaze returned to her, whatever she'd seen was gone.

"Know this, Dani. Wherever you are and whenever you need me, I will always come to you."

That had the sound of some sort of lifetime commitment and made her a little uneasy. Unsure how to respond, she just said, "Good, because I'm not leaving."

Logan was in hell. Holding Dani's soft body against his and breathing in her scent was killing him. He told himself he was only offering her comfort and friendship. Right. And the Taliban was nothing more than a bunch of choirboys being naughty.

Arousal stirred in his jeans, and he stepped away, putting a safe distance between them. "All right. If I let you stay, you have to promise you'll obey me. If I tell you to do something, you do it. If

I tell you not to do something, you don't. And you don't think about it either. If I give you a command, you don't ask questions, you don't take your time getting around to it, understand?"

Her eyes narrowed. If she could shoot fire at him from those Irish eyes, she likely would. It didn't reassure him that she would follow his orders without question, but, so help him God, she set his blood ablaze. *Not good, Kincaid, not good at all.*

"I don't blindly follow orders, but if I think they're appropriate for the situation—"

She didn't get it. If a soldier didn't obey his commander's directives during battle, he likely got sent home in a body bag. Logan swallowed hard. He already lived with the guilt of Evan's death. He wouldn't survive hers.

Not letting her finish, he moved into her space and glared down at her. "There are no buts. You have two choices. You give me your word you'll do what I say, when I say it, or you and Regan go to my house until this is over. Which will it be?"

Their faces were inches apart, and puffs of her warm breath wafted across his chin. Jesus, Joseph, and Mary, he had never wanted a woman like he wanted her this minute. What he wouldn't give to explore the heat and passion flaring in her eyes, and then when his fire was doused, he would explore the gentle side of her. The one he had seen sitting in a rocking chair and looking down at her nursing daughter with eyes full of love.

If he allowed it to happen, he wouldn't be breaking his personal vow, but he would dishonor his love and respect for Evan. That he would not do, no matter the temptation. Early in his life, he'd learned self-control, his SEAL training only made his willpower stronger. He could and would ignore his desires, was long used to doing so.

"You're not the boss of me." The stubborn lines of her mouth dissolved into a wide smile, and her eyes sparkled with merriment. "I just sounded like a six-year-old, didn't I?"

"That old? I was thinking more like three."

"No, that's the tantrum age, and trust me, you really don't want me throwing a tantrum. No one does it better than me." She walked away, stopping at the entrance to the hallway. "You have my word, tough guy. Whatever you say, no questions asked. I don't promise not to make faces at you, however." She stuck her thumbs in her ears, wriggled her fingers, crossed her eyes, and stuck out her tongue.

Logan grinned at her retreating back. This was the Dani he missed. When she was dating Evan, the three of them sometimes hung out together, and her love of life and humor had captivated him. There had been times when they'd invited him along and he had declined, not able to bear seeing her hand in Evan's or witnessing the quick kisses they often shared.

The devil whispered in his ear that Evan was gone, and there was nothing stopping him now from claiming her as his. He could be the one holding her hand and leaving kisses on all the places of her body he'd fantasized about.

Burying his traitorous thoughts down deep where they belonged, he picked up his leather tote and followed her down the hall. At the door to the nursery, he watched her lean into the crib and kiss Regan's forehead.

"Sometimes it hurts so bad to think she'll never know her father."

Guilt soured his stomach, and for a brief moment he hated his friend for dying. "You should write down everything you know and remember about Evan before it slips away from you. Someday, Regan will thank you for it."

Dani's sudden smile was like sunshine, warm and inviting. He caught himself taking a step toward her and stilled, planting his shoulder against the doorjamb.

"I'm already doing that, but even better, she'll have her uncle Logan to tell her stories about her daddy."

Someone should have posted signs warning of the minefield. Whichever way he stepped was going to be dangerous for him. He didn't know if he could handle being an active part of their lives in the role of uncle. What if Dani met someone and fell in love? It would happen eventually, and he couldn't stand on the sidelines again watching her with someone else. Been there, done that, could not bear doing it again.

Yet she'd just made him Regan's honorary uncle, and he didn't have the words to refuse her. Her smile slipped as she waited for a response.

"It would be a privilege to be Regan's uncle."

The brilliant smile returned. "Thank you." She kissed his cheek and walked past him.

Still attached to the doorway, he closed his eyes and prayed for strength. Her lips on his skin had felt as soft as he'd imagined. For close to three years, he'd kept his longing for her buried, and now it was surfacing like flotsam. Whoever this man was, he needed to be found and taken care of. Soon. Then he could go home and put temptation at a manageable distance.

"Logan?"

Pushing away from the door, he walked down the hall and followed her into a room.

"This is the guest room. It has its own bathroom through there." She pointed to a closed door and then frowned. "You're planning on staying here, right?"

He dropped his tote on the quilt-covered bed. "Until I catch this guy, I think it would be for the best."

"We."

Logan gave her his most intimidating glare. "Don't even think it. Your job is to stay safe, mine is to keep you that way."

She burst into laughter. Definitely not the reaction he expected. He crossed his arms over his chest and tried to stare her down. She laughed harder, plopping down on the bed and waving a hand in the air.

"Stop staring at me like that," she gasped. "I bet that fierce look sent your men ducking for cover."

It had. He bit down on his cheek to keep from smiling. "Doesn't seem to work on you though, does it?"

"I'm sorry. It's been a strange two weeks, and I think it's nerves more than anything."

"Understandable." He tucked his hands into his pockets to keep from reaching out to comfort her.

She glanced at the small bag he'd dropped on the bed. "You travel light."

The T-shirt, socks, and underwear he'd worn last night were in his tote along with several knives, another gun, a cell phone charger, and his toiletries. "Can't carry much on the V-Rod. I overnighted a trunk that should arrive any time." Along with clothes, it contained more weapons and a few of his favorite high-tech toys. As if on cue, the doorbell rang.

She started to stand, and he held out a hand to stop her. "I'll go to the door."

After signing the delivery form, he scanned the road and area in front of the house before closing and locking the door. Logan hefted the trunk and carried it back to his room.

Dani eyed it with obvious interest. "What kind of goodies do you have in there?"

"What makes you think there's more than just clothes?"

She snorted. "I was a SEAL's wife, remember?"

"I remember." As if he could forget. He set the case on the bed, wishing she would go away. He needed a few minutes alone to drill the reasons why she was off-limits back into his brain and lower regions.

Dani noted the change in his mood and wondered at it. She stood and walked past him, stopping at the door. "Why don't you get settled in while I start dinner? You can show me your toys later."

Evan had been a meat-and-potatoes man, but like Dani, Logan loved to experience all kinds of food. When the three of them had hung out together, she and Logan often teased Evan about his refusal to try a new dish. "I already know what I like, so why should I order something I'll probably hate?" was his standard reply. It was rare that they could even tempt him to taste one of their meals.

Cooking was her hobby, something she did whenever she came up against a wall when she wrote. Puttering around in the kitchen helped her think. Usually, by the time dinner was ready, she'd solved whatever plot issues were bedeviling her and had twice benefited—a great meal and the next scene for her story bubbling in her head.

Long used to enjoying her creations alone, she was excited to have someone to share them with. Tonight, she'd decided on steak Diane, loaded twice-baked potatoes, and spinach salad. Not that she wanted to impress Logan—it was one of her favorite meals.

Right, Dani, you went to all this work just for yourself.

Okay, so she wanted to show off a little. All the prep work had been finished before Logan arrived, so all she had to do was flambé the steaks, microwave the potatoes, and heat the dressing for the salad.

The dining room seemed too formal, so she set the table in the kitchen and debated whether to light any candles. Afraid it would send the wrong signal, she instead slightly dimmed the lights. Surveying the effect, she gave a little nod of satisfaction. Perfect. Not too dim to make it seem romantic but enough to take the brightness away.

Hearing Logan's approach, she poured a glass of wine and handed it to him when he entered the kitchen. "I think you'll like this. It's a Cabernet called Antler Hill from the Biltmore Estate here in Asheville."

He swirled the wine, sniffed it, and then took a sip and deemed it excellent. Evan had once told her that as a child, Logan had grown up dirt poor and neglected. Surprised at how knowledgeable he was of wines and fine foods, she'd found herself observing him whenever he hung out with them.

Though he was a warrior through and through, there was also something of a Renaissance man in him. His contradictions had so fascinated her, she'd used him as the model for the hero in one of her books. Evan had been amused when she'd told him, but she would die if Logan ever learned of it.

Dani made herself a soda water with lime, her favorite nonalcoholic drink aside from her hot green teas. After turning on the gas burner, she leaned back against the counter to wait for the pan to get hot.

Logan stood in the middle of the room sipping his wine, his eyes focused on her. Until he walked in, the kitchen had seemed spacious to Dani. Now she wasn't sure she had room to breathe.

When she'd first met the two SEALs, Logan had been the one to catch her interest, but he had faded into the background, allowing Evan to take center stage. And who wouldn't adore Evan?

No other man had filled her life with laughter the way her husband had. She even missed his silly jokes. Missed the way his hands felt on her body, missed his scent. Her big bear of a loving husband had won her heart, and her initial interest in his friend vanished. Now Evan was gone, and the man who had intrigued her for so long stood in her kitchen.

Dani wasn't sure if that was a good thing or not.

She waved a hand toward a chair. "Have a seat and watch magic happen."

The phone rang and she froze, her heart beating a wild tattoo in her chest. Logan set his wine on the table, came to her, and took the glass out of her hand. Pushing a button on the phone, he handed it to her.

She took a deep breath. "Hello."

"Danielle?"

Logan had put him on the speaker. Holding the phone away from her ear, she pushed the words past her lips. "This is Dani."

"Tell him to leave, Danielle."

"Who?" A dial tone was the only response. "He hung up."

She put the phone back in the holder. It was just so very wrong to hear her dead husband's voice. Unable to help it, she started shaking. Logan pulled her against his chest and wrapped muscled arms around her.

"Did you hear? He sounds so much like Evan."

"I heard," he said. "The voice is similar, but it isn't Evan."

"I know." She burrowed into his warmth. "But who is he? Who would sound like Evan?" Her eyes closed when his lips pressed down on her head.

"I don't know, but I won't let him hurt you. You believe me, don't you?"

Dani nodded against his chest. "I believe you." His hold on her was strong and soothing, and he smelled so damn good. A stirring of something she hadn't felt since the last time Evan had held her took her by surprise, and she pushed away. "I-I need to start dinner." It was only a natural response to the feel of a man's body after two years of being alone, she told herself. It didn't mean anything. He'd only meant to comfort her after the disturbing phone call.

She put the steaks in the cast-iron skillet, popped the potatoes into the microwave, and refused to wonder who the hell the man claiming to be her husband was. He would not ruin her night—she wouldn't allow it. Lighting the cognac on fire, Dani glanced at Logan to see if he was properly impressed. His eyes appreciatively followed her actions.

Evan would have preferred hamburgers, but Logan appeared to savor every mouthful of her meal. Seeming to sense her need to forget about her stalker for a while, he listened as she talked about living in Asheville.

"I haven't eaten this good since the last time you cooked for me." He pushed his plate away. "When was that?"

"The night before you and Evan left for your last mission." His eyes shuttered, and she regretted her words. She jumped up and grabbed their plates, putting them in the sink. "Do you want dessert now or later?"

He rubbed his hand over his stomach. "Later, if at all."

"Hazelnut coffee, homemade chocolate Amaretto brownies, and vanilla-bean ice cream."

"A week here with you and I'll be waddling like an overfed duck."

Dani leaned back against the sink and tried to imagine him fat and waddling. The picture refused to form. He stared back at her, their gazes held in some strange spell. Time seemed to stop. She

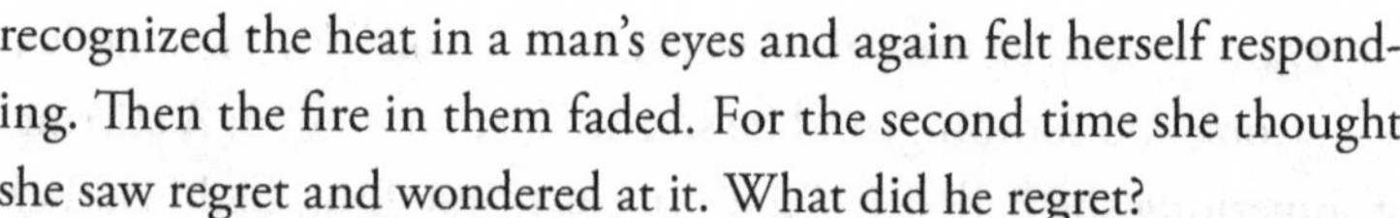

recognized the heat in a man's eyes and again felt herself responding. Then the fire in them faded. For the second time she thought she saw regret and wondered at it. What did he regret?

He stood. "I think I'll take a look around outside."

Nodding, she listened to the sound of his footsteps fading, the back door opening and then closing. After drying her hands, she walked into the dining room, peered out the French doors, and watched him walk down to the creek. He knelt and splashed cold spring water onto his face.

She'd truly loved only one man in her life, but as much as she wished otherwise, Evan was gone forever. And here was Logan looking at her with heat in his eyes.

"He wants me, Evan. How do you feel about that?"

How do I feel about it?

CHAPTER FOUR

Logan stilled, the sense of being watched finally penetrating his lust-filled brain. He scanned the woods, his eyes drawn to the massive oak tree. Nothing moved, but someone was out there. He palmed a knife from his boot and stood, the cold creek water dripping down his face onto his shirt. With his other hand, he pulled his gun from his waistband and held it down at his side.

At the edge of the woods, he stopped next to a tall pine tree, listened, and heard not a thing. Not good. At the very least, birds should be chirping, but it was eerily silent. Alert, watching for any unusual movement, he made his way to the oak tree. Circling it, he studied the ground.

At the base where a small patch of dirt wasn't covered by leaves, he found a partial print of the heel of a combat boot—the real thing or someone playing at soldiering? Logan knelt and studied it, regretting it wasn't a full print so he could estimate the size of the man. A fresh scrape on the bark indicated someone had recently climbed the tree, but whoever had been up there was gone now. Returning the gun to his waistband, he clamped down on the knife with his teeth and began to climb.

A little over halfway up he found a branch that joined with another near the trunk, forming the perfect place to sit. A broken limb confirmed Logan's fear that someone had been spying on Dani. He settled his back against the tree and turned his gaze to the cabin. A perfect view of her at the sink washing their dinner dishes greeted him.

"Shit," he hissed.

How long had the creep been watching her? The asshole probably had binoculars and had been observing her. Logan examined the back of the house to see into what other windows the man might have been looking. The French doors to the dining room were next, but he didn't give them much attention. The next set of windows would be Regan's nursery, and then Dani's room.

Had the man watched her sit in the rocking chair while she nursed Regan? Logan slammed his knife into the branch, burying it halfway up the blade. The motherfucker was a dead man. He pulled his knife out of the wood and carved a small hole in the branch above his head. Later, he would return and put a thumb-sized camera there. Quickly sliding down the tree, he headed back to the house, his long strides eating up the ground before him.

Storming through the kitchen, he passed Dani, ignoring her startled look, and marched to the door of Regan's room. Belatedly realizing the pounding of his boots on the wood floor might wake the baby, he stopped and took a calming breath, reminding himself the Iceman didn't lose his cool.

His gaze fell on the rocking chair in front of the window where Dani liked to sit. How many times had the pervert watched her?

"Logan?"

Not hiding his fury, he turned.

She took two steps back. "What is it? What's wrong?"

He welcomed the fear in her voice. She needed to be afraid. "Close the curtains in her room and yours. He's been watching you."

Her face paled and she put her hand against the wall. "How do you know?"

"I found his little nest. Close the damn curtains." He walked away before he could do something stupid like scoop her up in his arms and carry her far, far away to someplace safe.

The next morning, Dani sat in front of windows covered by yellow-polka-dot Dr. Seuss curtains and nursed Regan. She loved her home, but it was starting to feel like a prison.

Since she couldn't enjoy watching the horses race around in the pasture, she tried to remember if she had come into contact with any odd characters lately. No one she'd talked to stood out as suspicious. How long had he been watching her? She shuddered. Being spied upon by a faceless man was just damned creepy.

Regan finished nursing and gave a toothy little grin. Dani sat her daughter on her knee and burped her, then stood her up. "Mama's little girl."

Regan bounced up and down. "Mama!" she yelled, and bounced some more.

"She called you Mama."

Regan looked past Dani and grinned. "Mama!"

Dani glanced over her shoulder to see Logan leaning against the door. "She's been saying Mama for a while now."

He came and knelt next to the rocking chair, tapping Regan on the nose. "Hey, little girl."

Regan giggled and said, "Eairh."

Surprising Dani, Regan tried to go to him. She was normally shy around strangers, but she seemed to like Logan. He stood and Dani laughed at his panicked expression when Regan lifted her arms in a clear signal she wanted him to pick her up.

"You're such a sissy." He glared at her and Dani rolled her eyes. "Uncle Logan's a sissy," she sang.

"Issie," Regan said.

"See, she thinks you're a sissy, too."

Lightning fast, he snatched Regan out of her arms. Dani swallowed a laugh. Apparently men didn't like to be called sissies. Regan stared at him and grinned like a besotted fool. Dani understood Regan's fascination. Even dressed in a loose navy T-shirt and sweatpants he was hot.

Dani went to the curtains and parted them enough to peer out. "Do you think he's out there now?"

"No, I did a thorough search this morning and didn't see any sign of him."

She raised a brow. "And here I thought you just got up. I suppose you ran ten miles while you were at it?"

"No, only three."

"Jeez, Logan, you're getting lazy in your old age."

"More like I didn't want to leave you alone for too long."

"Oh." She peeked out the window again.

Having him here made her feel safe, but she resented it. He awakened needs she hadn't felt since Evan died. But Logan wasn't there for her; it was more like some kind of obligation he thought he owed Evan. How much had she disrupted his life by asking him to come?

Dropping the curtain, she spun. "I have to get out of this house."

He stopped making faces at Regan and focused on her. "Sure. Give me twenty minutes to shower and change, and I'll take you out to lunch. You can show me around a little if you want."

She wanted. "Make it thirty minutes. It'll take me that long to get ready."

Dani walked next to Logan as they strolled past a sidewalk café in downtown Asheville. The city, considered one of the most diverse in the country, had something for everyone. With open arms, the town welcomed artists, musicians, and anyone wanting to make a movie. *Cold Mountain* and *The Hunger Games*, both filmed around Asheville, were in her DVD collection, and she wondered if Logan would enjoy watching them with her. They passed a small group of men and women in flowing robes dancing around a large tree.

"What's that all about?" Logan asked.

"They're Wiccans. The tree is like three hundred years old, but it's dying. They're convinced they can heal it."

He snorted, causing her to laugh. She loved it in Asheville, witches and all. Her annual pass to the Biltmore Estate allowed her to visit any time she wanted. Often, she would take Regan and rent one of their bicycles with a baby seat and they'd spend several hours riding the winding paths, stopping at the pond to feed the ducks. The only other place she might like living as much as she did the mountains was the beach.

Two women dressed in business suits walked past, both eyeing Logan in open appreciation even though he cradled a baby in a carrier on his chest. Dani smiled in amusement. It didn't seem to matter to them that the woman walking with him could be his wife. He'd insisted on carrying Regan, and she had willingly let him. Just this morning, the man had been terrified of holding her daughter, and now he looked as if he'd been doing it for years.

A display of old, recovered windows caught Dani's attention, and she pointed to one. "Oh, I love it," she said of the one with a distressed frame and stained-glass panes. It would be beautiful hanging in front of her bedroom window. She could wake up every morning to see the sun shining through it, all the colors dancing over her walls and ceiling.

"It would be perfect in your bedroom," Logan said.

She glanced at him and grinned, pleased he saw it the way she did.

He pointed to a mirror. "That one there, you could use it in one of your Regency stories. Picture your hero visiting his mistress with that in her room."

The mirror was awful, and she loved it. Red velvet covered the frame, and the silhouette of a woman's nude body was painted in black along one edge. She visualized the scene he'd just described. In the movie running through her mind, the heroine barged into the room catching her betrothed in the act of making love to his mistress in front of the mirror. He would realize what he'd lost when the heroine called off the wedding and he'd have to—

"Dani!"

Jerked back to the present by the urgency in Logan's voice, she turned toward him. He pulled off the carrier, handing her Regan.

"Don't move from this spot," he said, and turned to leave. Stopping, he turned back and wrapped his hand around her upper arm. "Better yet, go inside the store and wait for me there."

He left her then, jogging away and disappearing around a corner. Where was he going? She started to follow, but glanced at Regan and stopped. Never would she do anything to put her daughter in danger, and she had promised to obey if he ever gave her instructions.

Turning, she entered the store. While anxiously awaiting Logan's return, she purchased the stained-glass window and—on a whim—bought the mirror. After arranging for the delivery, she browsed around—twice telling the overbearing clerk she didn't have any questions. Well, she did, but the salesman couldn't tell her where Logan had rushed off to.

Fists clenched at his sides and chest heaving, Logan stood at the end of an alley as the black Ford F-250 with dark tinted windows sped away. Damn it to hell. If he'd been just a few seconds faster, he would've had the license plate number.

The man standing across the street and watching them had caught his attention. For an instant, he thought he was seeing Evan. But the man was bulkier, and Evan would have never shaved his head. Unfortunately, the man had been too far away to see his features clearly. It wasn't Evan—it couldn't be. He had held Evan in his arms as he lay dying.

Angry strides took Logan back to the store where he'd left Dani and Regan. Who the hell was he? None of this made sense. A stalker who left teddy bears and resembled Evan—one who seemed to want to step into Evan's life, claiming his wife and daughter. It was bizarre and unsettling.

"Are you going to answer my question, Logan?"

He looked up from his pizza. They'd decided on the Wild Mushroom for lunch, and though the food was great, the music was so loud it hurt his ears. Also, the attitude of their waiter—along with the dreadlocks and rings in his eyebrow and nose—annoyed Logan to no end. The kid flirted with Dani as if Logan were invisible. *Her husband died for your right to look like an idiot.* He scowled at the waiter, satisfied when the boy scurried away.

"What question?" he asked, though he had heard her.

Dani sighed, then ignored him, tearing off a chunk of pizza crust and giving it to Regan to gnaw on. She was seriously annoyed, and he didn't blame her.

"She won't choke on that?"

Green eyes flashed with irritation. "No, the piece is too big. She'll just gum it. Stop stalling. What happened? Why did you take off like that?"

There it was again, the question he wanted to go away. Pushing the remainder of his pizza aside, he glanced at the baby girl with Evan's hazel eyes. "I thought I saw Evan."

The blood drained from Dani's face. Without giving it any thought, he slid around the table and pushed in next to her. "Dani, I didn't see him. Listen to me. I didn't see him. Whoever it was just looked a little like him."

She angrily pushed him away. "Stop it. They told me he'd been killed." Fat, heartbreaking tears rolled down her cheeks. "Do you think it was him?" she said, hope in her voice.

"No, I know it wasn't." Hurt that she didn't want his comfort, Logan reluctantly moved back to his side of the table.

She busied herself with putting Regan into the carrier. Once the straps were securely over her shoulders, she stood. "I want to go home."

After paying the bill, he escorted her and Regan to the car, all the while keeping an alert eye out for a man who resembled Evan. He glanced at Dani. Her day out had been ruined, and he didn't know how to make it better.

As soon as they arrived home, she'd disappeared into her room with Regan and the diaper bag, only coming out once to grab two jars of baby food. They'd been in there for hours. Logan stood in the hall and glared at the closed door. Was she all right? *Stupid question, Kincaid.* How could she be after learning the man stalking her not only sounded like her dead husband but also looked like him?

Lifting his wrist, he pushed the button that lit his watch dial. Two in the damned morning. He paced the hallway. On the way downtown, they'd stopped so he could overnight the teddy bear to Buchanan to see if he could lift any fingerprints. It would be a day or two before the results came back. There must be something else he could do in the meantime.

He liked missions where he knew his target and had all the background intel on the bad guy. There was never any doubt who he was going after, what the dude's habits were, or where he hung out. By the time he and his team finished studying him, they knew how many times he visited his mother and how many times he got laid, along with when, where, and for how long. With this creep, he was stumbling around in the dark, ineffective and useless.

It pissed him off.

With one last scowl at the door, he went to the kitchen and rummaged around in the refrigerator. He was hungry and tired of waiting for Dani to emerge from her room. She hadn't eaten since their pizza at lunch. How was she supposed to keep her strength up if she didn't eat? She was nursing, for God's sake. Didn't nursing mothers need nourishment?

Opening a plastic container that looked like leftover Chinese, he sniffed it. It smelled good so he set it on the counter. In the cabinet, he found a plate, cup, and coffee beans. The coffee started, Logan stared at the microwave until he found the express button.

"What are you heating up?"

One glance at Dani and his mouth went dry. She had on a soft, short robe the color of her eyes. Her hair was tousled, her feet bare. He did a double take. No, he hadn't imagined it. Her toenails were painted sky blue.

"Wicked Blue."

"What?" He had no idea what she was talking about, but he liked the sound of it.

She wiggled her toes. "The color. It's called Wicked Blue."

It was a good name. Who knew he would find blue toenails sexy? Unable to resist, his gaze traveled up long legs and over the curves her robe couldn't hide. A cold shower would probably be a

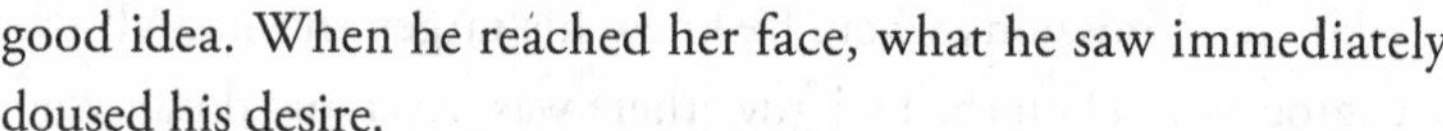

good idea. When he reached her face, what he saw immediately doused his desire.

"You've been crying."

One shoulder lifted in a shrug as she walked past him, picked up the container, and put it back in the refrigerator.

"Hey, give that back. I'm hungry."

"So am I," she said. "But I'm in the mood for comfort food."

"I was comfortable with that one."

That earned him a small smile, and his mind went to work thinking of other amusing things to say to wipe the tears from her eyes and keep her lips in an upward curve. Unfortunately, he was not a witty man. Evan was always the one with the humorous quips.

"I'm going to make you something special." She pulled a package of hotdogs out of the fridge.

"Seriously? Hotdogs are your comfort food?"

"Strange, but true. The coffee's ready. Why don't you make us a cup and then have a seat while I make you hotdogs like you've never had before."

He saluted her. "Yes, ma'am."

She gave him a look, but he definitely saw her lips twitch. He made their coffee, left hers on the counter, and took his to the table. Reaching over to a radio tucked into a corner, she turned it on, tuning it to a jazz station. He liked jazz, but only late at night. Did she feel the same about the bluesy music? She didn't seem to want to talk, so he sipped his coffee and sat back to watch her.

After filling a pot with water, she turned on one of the burners and dropped in a bag of rice. From the pantry, she took out a can of diced tomatoes, opened it, and poured the contents into another pot, then added ground pepper and some kind of spice.

"What was that?" he asked.

"Oregano."

The hotdogs were sliced and then added to the tomatoes. The rice started to boil, and she turned the burner up on the hotdog concoction. Logan had his doubts about whatever she was cooking up, thinking he would have preferred the Chinese leftovers. If it made her happy to eat hotdog soup at two in the morning, though, he would gladly go along.

When she stood on her toes and reached for the bowls, her robe rose up her thighs. He barely managed not to groan. If the woman had a clue what she was doing to him, she would wisely lock herself back in her room. The best thing to do was to close his eyes to the too-enticing view and concentrate on the music.

Though he wasn't sure, he thought he was listening to Miles Davis playing his trumpet. The sound was earthy and intimate, and he imagined making slow and easy love with Dani to the sounds coming out of the radio. How the picture formed in his mind was a mystery considering . . . well, considering.

His eyes popped open, and he shifted uncomfortably, glad he was wearing his sweats instead of tight jeans. She placed a bowl in front of him and sat across from him. Logan looked down at the contents, then up at her.

"This is the strangest use of hotdogs I've ever seen." She'd poured the mixture over the rice, and it smelled surprisingly good.

"It's my guilty pleasure," she said, and dug into her meal.

He spooned some and took a tentative taste. Okay, that was good. Following her example, he dug in, scraping the bottom of the bowl. It was the perfect comfort food: simple, tasty, and filling. He caught her watching him and raised a brow.

"You were a doubting Thomas," she said.

"You have me there. I couldn't imagine hotdog soup could be so good."

Her eyes shimmered in pleasure. "Hotdog soup? I like it. I've never been able to think of a name for it. Would you like some more?" Before he could answer, she rushed on. "No, let's have the brownies and ice cream we never got around to last night."

He glanced at the clock to see it was three in the morning. Sitting with her in the kitchen at a time when the world around them slept felt intimate. "I'll make us another cup of coffee."

Silently working together, they had the coffee and dessert ready and on the table at the same time. It almost seemed as if they'd done this many times before. Had she and Evan ever shared late-night kitchen forays?

"I mean it, Dani. I can't keep eating like this," he said, swallowing the last bite of brownies and ice cream.

She groaned and rubbed her stomach. "I wish I could run with you tomorrow, but I can't leave Regan alone. Suppose you go first and then watch her while I run off some of these calories?"

Had she lost her mind? "No, I'm sorry, but you can't. He's out there and I'm not letting you take off on your own, out of my sight."

The light faded from her eyes and she pressed her fingertips to them. "I forgot," she whispered. "How could I forget?"

She walked out of the kitchen without a backward glance and disappeared back into her room. Logan wearily stood and washed the dishes, and dried and put them away. He turned off the lights and slipped out the back door, sitting on the steps of the deck. Listening for night sounds, he heard the chirps of crickets and the hoots of an owl and knew there was no one lurking in the dark.

Dani slipped a T-shirt over her head and pulled on a pair of shorts. Sliding her feet into a pair of Black Dog flip-flops, she took a deep breath and followed the aroma of coffee to the kitchen. After getting up at six to feed Regan and play with her until she was tired enough to go back to sleep, Dani had crawled back into bed and slept until ten. She was tired, cranky, and in dire need of caffeine.

"Coffee?" Logan asked when she stumbled into the room.

"Hot tea," she grumbled, though she longed for the coffee. But she'd drunk too much the night before, or had it been that morning? As much as she loved nursing Regan, there were definite drawbacks. She aimed for the cabinet, but Logan stepped in front of her.

"Sit, I'll make it for you."

She frowned at him.

"Sit."

There was an edge to his voice. It seemed they both weren't in the best of moods. Was he angry because she had walked out of the room after they had finished their brownies? Was he that touchy? She shrugged and sat down.

Still in possession of a libido, even though it had lain dormant for almost two years, she gave him an appreciative once-over. A blue T-shirt stretched over broad shoulders and every time he moved, chest and arm muscles flexed. Tight jeans and black running shoes covered his bottom half. Did he have any idea what an awesome butt he had?

He turned with her cup of tea in his hand and caught her ogling his ass. Heat crept into her cheeks. His lips thinned and a muscle twitched in his jaw. Jeez, the man had muscles everywhere.

"Thank you," she muttered when he set the cup in front of her.

With typical SEAL efficiency, ten minutes later a plate of eggs, bacon, and toast appeared in front of her. "Aren't you eating?" she asked.

"I had my breakfast while it was still breakfast time."

"What's your problem, Logan?"

A cell phone rang from the vicinity of his marvelous butt. He pulled it out of his back pocket and looked at it. "I have to take this." He walked to the back door. Just before it closed behind him, she heard him say, "Hey, Maria."

Dani imagined a brown-skinned woman with lush curves and smoldering black eyes on the other end of the phone. Her long hair would shimmer blue-black in the sunlight. He'd greeted the caller with warmth in his voice, much different than the tone he had taken with her that morning. She pushed her half-eaten breakfast away.

As she washed the dishes, she watched Logan out the kitchen window. He sat on the deck railing with the phone to his ear, laughing at something the sensuous Maria said. Dani frowned. Of course, he had a life and the women he included in it were of no concern to her. Slapping the dish towel onto the counter, she turned away and left the kitchen.

CHAPTER FIVE

Not finding Dani in the house, Logan walked out to the front porch. Where the hell was she? He looked up the driveway and saw her coming toward him, the mail in her hand. "Damn it, Dani," he muttered. If she thought it was safe to go to her mailbox, then he still hadn't gotten through to her.

"Have you lost your mind?" he said, pleased with how calm he sounded.

She paused at the bottom of the steps and returned his glare. "Don't yell at me."

Okay, maybe not so calm. He paced to the end of the porch and took a deep breath, then turned and walked back. "I'm sorry, but you had me worried. I couldn't find you anywhere in the house, and where are you? Outside. By yourself. What if he'd been waiting for you?"

Coming up the steps, she stopped in front of him and rested her hand on his arm, her touch calming him. How did she do that? Someday he would try to understand how he managed to stay ice cold under fire, but lost all sense of direction around her. Up was down and out was in. He needed a Dani GPS.

"I just went to get the mail. It wasn't like I took off down the road. You were so involved in your conversation with Maria that I thought you wouldn't even notice I was gone."

Logan didn't miss the drawn-out emphasis she put on Maria's

name and didn't know what to make of it. "I noticed," he said, and followed her into the house. "Next time, I'll get the mail."

"I was perfectly fine. Nothing's going to happen in broad daylight with cars passing by."

"You don't know that. We don't know who he is or what he's capable of. So nothing unusual happened?"

"No, Logan, nothing unusual happened. A black truck slowed down, but that happens sometimes. I'm going to take a shower."

She turned to leave, and he caught her by the arm. "What kind of black truck?" She looked at the fingers digging into her flesh. He loosened his hold. "Describe it. In detail."

Her gaze lifted to his. "You're scaring me."

About fucking time. She had yet to take this as seriously as she needed to, and that was always the mistake of a cherry soldier. They just didn't get it, until they did or died. If something happened to Dani, he would never get over it.

"The truck, describe it."

She pulled her arm away. "It was just a black pickup with dark tinted windows. The kind of truck every third good ol' mountain boy drives."

Christ Jesus. The bad guy had been close enough to grab her. Up was down and out was in. If he had a damn Dani GPS, he thought stupidly, he might not have lost all sense of right and wrong. But he didn't, so when he pulled her into his arms and soundly kissed her, he blamed her for his taking a wrong turn.

Logan was vaguely aware at first that her hands pushed against his chest, but when sanity began to creep back into his brain and he tried to pull away, she grabbed him around his neck and held tight. Her lips were soft, the inside of her mouth hot. He stopped thinking, closed his eyes, and lost himself in the kiss. He licked her teeth, he licked at the insides of her cheeks, and he sucked on her tongue. He did all that once and it was so good, he did it again. She tasted like heaven and he was in hell.

Remember Evan. The two words were as effective as being doused with ice on an already cold day. He stumbled back. "I'm sorry, I didn't want to do that."

Hurt flashed in her eyes. "Bastard," she said, and walked away.

"You don't understand," he told the empty room. He did want to. Wanted very much to do it. Had since the day he first saw her in Sinner's Bar. But she belonged to Evan.

What Logan wanted didn't count.

Restless, he decided to go check on the camera he'd placed in the oak. Since Dani's stalker had just driven by, it was a safe bet he wouldn't be in the tree. Although Logan wished the man were there so this could end today and he could go home, safely putting seven hundred miles between him and temptation.

Dani slammed the bathroom drawer closed. Why had Logan kissed her if he didn't want to? Adjusting the water temperature to warm, she stepped into the shower and lifted her face to the spray. She tried to recall the look in his eyes right before the kiss. He'd been angry, but also worried about her. Which emotion drove the kiss, the anger or his concern? Did it matter?

He was the most exasperating man. One minute he looked at her as if he might devour her and the next his expression turned guarded, his eyes distant. The kiss surprised her and so had her reaction. The last man whose lips had touched hers had been Evan, and that had been long enough ago to forget how good it felt to be held in a man's arms and feel his mouth on hers.

She rinsed the shampoo out of her hair, her question still unanswered. Why had Logan kissed her if he didn't want to? Ever since he had arrived, needs long dormant were stirring. She had no interest in marrying again, at least for a long time. The life she'd created for her and Regan was near perfect, and she didn't need anyone messing it up.

What she wanted was a torrid, mind-blowing affair with a hot, mouthwatering man. And she wanted that man to be Logan. A frustrated chuckle escaped. If he knew the direction her thoughts were taking, he would jump on his "it goes very fast" Harley and disappear before she could say Davidson.

In her bedroom, she grabbed a T-shirt and threw it on the bed. She stopped, looked at it, and smiled. Change of plans.

Once she was dressed, she went to the living room, pausing in the doorway. Logan sat on the couch, holding Regan. He brought a spoon to Regan's mouth, and her daughter—obviously still in the throes of adoration if her intent focus on Logan meant anything—obediently opened her mouth.

"That's my girl," he purred.

Regan gave him a smile Dani had never seen before. *My God, the little stinker's flirting with him.* Smothering a chuckle, she stepped into the room. Regan noticed her first.

"Mama!"

Logan glanced up, did a double take, and gave Dani a slow perusal, causing her body to ripple in awareness. Judging by the heat in his eyes, the little spaghetti-strap sundress made of fine white gauze was met with approval.

"Ah," he said, drawing the word out.

He seemed lost as to where to go from there, so she took pity on him. "Thanks. I'll take over now." Holding out her arms, she said,

"Come here, silly girl." Regan's face scrunched up and her little lips trembled.

The corners of his eyes crinkled in amusement. "I think she wants me to finish feeding her."

"Have at it, then." Dani walked to the window, feeling the soft fabric swirl around her legs. She brushed her fingers over the skirt. The dress came to just below her knees, but had a slit to halfway up her thigh. Strappy red sandals, a thin red leather belt, and red dangling glass-bead earrings completed the look and were a daring contrast to the white gauze dress. The outfit said, *Look at me, I might be feeling naughty.* Would Logan get it?

She slid a finger under a blind and lifted it. It was a beautiful day, and she wanted to be out in it. There was a restlessness inside her, had been for a while, even before this stalker business started. The dress she wore had been purchased on impulse—on a day she'd needed cheering up—even though she'd doubted at the time she'd ever wear it. She glanced at Logan over her shoulder just in time to see him almost spoon Regan's baby food into her ear.

Dani didn't know whether to swoon or laugh. Logan—heat flaring in his eyes—was so focused on her that he had totally missed Regan's mouth. Regan giggled when the spoon touched her earlobe. He jerked his eyes down and saw he was close to pouring pureed sweet potatoes down her ear.

Fascinated, Dani watched as red crept up his throat and onto his cheeks. She managed not to laugh. Oh, but it felt good to want to. He busied himself with feeding Regan, something Evan would never get to experience.

From the time she was born until the day two Navy men in dress uniform stood on her doorstep and asked to come in, her life had been blessed. Her parents were old money, lots of it. Not one of her friends' parents could stand to be in the same room with each other, and she'd always felt special that hers deeply loved each other. It had been one reason her three best friends spent most of their time at her house. Her home was a happy one.

In addition to a mother and father who supported her in all ways, she had a trust fund left to her by her grandparents and a career she was good at and loved. Then Evan came along, completing the picture to perfection.

A hard lesson had been learned, though: beware of a life too good to be true. She'd never known loss or heartbreak, had never dreamed it could happen to her. Nothing had been right since the Navy chaplain took her hands in his and gently told her that her husband had been killed.

She wanted to feel again, wanted a man to want her, wanted to be touched, whispered to, and held tight in strong arms. Unfortunately, she wanted a man who didn't want her. Well, maybe there was some kind of chemistry going on between them, but he didn't seem happy about it.

Dani glanced down at her dress, saw that because of the way she stood, the slit was open, exposing her leg. Good God, she was dressed for trolling and was suddenly disgusted with her behavior.

If she was appalled, what must Logan be thinking? He was here as a friend to help her, not to provide stud service. But he was the one who'd kissed her and lit the match that started the fire. *Fine, it's his fault I'm acting like a slut.* She glared at him, but he was too busy feeding Regan to notice.

Without a word, Dani walked out of the room—something she seemed to be doing a lot since he'd arrived. After changing into a pair of jeans and a T-shirt, she returned to find Logan on the floor playing with Regan. He glanced at her, but made no comment. She sat on the floor and for the next hour tried to forget her sorrows, her stalker, and the longings Logan stirred up.

Logan tickled Regan, amused by how giggly she became each time he touched her. "I'm gonna get your tummy." He flicked his finger over her stomach. She was on her back, her feet and hands thrashing in the air, her shrieks of laughter piercing. If he tried to remove his hand, she grabbed his finger and put it back.

"More?" He tickled her again while keeping a covert eye on Dani. The dress she wore earlier should be declared illegal or at least come with a warning: *Beware, may cause loss of breath.* Her abrupt departure and change of clothing indicated something was going on in her mind, but damned if he knew what. He hadn't missed the look she sent his way right before striding out of the room, one that said he was a shithead for some reason.

Now, she seemed to be attempting a happy front, but tension poured from her so thick he could cut it with his knife. Unfortunately, after Regan fell asleep he was going to ruin whatever peace she had left. Regan pulled his finger into her mouth and sucked.

"She's getting sleepy," Dani said, and popped a pacifier into Regan's mouth.

Logan leaned back against the sofa and let out a sigh. "Thank God. Where does she get her energy?"

Heartfelt love filled Dani's eyes as she gazed at her daughter. Had his mother ever looked at him like that? A no-brainer question. Never. The only person Lovey Dovey cared about was Lovey Dovey. One unwanted child had been an inconvenience. Then along came Maria and by the time she was three, Lovey Dovey, had decided two brats were intolerable.

His sister had come within a hair's breadth of being a throwaway, a little girl given over to social services to be placed in foster care. Only because he had been fifteen and working after school, giving Lovey Dovey his earnings, had she reluctantly agreed to give Maria to him. His threat to disappear forever, taking Maria with him, had the desired results. Lovey Dovey's fear of losing her booze and cigarette cash was the only reason his baby sister hadn't been lost to him forever.

"Lovey Dovey could take lessons from you on how to be a mother."

"Who?"

Hell and damn, why had that come out of his mouth? "My mother."

"Your mother's named Lovey Dovey?"

The incredulous look Dani gave him was expected. Who the hell had a mother named Lovey Dovey, anyway? Logan hated talking about his parent—rarely did to anyone. But he'd opened that door.

"She was born Gretchen Kincaid. When she decided she was going to be a famous stripper like Gypsy Rose Lee, she legally changed her name to Lovey Dovey. She kept the name, but the dream got lost in the dregs of a tequila bottle."

Dani didn't seem to have a response, and he was glad for it. He had nothing more to say about the wretched woman.

Nodding at Regan, he said, "She's asleep. Why don't you put her to bed, and then we need to talk."

"About what?"

"Your stalker."

Her expression turned guarded. "Do you know something?"

"Yes. Put Regan in her crib; then I'll tell you."

She gently gathered up her daughter, and again he compared her tenderness to his mother's cruel touch, especially with Maria. To Lovey Dovey, Maria was competition. By the time his sister reached her teens, it became obvious she was going to be stunning. Lovey Dovey's hatred of her daughter grew with each passing year.

Pushing away thoughts of the woman who birthed him, he went to his room and retrieved his laptop. By the time Dani returned, he was ready for her. She stopped in the doorway and eyed the computer sitting open on the coffee table.

"Come here, Dani," he said softly.

Her gaze shifted to his, and he held out his hand. She came to him and slid her hand into his. His heart thumped hard in response to her touch. Her hair—a riot of curls hanging halfway down her back—brushed over his arm, and he closed his eyes for a moment, willing his skin not to twitch. It didn't work. *Concentrate on the mission, Kincaid.* He needed the Iceman, but it appeared he'd gone AWOL.

This morning he'd downloaded images from the camera he put in the tree. Because she hadn't let go of him, he operated his computer with one hand. "Have you ever seen this man before?"

She leaned her nose close to the screen and studied the photo. "With all the camouflage paint on his face and the ball cap pulled down over his eyes, he could be anyone."

Logan clicked on the next photo. "Look familiar?"

Her eyes widened on seeing the black Ford F-250 truck. "Is that his?"

"No, just a picture I downloaded, but he drives one like it, except his has dark tinted windows."

The color drained from her face. "That was him who drove by this morning?"

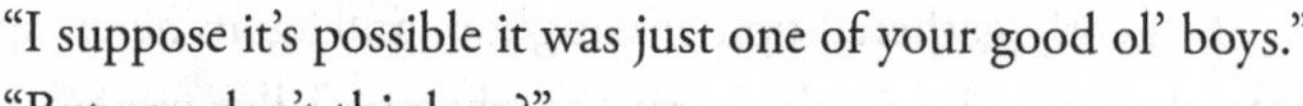

"I suppose it's possible it was just one of your good ol' boys."

"But you don't think so?"

The urge to assure her the man hadn't been within feet of her warred with his need to explain the danger she'd be in if she wasn't careful. He flipped the computer lid closed. "No, I don't. It was stup—"

"I know what you're thinking. I'm sorry." Her shoulders slumped, and she stared at her hands.

He hated seeing her this way and waited for her to look at him before he cocked a brow. "You're sorry you know what I'm thinking?"

"No, I'm sor—oh, you're teasing me." She narrowed her eyes. "Aren't you?"

Against all good judgment, he wrapped his arms around her and leaned back on the sofa, pulling her with him. She came willingly, snuggling against his side. Holding her felt so damn right.

"Yeah, I'm teasing." Resting his chin on her head, he inhaled her scent. "Your hair smells like honey."

"It's honey and green tea."

He tilted his head and peered down at her. "You put honey and green tea in your hair? Isn't that kinda messy?"

She grinned. "No, silly, the shampoo fragrance is honey and green tea."

To see her smiling again was worth being called silly. "I like it." He leaned his head back and closed his eyes. Christ, he wanted to kiss her again.

"Well, if you like this one, wait until you smell my vanilla-bean-and-apple-pie-scented shampoo."

Did she change shampoo scents the way she changed toenail polish? God help him. If she came near him smelling like vanilla ice cream and apple pie, he refused to hold himself responsible for licking her from her toes to her mouth.

"Did you just groan?"

Had he? "I don't think so."

These minutes, sitting on the sofa with her curled up next to him, all warm and sweet smelling, made him dream of a life with a woman who loved him and only him. Dani wouldn't be like Lovey Dovey and bring strange men home, a rare one or two of them nice, but most from whom he'd had to protect Maria.

"I think you did." She pushed her hand under his T-shirt, sliding her fingers over skin that was aching for her touch. Her face lifted, her mouth inches from his.

I'm sorry, Evan, he offered just before he kissed her.

Logan memorized the spicy taste of her because he couldn't let this happen again. But for a few minutes he allowed his desire free rein. He angled his head and deepened the kiss. Her lips were full and soft, perfect for kissing. Cradling her neck with his palm, he held her close while his tongue explored her mouth. Under his shirt, her hand was busy with its own exploration, and when she flicked a finger over a nipple, he groaned.

This time he was certain he had because he heard it, the sound a red flag to his lust-filled brain. He had to stop. He didn't want to stop. One more minute—he would allow himself one more minute.

When she sucked on his tongue, he forgot about time and minutes. Tangling one hand into hair softer than silk, he slid the other over the curve of her breast. She sighed into his mouth.

He felt the vibration of her sigh down to his bones. Tentatively, her fingers traced the bulge in his jeans, and he vibrated again.

Amazing.

Logan pressed her palm down on his cock. She tried to curl her hand around him, but the tight denim prevented her from grasping him. As she reached for the zipper, he vibrated a third time.

Christ, it was his damn phone. Lifting his head, he looked at her, taking in the dilated eyes, and the mouth, pink and moist from his kisses. He could have Evan's wife this minute on her sofa. Disgusted with his breach of honor and his disrespect to his best friend and SEAL brother's wife, Logan untangled his hand from her hair and mumbled an apology.

He pulled his phone out of his back pocket, looked at the caller ID, and punched TALK. "Hello, sweetheart."

CHAPTER SIX

Sweetheart?

Dani left the room, allowing him to talk to the buxom Maria in private. Seeing the woman's name on his phone reminded her there was a prior claim on Logan. "Hello, sweetheart," she mimicked as she slapped a package of shaved Black Forest ham down on the counter. What incredible timing. The lady must be clairvoyant.

To make matters worse, he had apologized for the kiss. Again. So, why was he kissing her if there was another woman in his life?

After putting a layer of baby Swiss cheese on top of the ham, she turned on the broiler. She sliced a kosher dill pickle and put the slivers on their plates. God, he was a good kisser. Somehow she needed to learn what his relationship with this Maria was. If it was serious and a commitment existed between them, then there would be no more kissing. Or fondling. Or the other stuff that followed fondling.

On the other hand . . .

The Georgia peach slices added the perfect finishing touch. Envisioning how the plates would look with the toasted ham and cheese hoagies added to them, she smiled with satisfaction. Not able to resist a fat, ripe peach, she picked up a slice and popped it into her mouth, the juice running down her chin. She turned to get a paper towel and shrieked.

How long had Logan been watching her? He looked so manly leaning against the doorway with his arms crossed over his chest. Smoldering chocolate-colored eyes followed the juice sliding down her chin. She stuck out her tongue and licked at the peach juice. His nostrils flared as he lifted his eyes to hers.

Heaven help her. The man was a living, breathing, walking advertisement for "Why I Want to Have Sex." She shivered and hoped he didn't notice.

His gaze slid over her body. "Are you cold, Dani?"

The words rumbled over and through her. Good God, even his voice dripped sex, and jeez, the way her name slid over his tongue sent heat spiraling through her. Her favorite Regency word came to mind. *Wanton*. Yes siree, she was one of those.

"Uh . . . no. I'm fine. Really. Are you hungry? I've made lunch. Well, almost. Just have to stick this under the broiler." She shoved the cookie sheet with the hoagies into the oven and slammed the door shut.

"Didn't mean to do that," she muttered. Amusement shimmered in his eyes. She might slap his face yet. "Beer?"

"Sure."

"Grab one from the fridge." Opening a drawer, she picked up a bottle opener, but before she could give it to him, he'd twisted the cap off. Evan used to do the same thing. She stood like an idiot as tears welled in her eyes. God, what was wrong with her?

He set the beer on the counter, took the opener from her hand, and put it back in the drawer. "Dani?" His hand came to rest on her shoulder. "Are you upset because I kissed you? I shouldn't—"

Damn him. "Do. Not. Apologize." Turning her back on him, she slid a mitt onto her hand and removed the hoagies from the oven. "Please don't say you're sorry. Obviously, we're attracted to each other, and I'm okay with that." She glanced over her shoulder. "But you're not for whatever reason, so no more kissing."

He focused on her in that direct way of his. "It's a matter of honor." Picking up his plate and beer, he sat down at the table.

They ate in silence, her mind churning with questions. Did he mean Evan, that he felt it was wrong to kiss his fallen comrade's wife? With Logan's strong sense of loyalty, that was a good possibility. Or was he thinking of Maria? If he meant he couldn't kiss her because he was already involved with someone, she could respect that.

It was unfortunate he was involved with someone, because he was the first man since Evan to whom she was attracted. She also believed Evan would applaud her choice, had even teased her that Logan had a crush on her. More than anything, though, Evan had wanted her to find a way to be happy if something happened to him.

"I want you to promise me something, sugar," he'd said on his last night before deployment.

"Anything," she'd said, inhaling his scent and missing him before he'd even left.

"If I don't come back, you have to promise me you'll find a way to be happy again."

She'd pressed herself against him, hating talk of the danger that loomed over him as long as he was a SEAL. "Please always come back to me, Evan."

"I'm going to do my best, sugar, but this has to be said. If anything ever happens to me, Logan will always be there for you if you're ever in need. You'll have to ask him to come to you, though. He won't willingly trespass onto my property."

She giggled and punched him. "I'm not a piece of property."

"No, you're my heart." He kissed her like there was no tomorrow.

"Sugar," she murmured.

"Pardon?"

Dani slid a pickle across her plate, transfixed on the wet trail it made. It seemed to upset Logan whenever she mentioned Evan, but damn it, she wanted them to be able to speak of her husband and his friend.

"I was just remembering how Evan liked to call me sugar. I think it was a Texas thing."

His eyes shuttered and he stood, taking his plate to the sink. Had Evan been right? Had Logan harbored secret feelings for her, and did he still? No, he might have once, but he had the delectable Maria now and was obviously over any attraction there might've been for her. Didn't explain why he had kissed her twice, though.

She sighed and carried her plate to the sink. Logan took it from her and busied himself washing the dishes while she dried and put them away.

"Is there anywhere you would like to go?" she asked after they finished.

He leaned back against the counter and shrugged. "I'd like to go by—"

He pulled his phone out of his back pocket, but she was at an angle where she couldn't see the caller ID. Jeez, was *she* calling again, already?

"Hello, Suzanne," he said, and walked out the back door, shutting it behind him.

Suzanne? Well, he had been in the Navy and maybe practiced the old adage of a girl in every port. His tone of voice had been different with this one, however. With Maria, he sounded soft and sweet, but with Suzanne, clipped and distant. Dani pictured a slim, blue-eyed woman with sleek, streaked blond hair and a cool, sophisticated demeanor.

If he had the black-haired Maria and the bleached-blond Suzanne, it seemed to her that she could round out the colors with her red hair. Now there was a stupid thought. She had no intention of joining a harem.

"You Had Me from Hello" by Bon Jovi chimed from the wall speakers. Dani went to the door and peered into the peephole. Smiling, she unbolted the locks. "Hey, Jared. Come in. Where's Scott?"

One of the best-looking men on the planet walked in and grabbed her in a bear hug. She pushed her hands into his rakishly long golden hair and smacked him on the lips.

"Scott dropped me off. He had to run to the post office, but he'll be back shortly." He handed her a plastic container.

Dani opened the lid and inhaled the tantalizing scent of warm zucchini bread. "Yummy," she said, pulling off a chunk and popping it into her mouth. "Oh, wow. This one is the best yet."

He laughed. "You say that every time."

"Because it's true every time." She turned to go back into the kitchen, and he followed her, as at home in her house as she was in his.

Jared shared her love of cooking, and they often made meals together, much to Scott's enjoyment. Anyone looking at Jared would not be surprised he was a personal trainer. He was big, muscled from head to toe.

The surprise would be his culinary skills. As more of a hobby than a job, he worked part time as a private chef. For some pretty big bucks, he would go to a client's home and create a night of culinary magic. Whenever he had a booking scheduled, he would practice his menu on her and Scott.

Jared and Scott had been her salvation after Evan's death. One or the other had stayed with her and held her while she cried. Jared had encouraged her interest in cooking, while Scott critiqued her books. Both had paced the waiting room when she gave birth. She couldn't ask for better godparents to her daughter. They were the brothers she'd never had, and she loved the hell out of them.

Setting the zucchini bread on the counter, she peeked out the window to see Logan still talking on the phone. From the expression on his face, he didn't seem to be enjoying the conversation. That pleased her to no end.

The phone rang and Dani froze.

"Dani?"

Jared's concerned voice penetrated the haze. She answered the phone, pushing the speaker button. "Hello."

"I'm disappointed in you, Danielle."

She glanced at Jared, saw the questioning look in his eyes, and put a finger to her mouth to hush him. "I can't imagine what I've done to disappoint you. Will you tell me your name?"

"The Bible says a wife should cleave unto her husband. Why is there a strange man in your house, Danielle? I very nicely asked you to send him away, yet he's still there. The Bible says a wife should love, honor, and obey her husband. If you can't manage such a simple thing as obey, Danielle, then how can I trust you to love and honor me? The Bible says thou shalt not kill, but Papa Herb—oops, almost spilled the beans," he said, and giggled.

A chill slithered down Dani's spine. Whoever this was, he was crazy. "Papa who?" she asked, only to hear a dial tone. "Crap," she said, and hung up the phone. "I could use a hug, Jared."

He wrapped his big body around her. "Dani, love, what's this about?"

Logan pushed the phone into his pocket and glared at the sky. When would the blasted woman give up? He had said it was over nine ways to Sunday even though in his mind there hadn't been anything between them in the first place. Four dinner dates spread out over two months did not constitute a relationship.

Just as he turned to enter the house, the hair on the back of his neck stood up. The bad guy was watching him. Logan slid his hand behind him and touched the gun, reassuring himself it was there. Knowing that if he headed for the woods, the man would disappear, he walked back into the kitchen.

"Dani, love, what's this about?"

Logan stilled in the doorway and speared the man daring to call Dani his love with a look that would have sent his team members scurrying. The man pushed Dani behind him and magically grew bigger. Logan knew that trick and performed his own body expansion. They exchanged hard stares, sizing each other up. The dude was obviously trying to appear menacing, but he sported gym muscles, nothing more.

Who the hell was he? "Dani, introduce your friend."

She peeked around the man's massive arm. "Logan, meet my neighbor, Jared Cooper. Jared, this is my friend, Logan Kincaid. He was Evan's SEAL commander."

A smile appeared on Jared's face and he stuck out his hand. "Heard a lot about you, Kincaid. Good to finally meet you."

She had talked about him? Over an exchange of handshakes, Logan couldn't resist saying, "Haven't heard a thing about you, Cooper, but good to meet you anyway."

Jared's eyes narrowed before crinkling up at the corners, his smile turning to a wide grin. "Dani, my girl, your boyfriend's jealous." He draped an arm around her. "The joke's on him, my love."

The two of them looked at each other and burst out laughing. Irritated, Logan scowled. What was he missing? Exactly what joke was on him? And why the hell was she cozied up to this dude? Without thinking, Logan deftly hooked an arm around her, pulled her to him, and tucked her up under his arm where she belonged.

Music flowed out of ceiling speakers. Jared smiled. "That's Scott."

Logan tightened his hold on Dani. If another iron-pumping jock walked into the room and called Dani his love, he was going to hurt someone.

Jared disappeared, returning with his arm around the shoulder of a slim man who reminded Logan of Clark Kent. For the first time since he'd walked in and found Dani in another man's arms, Logan relaxed. Not that it was any of his business to whom she gave her affection. He just didn't want to be around when it happened. The black-haired newcomer looked at them with interest. Realizing he still had her tucked into his side, Logan stepped away.

"Logan, this is Scott Parker. Scott, meet my friend, Logan Kincaid."

An hour later, Logan stood at the door with Dani as Jared and Scott took their leave. He held a crying Regan in his arms. She had made it clear she didn't want them to go.

"Don't cry, pumpkin," Logan said, bouncing her in his arms. "You're going to see them tomorrow."

"Here, give her to me. She played hard. She's tired and hungry."

He handed the baby over. "I like your friends."

"Especially since they agreed to babysit tomorrow so you can take me for a ride on your motorcycle. I can't believe I let you talk me into it."

"I promise, you're gonna love it." He followed her into the kitchen. "After you feed her, we need to go to the Harley dealership and buy you a helmet."

Dani held on to Logan for dear life. For the first ten minutes, she had kept her eyes squeezed shut. He'd elected to ride south on the Blue Ridge Parkway to the Pisgah Inn for lunch. Once on the parkway with its gentle curves and slow speed limit, she ventured to open her eyes and, surprisingly, began to enjoy the ride. She didn't loosen her grip on Logan's waist, however, but stayed pressed against his back so tightly their helmets kept bumping.

Even during the summer, it was chilly on a motorcycle at that altitude, and she was thankful for the jacket he had insisted on buying her along with the helmet. She also thought the black leather looked badass cool on her.

They rode past a lookout, and although she'd driven on the parkway before, she had to agree it was different on a bike. It was better. It was beautiful with the blue-tinged mountains rising above her—no car roof to block the view—and the many shades of green on the valley floor thousands of feet below. Taking in a deep breath, she inhaled the spicy scent of the spruce pines. As they came out of a curve, a waterfall appeared and she grinned in delight, craning her head to look at it until it disappeared from sight.

Heaven on earth, she decided.

She braved letting go of Logan with one arm and lifted the visor on her helmet so she could feel the cool wind on her face. For the first time since her stalker appeared, she felt free, even if it was only for a few hours. Laughter bubbled up and escaped.

Logan reached back and squeezed her knee. "Having fun?" he yelled over the roar of the bike and wind.

Yes. Yes, she was having fun. She nodded, bumped his helmet with hers, and realized he couldn't see her. "Yes!"

He gave her knee one more squeeze, then put his hand back on the handlebar. At the next curve, she leaned with him, growing more confident and no longer resisting by trying to keep her body upright.

"There you go, you got it now," he said.

Dani grinned big and wide. She was a certified biker chick.

Logan slowed the bike and pointed. A mother deer and her spotted fawn stood at the edge of the tree line staring back at them. Could this day get any better?

Her happiness with the day had been stolen. The pan-fried trout Dani had thought delicious an hour ago now set heavy in her stomach. After lunch, they'd sat in the rocking chairs on the deck behind the Pisgah Inn, at five-thousand-feet elevation, sipping coffee and marveling over the view of the vista spread before them. From the moment she'd thrown a leg over the bike and wrapped her arms around Logan's waist, the day had been perfect.

Now it wasn't.

Logan stared at the motorcycle, his hands fisted at his sides. Dani looked away from the two slashed tires and surveyed the parking lot. Her stalker was there, or had been. He must have followed them, must have watched them go into the restaurant. She wrapped her arms around her waist, a shiver passing through her.

Logan pulled her next to him. "He's gone now."

She willingly went. "How can you be sure?"

"He wouldn't stay after doing this, wouldn't risk getting caught." Logan did his own survey of the area, and her gaze followed his.

No menacing black trucks in sight, but what if he had a different truck or car? Something they weren't aware of? She glanced at Logan. His eyes had the cold, deadly look of one aching to get his hands on the man who dared to do this to his bike.

"So, what now?" she asked.

"I'll call the Harley shop and arrange for my bike to get picked up. Call your friends and see if they can come get us." He unzipped his jacket and pulled out his cell phone.

She caught a glimpse of the handle of his gun, a grim reminder of his reason for being here and something she'd wanted to put aside for a few hours. Not a wise thing to do for many reasons. As soon as this was over, he would go back to his life. A pain arrowed its way through her heart. She would miss him. Better to stop this deepening affection before it grew into something unmanageable.

Unzipping one of the leather jacket's pockets, she removed her cell and punched in Jared's number. Scott answered, and after she finished talking to him, she waited for Logan to finish his conversation.

"Why do you think he slashed your tires?" she asked after he ended his call.

"He wants you, and I'm in the way. The question is, why? Why does he refer to you as his wife?"

"I. Am. Not. His. Wife. He's not Evan."

Logan reached out an arm, then pulled it back and slid both hands into his back pockets. He seemed focused on her ear, as if he didn't want to meet her gaze. His eyes had the look of a brooding man, a man who perhaps regretted his offer of help.

She was half-tempted to send him home and deal with her stalker herself. She would have, too, if she wasn't frightened out of her mind, not just for her safety, but more important, that of her daughter's.

No more wishing he would kiss her again. It would be best to consider his presence strictly business. He was here to do a job, and when it was successfully completed, he would return to his life with the magnificent Maria. Or perhaps the ice princess, Suzanne. Whichever, it wouldn't be Dani Prescott.

Suddenly, his gaze left her ear and focused on her, so intently that she grew uncomfortable under his stare. Why was he looking at her as if she were someone he'd never seen before?

"Logan?"

Not answering, he turned away. Dani stood next to the bike and watched him walk to the edge of the drop-off. He looked out over the panorama of mountain peaks, the valleys below, and the vast sky. What the hell was wrong with him? Did he blame her for the mess they were in? If he didn't want to be here, all he had to do was say so.

She sat on the bike's seat and prepared to wait for Jared and Scott. Logan hadn't moved from his spot at the edge of the mountain, his rigid posture warning her to keep her distance. Fine, if that was the way he wanted it, she would oblige him. She just wished she knew what his problem was.

CHAPTER SEVEN

Logan was disgusted with himself. He had let his desires get in the way of the job he was there to do. Men got killed when their commander didn't keep his mind on the operation. Since the risk if he FUBARed this mission was Dani's safety, allowing his longings to divert his attention was unforgivable.

Take today. All he'd wanted was to give her a few hours of fun, maybe help her forget for a while about the deranged man fixated on her. Had he once considered that the man would follow them? Had he watched in his rearview mirrors any more than an ordinary person might? Had he been at the top of his fighting form, aware of his surroundings and anything that seemed out of place?

No.

Starting now, beginning this very second, she was a job, nothing more. It was the only way he knew how to shut down his hunger for her. Christ, but the few hours of fun that morning had been remarkable. He recalled her laughing with the joy of it, the intimacy of squeezing her knee, the moment she first leaned with him into the curve. These were the things that made him inattentive and would get her hurt if he didn't get a grip.

It was high time to get his game face on and allow no distractions. There would be no more mistakes. He glanced over his shoulder. Dani sat on his motorcycle, her eyes alert to the activity in the parking lot, looking everywhere but at him. He walked to her.

"Why don't you go inside where you'll be more comfortable? I'll wait here until help arrives."

She shrugged. "If you think it's best."

He kept his eyes on her until she was safely inside, and then he took his place on the V-Rod. It would be about two hours before anyone showed up, plenty of time to make some phone calls.

The next day, after arranging for Scott to stay with Dani, Logan borrowed her Jeep. He made a visit to the Asheville police department and explained the situation to Detective Langley.

Langley assured him the patrol cops would be on the lookout for a black Ford truck driving anywhere near Dani's house, but that was the best they could do until the man broke the law. Although it didn't sit well with Logan, he understood their position. As for himself, he had a lot more freedom than the cops.

Next, using the yellow pages he had torn out of Dani's phone book, he started visiting motels, beginning with the closest to her house. On his fifth stop, he hit pay dirt. At the Mountain View Motel, the desk clerk nodded when Logan described the truck.

"Had one like that in the parking lot off and on for the past month. Guy comes and goes. Checked out yesterday."

Logan tempered his excitement. Didn't mean it was their guy. "What was his name?"

"John Smith."

He raised a brow. The clerk stared back at him, his expression blank. Logan opened his wallet, pulled out a twenty, and slid it across the counter where it disappeared into the man's pocket.

"His name?"

The clerk smirked. "John Smith."

"I'm not fond of games." Logan resisted the urge to wipe the ill-advised grin off the smartass, but his wish to do so must have showed.

The man's smirk disappeared and he took a step back. "That's the name he gave me, mister. Shit, half the men checking in here are named John Smith. I could hold a Smith family reunion most any day of the week."

Damn. Logan picked up a pen and a flyer for pizza delivery and wrote his cell number on it. "If he comes back, you call me." He turned to leave.

"Why should I?"

He stepped back to the desk. "Because if you don't, you'll wish you had. But if you do, I'll make it worth your while."

"You a bounty hunter?"

Logan's chuckle held no humor in it. "You might say that." At the door, he paused. "Do you get the license plate numbers?"

The clerk nodded. "Don't know why I bother, though. Most are made up."

"So you don't get the plate numbers yourself?"

"Too much trouble. I just ask them to write it down when they sign the registration form."

Logan let the door close and returned to the desk. "What number did John Smith give you?"

Pulling a spindle speared to the top with sheets of paper from under the counter, the man thumbed through them, finally handing one over. Logan glanced at it, then folded it and put it in his pocket.

"Hey, I might need that someday," the clerk said.

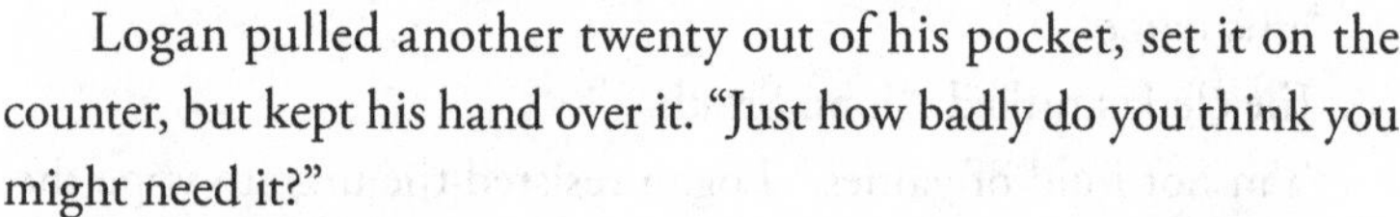

Logan pulled another twenty out of his pocket, set it on the counter, but kept his hand over it. "Just how badly do you think you might need it?"

"Not all that bad."

Once outside, Logan scanned the area. Why the dive bore the name Mountain View was a puzzle. The only view was that of a biker bar, a laundromat, and an abandoned auto-repair shop. The only cars in the motel parking lot were an older-model Chevy, Dani's Grand Cherokee, and a Volkswagen bus with daisies and peace signs hand-painted on it, parked in front of one of the rooms.

He unlocked the Cherokee's door, slid inside, and tapped his fingers on the steering wheel. *Where are you, John Smith?* Taking out his phone, he called Buchanan, gave him the probably fake plate number, and told him to run a check.

"Got a state to go with that number, boss?"

He glanced at the paper. There was a place for an address, but it was blank. "No, just a name and that number."

"What's the name?"

"John Smith."

Logan hung up on Buchanan's laughter. He spent another hour checking out motels with no luck. Frustrated, he turned for home. Correction. Dani's home. What he should do is go back to Pensacola and send Buchanan to Asheville to protect Evan's wife. Along with that thought came the urge to bloody Buchanan's nose. Romeo couldn't resist a pretty lady, and Logan had overheard one woman refer to Buchanan as one hot hunk of a man. Not happening.

He slammed his hand on the steering wheel. Where the hell was this asshole? Had Buchanan been able to lift any fingerprints off the bear? Logan shook his head in disgust. He should've asked when he had him on the phone. More proof he was so far off his game, he wasn't even in the right ballpark. The Iceman never missed important details like that, but his other persona was still AWOL.

What he needed was intel, and he should have spent the past few days gathering information and searching for John Smith instead of acting like a besotted fool. As he steered the Cherokee around a curve on the road to Dani's house, he mentally compiled and prioritized a list of things he needed to do.

Dani's Jeep jerked forward as the crunch of metal against metal grated in Logan's ears. His gaze jerked to the rearview mirror, a black Ford truck filling his vision. He floored the gas pedal in an attempt to pull away, but the Jeep was already veering toward the embankment.

The black truck caught the left side of the Jeep's bumper, and the driver increased his speed, causing Dani's SUV to veer off the road. The Jeep's right front wheel dipped as it slid over the edge of the slope.

Shit. As he sailed through the air, he regretted his treatment of Dani since the slashing of his motorcycle's tires. The last thing he'd seen in her eyes was hurt at the cold shoulder he'd given her. It was fucking sad her last memory of him would be how he'd turned his back on her.

The Jeep hit the ground about halfway down the incline, then tumbled end over end, taking down small trees on its wild ride. Logan's last thought was that the Iceman would have seen the danger coming.

Dani lifted the blinds and peeked out. It would be dark soon. Where was Logan?

"A watched pot never boils."

She dropped the blinds and looked at Scott. "What does that have to do to with anything?"

He muted the baseball game. "Just saying. Peeking out the window every two minutes isn't going to make him appear. You're as squirrelly as a nut-hiding squirrel."

Dani laughed—his intention, she was sure. "Sorry. I know Logan's perfectly capable of taking care of himself better than most. It's just that he should have been back by now."

"Mr. I Can Kill You With My Little Finger is just fine, darling. Why don't you fix us a cup of that special blend of green tea of yours and come sit with me? The Marlins are tied with the Braves in the bottom of the sixth."

"Okay." Not that she would be able to enjoy watching a game with Scott as much as she usually did, not until Logan was safely home. Something was wrong. He would have called if he were going to be this late. Unable to resist one more look out the window, she saw Jared's car turn into her driveway.

"Jared's here."

Scott's face lit up. Dani tried not to envy that he was in a loving relationship. She cherished her friendship with Scott and Jared, enjoyed being around them, but sometimes it was hard. Their happiness was a reminder of all she had lost.

"Sorry, would have been here sooner, but had to go around the long way," Jared said, giving her a kiss on the cheek as he entered. "Cops had the road closed because of an accident."

Was it possible for one's heart to take a dive to one's toes? Yes. Yes, it was. "Something's happened to Logan," she said, grabbing Jared's hand. "Scott, stay with Regan. Lock the door and don't open it for anyone but me, Jared, or Logan." She dragged Jared outside.

"Whoa." Jared pulled her to a stop. "What the hell, Dani?"

"It's Logan. I know it is. Please, I have to go to him."

He put his hands on her shoulders. "I hope you're wrong, but you have to calm down. If it's him, you won't do him any good like this."

He was right. She took deep, calming breaths and then pushed away. "Let's go."

Jared followed her to his Mustang and opened the passenger door before jogging around to the driver's side.

Several miles down the road, Jared slowed as they approached a police car positioned across the two-lane country road. The cop leaning against the hood held up a hand, then approached them. "Sorry, this road is closed for at least another hour. You can go around by taking Rambling Creek Road, left on Graveyard Street, then another left at Two Branch Road. That'll bring you back to Woodvine."

Dani shivered at the officer's mention of Graveyard Street. Every time she drove by it, she wondered who would willingly live on a road with such a name. She opened the door and jumped out of the Mustang.

The officer stepped in front of her. "Ma'am, please get back in the car."

Jared stepped up beside her before she could scream at the cop to let her by. He placed his hand under her elbow and gently squeezed. She pressed her lips together and let him explain.

"Can you tell us what kind of car it was?" Jared asked.

"A red Grand Cherokee."

"Oh God," Dani whispered, and grabbed hold of Jared's arm.

"That's her car, officer. She loaned it to her friend. Is he—"

"He's alive," the cop interrupted. "Come with me."

Ahead, Dani saw an ambulance, a fire truck, and several police cars parked on the road, but there was no sign of her Cherokee. Had they towed it away already? When they were within a few yards of

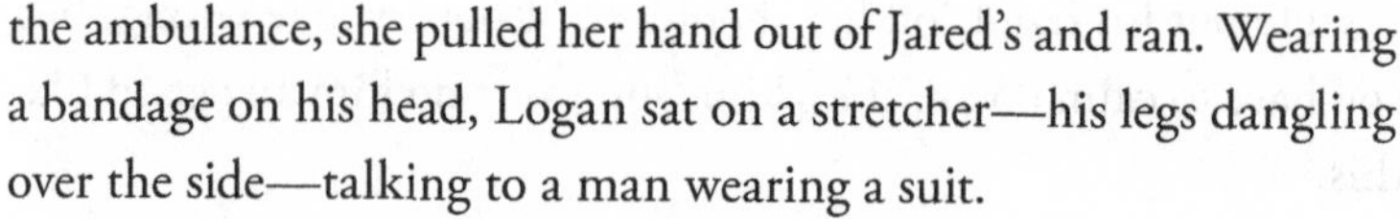

the ambulance, she pulled her hand out of Jared's and ran. Wearing a bandage on his head, Logan sat on a stretcher—his legs dangling over the side—talking to a man wearing a suit.

"Logan!"

He grimaced, not looking pleased to see her. "Sorry about your Jeep, Dani."

At the mention of her name, the suited man gave her a curious look. Who was he? Relief flooded her when Logan said he was only worried about her reaction to the damage to her car. Needing to touch him, she lightly rested her palm on his shoulder. When he didn't wince, she let her hand remain there. He had several cuts on his face and arms, but thank God they seemed to be superficial.

"Bloody hell, Logan, I don't care about the damn car."

Logan gave a half smile and looked at the other man. "She writes historical romances, thus her liking for words like 'bloody hell.'"

The man grinned. "My wife reads them. Sometimes she reads a paragraph or two out loud. You romance writers sure know your stuff. I've had some interesting evenings thanks to you and your like."

Dani laughed. Logan was okay, and everything in her world was right again. "Dani Prescott," she said, offering her hand. She liked this man, whoever he was. She guessed him to be nearing forty, possessing alert, watchful eyes and a sense of humor.

"Kevin Langley, Detective, Asheville Police Department."

"Oh." Why had a detective responded to a car accident?

Logan rubbed his head. "Sorry. I should've introduced you two."

Dani studied him. He didn't look good. His face was pale, and his eyes didn't seem quite in focus. "Shouldn't you go to the hospital?"

"No reason," Logan said, and stood, only to sway.

She slipped under his arm to help support him. One thing she had learned from Evan, these blasted SEALs had their pride. As expected, he tried to push away, wanting to prove, she was sure, that he could stand on his own.

"Please, I'm attached to you for my sake," she said. "You scared the daylights out of me."

He sagged against her. "All right."

She turned to the detective. "I won't be able to sleep tonight worrying about him. You're a cop; can't you make him go to the hospital? Jared and I will follow the ambulance and bring him home if they say he's okay."

Logan's protest was miniscule, telling her she was right to insist he get checked out. "Where did they take the Cherokee?" she asked Langley. Logan and the detective shared a look she didn't much like.

"Show her," Logan said.

Reluctantly letting go of Logan, she followed the detective to the edge of the drop-off, where down below her Jeep rested nose first in a creek. A massive tree branch dissected the car in half.

"He could have died." The detective caught her when her knees gave out. He let her slide down the side of his body until her butt planted itself firmly on the ground, and then he sat next to her.

"But he didn't, Miss Prescott. The branch punctured the airbag, and he thinks his head hit the steering wheel. Seems a black Ford truck came up behind him and pushed him over the edge."

Oh God. Oh God. She wrapped her arms around her stomach and pressed her forehead against her knees. Because of her, Logan had almost been killed.

"So you have no idea who this character is?"

Dani lifted her head and stared down at her car. Whoever he was, he had meant to kill Logan. "No, but I wish I did. I would kill him myself."

Langley chuckled. "I didn't just hear that. Can't say I blame you for wanting to, but you need to leave catching the perp to the police."

"Logan's not going to sit around twiddling his thumbs waiting for you to catch this guy."

"That doesn't surprise me, considering who he is."

"He told you?"

"This morning when I had the gall not to take him as seriously as he thought I should. Don't get me wrong. I believed him, but your boyfriend thought I should make this my top priority."

"He's not my boyfriend."

"If you say so. Anyway, Kincaid's got top-secret clearance and knows things that would give me nightmares. Add to that, he's got access to the kind of toys my department doesn't even bother dreaming about, they are so far out of reach. So yeah, to some extent, I'm gonna look the other way where your ninja boy's concerned."

He glanced down the ravine at her Cherokee. "Whoever this nutcase is, he upped the stakes with this little stunt. But, Miss Dani, if your not-boyfriend so much as puts a scratch on this character except in self-defense, I'll throw his ass in jail. I'm trusting you to see he toes the line."

Like she could stop Logan from doing whatever he thought necessary to protect her. Keeping the thought to herself, she put her hand on the detective's shoulder and levered herself up.

"For now, all I care about is getting him to the hospital. He needs to have a doctor look at that bump on his head." She brushed off the seat of her jeans and returned to Logan's side.

Dani sat beside the bed and sipped a cup of coffee. She'd insisted Logan take her bed as there was a comfortable chair in her room where she could keep an eye on him. A vanilla-scented candle burned on the night table, allowing her to see his face. Considering the kind of work he did, a mild concussion was probably nothing to him, but it scared the hell out of her.

She mentally reviewed the things she needed to watch for. Thankfully, there had been no sign of nausea or slurred speech. She chuckled. His speech had been perfectly fine when he'd declared he had no intention of spending the night in the hospital. He'd claimed his head hardly hurt, but knowing Logan, if he would admit that much, then he did have a headache.

"Are you going to sit there and stare at me all night?"

Startled, she spilled hot coffee on her hand. "Ouch!" She set the cup on the table and wiped her hand on the afghan spread over her lap. "You're awake."

Sitting on the edge of the bed, she placed her hand on his forehead. No fever, thank God. Was fever a symptom? Crap, she should have gone into nursing. "How do you feel?"

He reached up and turned on the bedside lamp, squinted when the light hit his eyes, and turned it back off. "I'm fine." The doubt must have shown on her face because he added, "Really."

"He tried to kill you." She shuddered at the thought of a world without him in it. She had lost Evan; she could not lose Logan, too.

Pushing himself up against the pillows, he took her hand. "I'm still here, aren't I?"

His hand, so big and strong, comforted her. He knew things—was trained to vanquish enemies. He would not leave her.

"Logan," she whispered.

"Mmm?"

"Would you hold me?"

He pulled her to his bare chest. The light dusting of dark hair tickled her nose as she burrowed her face against his skin. He had showered when they arrived home, and he smelled like the bay-rum-scented soap she kept in the guest bath. God, how she missed the feel of strong arms wrapped around her and couldn't resist snuggling up against his side.

The burning candle cast flickering shadows on the ceiling and over his face. Set on low, the soft swish of the ceiling fan and the beat of his heart beneath her ear were the only sounds in the room. If he weren't injured, she would have tried to seduce him. Since that wasn't going to happen and she was too keyed up to sleep, she wanted to talk. Would he tell her about his life if she asked?

"Is your mother still alive?" The silence stretched and she thought he wasn't going to answer. Then the hand at her back started to move, slowly caressing her as he began to talk.

"No, she died three years ago, and I may sound like a coldhearted bastard for saying this, but it was a relief."

"Why?"

His hand stilled and his chest rose as he sighed. He obviously didn't like talking about his mother, but Dani hoped he would continue. She also wanted him to keep rubbing her back. His hand started moving again. "That feels good," she said.

"Are you sure you want to hear this? It's not a pretty story."

She lifted her head and looked at him. "Please."

He held her gaze for a moment and then pressed her head back down on his chest. "My mother was the town drunk. Not satisfied with only one title, she also claimed the distinction of being the town whore. It's a toss-up as to which she did best.

"She brought home men who smelled so bad I had to scrub the stench from the walls after they left. She brought home men so drunk they passed out and fell on their face before they could get between her legs. Those were my favorites because I could just drag them outside and dump them on the street. The worst were the ones I had to protect Maria from."

The marvelous Maria? "Who's Maria?"

"My sister."

"Oh." The degree of happiness she felt at this news surprised her. Thinking that she had been jealous of his sister, she bit down on her bottom lip to keep from smiling. God, the adjectives she had assigned the poor girl. Dani sat up and tucked her legs under her. "Tell me about your sister."

"I don't usually talk about her. Not because I'm ashamed of her, but because she's special. There was no one on my SEAL team I wanted fantasizing about her. If they knew about her, they would want to see a photo. Once they did, they would've drooled on it, and I would've had to kill them." He grinned, but she was sure he was dead serious.

"Would you show me her picture sometime?"

"Go in my room and get my wallet off the dresser."

Dani scrambled off the bed, grabbed his wallet, and returned, handing it to him. He opened it, removed a photo, and then turned on the lamp. The girl staring back at Dani was drop-dead gorgeous. Long dark hair fell over her shoulders and down her back. Her eyes were almond shaped, her cheekbones high, and her full lips parted in a beautiful smile. But it was her black eyes sparkling with humor and mischief that told Dani she would like this girl.

"I see why you didn't want to show this picture to the guys. They would've driven you crazy wanting to meet her."

"Buchanan and Turner have met her. It was impossible to keep her a secret once they came to work for me, but I made sure they knew the danger of thinking of her as more than my sister."

"How old is she?"

He took the picture and looked at it, his eyes turning soft and loving. "Just turned nineteen. She's a sophomore at Florida State."

"So, it's just you and Maria?" She wanted to hear more about the two of them. From what he'd said, they hadn't had an easy life.

"Yeah. I have no idea who my father is or Maria's. They were probably Navy men since Lovey Dovey mostly worked the bars surrounding the naval air station. When I was fifteen, there came a day when there was no milk in the house for Maria. A baby needs milk, so I tried to steal some at the convenience store near my house. I got caught by the owner. It was the luckiest day of my life. Mrs. Jankowski grabbed my hand and marched me home to discuss my sticky fingers with my parents. She took about thirty seconds to assess the situation before appointing herself my and Maria's guardian angel."

"What happened then?"

He chuckled. "She gave me a choice of going to jail or coming to work for her. Not knowing a fifteen-year-old would likely be turned over to social services and not sent to jail, I chose her. She kept Maria supplied with milk, put me to work in her store, and taught me the meaning of honor."

Fascinated, she asked, "So, you adopted her as the mother you wished you had?"

A fond smile curved his lips. "Something like that. She was a taskmaster, giving no quarter. As soon as school was over, I had to go home, get Maria, and bring her to the store. Mrs. Jankowski set up a little play area in her office for Maria, and as soon as we arrived, I sat at her desk to do my homework. Once it was done, she looked it over, and if it met with her approval, I was put to work. I swept floors, carried out trash, stocked shelves.

"At first I hated her. No one had ever made me do my homework before, but about two months into my captivity, miraculous things began to happen. Science started to get interesting, turned out I had a knack for math and languages, and geography was fascinating. My grades went from failing to average to above average to the day when I got my report card and stared in amazement at all the A's."

"Mrs. Jankowski sounds like an incredible woman. Is she still alive? I'd like to meet her someday."

He smiled and Dani studied the man who had made something of himself in spite of all the strikes against him. Tears burned her eyes. What a sad, lost little boy he must have been before his savior rescued him and his sister. And then to discover his talents, grasping onto learning everything he could from his studies as a means to escape his environment. He had transformed himself from a throwaway kid to her Renaissance man. Oh God, he wasn't hers, she didn't want him to be, but she could easily fall for him.

That scared her.

He wasn't a sweet, lovable bear-of-a-man like Evan. He was hard and unyielding—arrogant. There was nothing sweet about him. But, merciful heavens, she wanted him. He made her pulse race and her body want. It was lust, that was all. Lust could be assuaged.

His hand came up to cradle her face. "Someday, perhaps," he said as his thumb slid gently across her bottom lip.

Someday what? Lord, the man had the ability to steal her wits. Hypnotized by the desire she saw in his gaze, she lowered her mouth to his. His eyes darkened as his arm wrapped around her back, pulling her hard against him.

"Dani," he whispered, making her name sound like something precious.

"Please." *Oh God, please don't stop.*

He reached up to turn off the lamp and stilled. She felt the change in him under the palm she rested on his bare chest. His muscles tensed, the arm at her back fell to the bed, and he took a deep breath.

What had she done wrong?

CHAPTER EIGHT

Logan blamed his lapse on his head wound.

How Dani had wormed his past out of him, he didn't know. He talked of it to no one. Only Maria and Mrs. Jankowski were privy to most of the story because they were a part of it. Maybe the pain pills he'd taken at the hospital had given him a loose tongue.

The way those green eyes had turned all watery and soft on his behalf had been his undoing—that and the apple pie scent of her hair. He shouldn't have left the lamp on. If he hadn't turned his head to find the switch, he wouldn't now be looking at Evan's picture. He was about to dishonor himself with his best friend's wife.

Mrs. Jankowski had drilled into him a keen sense of ethical conduct. "Honor," she'd often said, "is how a noble man lives his life. He does not steal, he does not bully those weaker than him, and he does not covet another man's wife."

It was years before Logan accidently learned Mrs. Jankowski's husband had left her for their neighbor, and likely the reason she considered the last item on her list important. And because a young boy liked the idea of being a noble man—something he'd believed beyond his reach before Mrs. Jankowski barreled her way into his life—he had adopted her principles as his own.

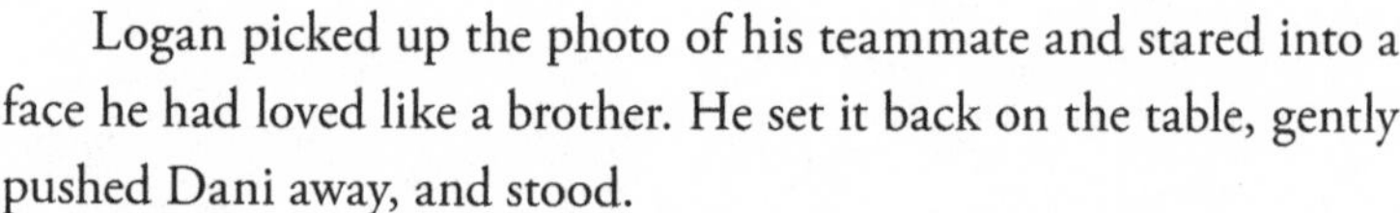

Logan picked up the photo of his teammate and stared into a face he had loved like a brother. He set it back on the table, gently pushed Dani away, and stood.

"Why?"

He had reached the doorway when she asked her question. He stopped, turned, and met her gaze. She knelt in the middle of the bed, her eyes full of hurt. Mrs. Jankowski would not be proud of him at this moment.

"It's a matter of honor," he said, and returned to his room.

The next morning—always up by six—Logan was in the kitchen making breakfast when Dani stumbled in, made a cup of coffee, and then disappeared back into her room. "Good morning to you, too," he muttered. Was she angry about last night?

She could have at least asked how his head was. Christ, he was really mucking things up. Since arriving, he'd insulted her, wrecked her car, and was no closer to catching the creep stalking her. He shoveled eggs into his mouth and again considered bringing Buchanan up to guard her. No. No way was he letting Romeo anywhere near her.

Irritated about everything, he decided he shouldn't be the only one not having a good day. He called Jake Buchanan to give him hell.

"What time is it?" Buchanan asked, sounding half-asleep.

"I don't give a damn about the time. I want to know if there are prints on the fucking bear."

"What bug crawled up your butt? I left you a message last night telling you what we got."

Damn, he hadn't bothered checking his messages. "Humor me here and tell me again."

Logan heard a big sigh from Buchanan and then a female voice in the background. Typical Romeo.

"Can't this wait until I pour about five cups of coffee down my throat? Better yet, why don't you hang up and listen to my voice mail? I've got a bit of sweetness here, wanting my attention."

Meanness crept into Logan's voice. "If you still want to be employed tomorrow, tell me about the damned fingerprints."

"Yes, sir." Logan could almost hear Buchanan's salute. "We lifted a thumbprint. Strange thing is, there were no matches, but the whorls and pattern lines are similar to Prescott's. The print's not Evan's, but almost could be. What does it mean, boss?"

Damn. He'd started having a suspicion, but had hoped it wasn't true. "It means you send your guest home, and then spend today delving into Evan's life. His parents, birth certificate, everything, no matter how insignificant you think it is. Put Turner on a plane and send him to Dallas. Tell him to track down anyone who might remember the Prescotts—old neighbors, church, whatever. You got that, Romeo?"

"Not having fun in Asheville, boss?"

"Go to hell," Logan said, and clicked off.

The rest of his eggs had congealed into an unappetizing mess by the time he hung up. He crammed two pieces of bacon and the last of his toast into his mouth, and then walked outside. Taking a deep breath of the crisp, early-morning mountain air, he tried to find his balance. The woman hiding in her room was throwing his world out of alignment. He just didn't know what to do about it.

Logan stood on the deck and watched the sun come up over the mountain. When it was light enough to see the oak tree, he focused on it, but didn't sense anyone there. *Who the hell are you?* The back door creaked open and he turned.

His gaze hungrily slid over Dani, taking in the white T-shirt that showed a slit of stomach above the waist of a pair of cutoff jeans, lingering a moment on the silver belly ring, and then on down to the latest toenail color, a purple so dark it was almost black. Did she change the color of polish to suit her moods? Should he take the near black as a warning?

"When you're done ogling me, maybe you'll tell me why you're looking into Evan's background."

Yep, black toenails didn't bode well. Not wanting to answer her question yet and since ogling her obviously annoyed her, he made a slow perusal in reverse direction, from her toes up. When he reached her eyes, he cocked a brow. "Sorry, did you say something?"

"You're an ass," she said, disappearing back inside to the sound of the slamming door.

He couldn't deny the reality of their situation, and the sooner she accepted it, the sooner she would stop looking at him with hurt in those Irish green eyes. Not only was she Evan's wife, but Logan Kincaid wasn't good enough for her. How could a woman born into a house with seven bathrooms ever love a man who grew up in little more than a glorified shed with one barely working bathroom, a man whose mother spread her legs for any man with a few bucks in his pocket?

Never going to happen.

Dani aimed a kick at the foot of her bed. "Crap!" She hopped in a circle and then sat, holding her toe. Madder at herself than Logan for letting him get under her skin, she threw herself back on the bed. When his gaze had roamed over her body, she'd seen the hunger in his eyes, had wanted to tear off her clothes and jump on him right then. He wanted her, but didn't like it.

Why couldn't they have hot, mind-boggling sex? She wouldn't expect more from him. But no, he had his damn honor. "Stupid man."

"I assume you mean me."

She lifted onto her elbows and glared at him. He stood in the middle of the doorway, his hands in his pockets. God help her, one look at him and she was ready to drool. "Do you make a habit of eavesdropping on other people's conversations?"

He shrugged. "I'm not sure talking to yourself constitutes a conversation, but I could ask the same."

She sat up. "You have me there. I heard the end of your phone call. Was that Jake on the phone, and why are you investigating Evan?"

Startling her, he walked in, slid his arms under her legs, and picked her up, carrying her toward the living room. Holy Batman, he was strong. "What are you doing?"

"I can't talk to you when you're on your bed. My mind doesn't work right."

She was face-to-face with him, and if she dared, she could close the inches between them and kiss him, but she still smarted from his rejection. He had removed the bandage from his forehead, and she gently put her finger next to the cut. "Do you have any idea how lucky you are? God, when I think what could have happened."

He stilled and focused on her. "If I were truly lucky—" He gave a little shake of his head before continuing down the hall.

"If what?"

Stopping in the doorway to the living room, his gaze fell to her mouth. "I would have the right to do this." His face lowered until his lips covered hers.

She wrapped her arms around his neck and closed her eyes. He feathered kisses over her mouth, soft brushes that tingled wherever he touched, her top lip, the bottom, the corners. When she sighed in pleasure, his arm tightened around her back and he deepened the kiss.

When he nipped on her lower lip, she opened her mouth for him. Their tongues tentatively touched, and then tangled. He tasted of coffee and mint toothpaste.

He pulled her tight against his chest and made a low growling noise deep in his throat. The sound excited her until it mixed with the cry of a baby. Tearing his mouth away, he practically threw her on the couch.

"Christ, Dani, you're killing me here." He backed up until he fell onto the chair behind him.

Why did he look so miserable? He was unfathomable, a mystery, and he intrigued the hell out of her. In bed, she just knew he would take her to the stars, perhaps even to the outer edges of the universe. Making love with Evan had always been tender and beautiful. Sometimes she had thought her husband held back, afraid of hurting her. With Logan, it would be hot, wild, and out of control. There would be no holding back for him.

The man had unleashed something feral inside her, and she did a thing she never would have dreamed of ten minutes ago. She stood and went to him, braced her palms on the back of his chair, and lowered her face to within inches of his.

"I don't want to kill you, Logan, I only want to fuck you." When he parted his lips in surprise, she covered his mouth with hers and licked his tongue.

As she left the room, she glanced over her shoulder and winked. If ever a man looked lost, it was Logan at that moment. She almost felt sorry for him. It wasn't until she was sitting in the rocking chair and nursing Regan while staring at Dr. Seuss curtains that she realized he had never answered her question.

Why was he looking into Evan's childhood?

Dani sat in the sales office at the Jeep dealership and stared moodily at the two men bargaining over the price of her new Cherokee. Logan had to be the most stubborn man she had ever met. Never mind that she could afford to buy her own damn car; never mind her insurance would cover the cost. Logan was adamant that as he had wrecked her Cherokee, he would buy her a new one.

Exactly what services he provided the government and Fortune 500 companies other than security, she had no clue. Based on his SEAL background, there were probably some black-ops jobs in there, too. Even though she was certain he was doing well, he worked hard for his money and shouldn't be spending it on her. The last thing she wanted to do was take anything from the boy who'd grown up with nothing.

Once the two he-men finished their grunting—finally settling on a price that seemed to satisfy them both—Logan whipped out his phone, called his office, and told someone named Barbie to arrange a bank transfer. A few minutes later, the salesman accepted a call from Logan's bank confirming that the money was on its way. The keys were dropped in her hand, and just like that, she had a new car.

"Jeez, Logan, next time I need something done fast and efficiently, I'm putting you in charge," she said after the salesman left to put a temporary tag on the Jeep.

No answer, not even a glance at her as he picked up Regan's carrier and walked out of the office. Dani narrowed her eyes at his back.

In the parking lot, she stared at the sleek black Grand Cherokee Summit, loaded with every option imaginable. It really was a beauty. They moved Regan's car seat to The Black, the name Dani decided to give the Jeep. After leaving the keys to Scott's car with

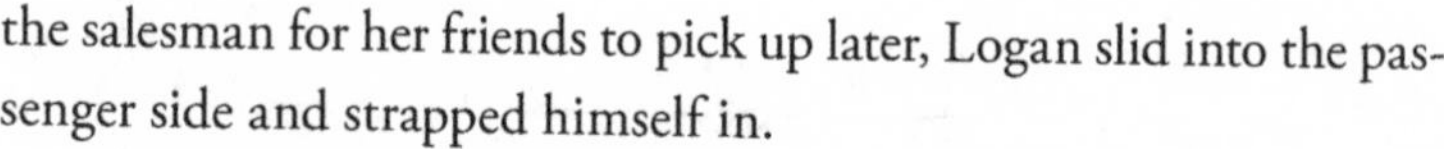

the salesman for her friends to pick up later, Logan slid into the passenger side and strapped himself in.

Dani opened the driver's door and poked her head in. "Aren't you driving?"

He stared out his window, giving her the back of his head. "Nope."

The blasted man had been like this ever since she'd made her daring announcement. It pleased her while at the same time irked her. She had gotten to him, but his resolve to ignore her grated.

"Fine." She slammed the door and immediately regretted her show of temper and for hurting The Black. "I'm sorry," she said, and patted the glossy door. Once Regan was safely secured, Dani slid behind the wheel, turned the key, and backed out.

"Where to now, ninja boy?"

She kept her face forward, but watched him from the corner of her eye.

He turned his head toward her. "Ninja boy?"

"Hmm?" All morning, he had warily watched her the way one would a copperhead snake. She considered biting him, but reached over and squeezed his forearm instead. "Oh, thanks for the car. I love it."

His eyes lowered to her hand, then back up to her face. "Least I could do."

There were things she wished he'd do. She shifted into drive and eased through the dealership lot. "I don't want to go home yet. What would you like for lunch?"

"Whatever you feel like."

Dani stopped the car. "I'm not moving another inch until you adjust your attitude. You've been pissy all morning. Enough already."

His lips thinned and he put his hand on the door handle. He was going to get out. If he did, when he finally made his way back to her house, he was going to find all his clothes and spy toys in a pile in her yard.

"I swear to God, Dani, you're making me crazy. Just take me to the Harley dealership so I can pick up my bike."

She bit back a smile. She was getting to him, all right. Evan had been so easygoing, always happy. Whenever she thought of her husband, she thought of peace and comfort, a big, cuddly man who always looked on the bright side of things. Logan was leaner and meaner, a challenge that stirred her blood. Living with him would not be a walk in the park, but it would be damned interesting.

Why was she thinking of living with him? All she wanted from him was a hot affair, and then they would each return to their lives when all of this was over. Her heart gave a painful little flutter, but she ignored it and put her mind to new ways of making Logan crazy.

Logan leaned on the deck rail and took a deep drink of his beer. So all she wanted was a good fuck. Dani wasn't Lovey Dovey. Somewhere in his brain he knew that. But when she'd leaned over him and made her little announcement, he'd suddenly been fifteen again.

Squeezing his eyes shut, he willed the memory away, refusing to go there. The only good thing to come of that morning was his decision to escape. It was the day he'd decided to join the military as soon as he was old enough. He'd started studying each branch, and when he had read about the SEALs, he made up his mind that he was going to be one.

They were tough. They were dangerous. No one messed with them, especially their mothers.

He'd learned everything he could about the SEALs. For the next three years, whenever he had free time, he practiced the drills.

He ran, worked out, swam for miles in the ocean, learned to hold his breath for three minutes while sitting on the seafloor, and two minutes while swimming with a pack on his back. When he turned eighteen, he put Maria in the care of Mrs. Jankowski, and severed all ties with Lovey Dovey.

Good riddance.

He lifted the bottle to his lips, angry he couldn't get Dani's words out of his mind. The rational part of his brain knew she didn't understand the impact of what she'd said, but he still resented her for making him feel like that boy again.

The boy from the wrong side of the tracks had no intention of accommodating Little Miss Rich Girl. If all she wanted from him was a fuck, then she could find someone else. He wanted her too much, loved her too much to be a one-night stand.

Christ, he was royally FUBARed. He couldn't take less because one taste of her would never be enough, and he couldn't take all of her because of his honor and respect for a fallen comrade. That was before he even considered the differences in their backgrounds and the whore's blood pumping through his heart.

The back door opened and Dani poked her head out. "Dinner's ready." She disappeared back inside.

Logan sighed. It had been like this between them all day. She didn't understand why he was acting like an ass, and there was no way he'd ever tell her. Even now, whenever the memory surfaced, he felt dirty. Finishing off his beer, he took a deep breath and willed memories of his mother to hell, where they belonged.

Inside the cabin, he stood in the mudroom and inhaled deeply. Lasagna or spaghetti and garlic bread. He hoped for the former. Another inhale. Apple pie? His mouth watering, he entered the kitchen. If he ever married Dani, he would have to run ten miles twice a day. He gave a slight shake of his head to banish that kind of thinking. Somehow, he had to find a way to wipe the picture of domestic bliss with her from his mind.

"Sit and eat before everything gets cold."

Logan saluted her. "Yes, ma'am."

Brilliant green eyes flashed fire, but she stayed quiet. Logan took his seat and dug into the lasagna with gusto. The garlic bread dripped with butter and never had he tasted better. An extra benefit, there would be no kissing after eating it. He took a moment to consider if that was intentional, but the food was so damn good, he didn't ponder the question long.

There had been so many years in his life when food had been scarce, sometimes nothing more in the house than a package of hotdogs or bologna. Bread had been an extravagance. If he wanted to eat something besides a cold hotdog, it was up to him to cook. By the age of seven, the kitchen was his territory. Sometimes, he stole money from Lovey Dovey's johns to buy food when they were too drunk to notice. Other times, he stole from his mother.

Logan pushed his empty plate aside. "That was unbelievably good."

"Hope you saved room for apple pie and coffee."

He groaned. "Later." They had eaten their dinner in silence, and he couldn't stand it any longer. "Look, I'm sorry. I know I've been a jerk today."

Her gaze narrowed. "You've been the biggest asshat today I've ever had the displeasure to know."

Suddenly he felt like laughing. How could he not love a woman who didn't think twice about giving as good as she got? Lovey Dovey had gotten it all wrong. Cowering, simpering, and acting like a woman without a brain wasn't the way to go.

His gaze soaked up the woman who didn't hesitate to knock him down a peg or two. Auburn hair curled around her face and

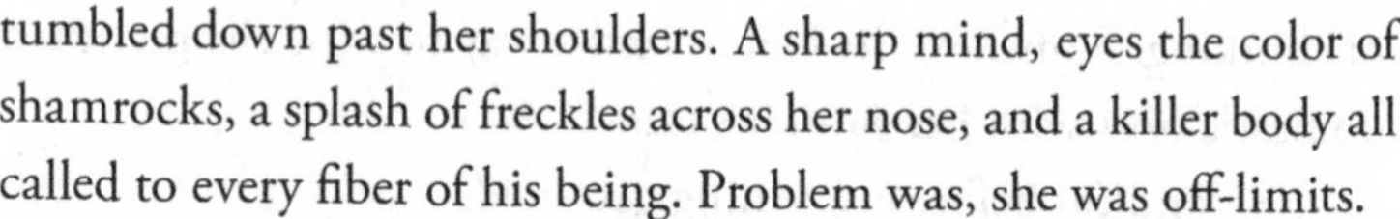

tumbled down past her shoulders. A sharp mind, eyes the color of shamrocks, a splash of freckles across her nose, and a killer body all called to every fiber of his being. Problem was, she was off-limits.

She ran her finger around the rim of her glass. "Do you want to talk about it?"

Not in this lifetime—or even the next—and especially not to her. "There's nothing to talk about. I'm just frustrated is all. I'm spinning in circles with this guy and getting nowhere." Her eyes searched his, and he didn't think she believed a word he said.

She shrugged. "We'll have it your way for now. There's a ball game on, Cubs and the Braves. Wanna watch it?"

"Only if you're for the Braves. I'm a Cubbies fan, so I need someone to make fun of when they send Atlanta home with their tail between their legs."

"Ha, so not happening."

Halfway through the game, Dani uncurled her legs and propped her feet on the coffee table. Logan noticed there was no color on her toes. Why was that? He had learned to gauge her mood by the color of her polish. What did bare toes mean? A piece of popcorn hit his forehead. He jerked his gaze up to see Dani getting ready to throw another one.

"Why are you staring at my feet like that?"

Grabbing a handful of popcorn from the bowl on his lap, he threw it at her. Her grin was wicked and her eyes glittered with mischief.

"Food fight!" she yelled, and ducked behind her chair, taking her bowl with her. Missiles in the form of popcorn flew his way.

Logan stared at the empty chair. "Exactly how old are you right now, Dani?"

Her head poked up. "You mean right now, this minute?"

He nodded.

"I'd say about five." She giggled, threw more corn at him, and ducked.

Logan had no idea how to play. Just another thing Lovey Dovey had never taught him. But like everything else he knew how to do, he could damn well learn.

Going into soldier mode, he surveyed his surroundings and decided on a surprise rear attack. With his bowl in the cradle of his arm, he slipped behind the end of the sofa. Her head edged up over the chair, and he tossed some popcorn at her. Delighted laughter flowed from her. When she ducked, he slid the sofa away from the wall and started crawling behind it.

"Where are you?" she called in a singsong voice.

"Right here," he said from behind her, and dumped the contents of his bowl on her head.

She screamed. He tackled her and had her facedown on the floor before she knew what was happening. Straddling her, he wrapped his hands around her wrists and held them above her head. Leaning down, he pressed his mouth to her ear. "Surrender or bear the consequences."

Her hysterical laughter caused her butt to jiggle against his groin. Logan managed to suppress a groan, but couldn't resist the urge to press his lips on the soft white spot below her earlobe. He touched the tip of his tongue to her pulse point and felt the throb of her lifeblood.

She quieted and arched her neck, giving him better access. All the reasons why he shouldn't be doing this forgotten, he nipped at her skin, then soothed the little red marks with soft kisses. She pushed her bottom against him and wiggled it. So damn good, even with their clothing between them, she felt so damned good.

"Logan?"

He flipped her over. "I'm here."

Still straddling her, he lowered his mouth to hers. She tasted delicious—like buttered popcorn. Never again would he eat the stuff without thinking of Dani. She slid her hands under his shirt, trailing a path up his sides and over his ribs. Did his skin feel as hot to her as it did to him? Lifting up, he stared down at her. Her lips were moist from his kisses, her eyes were the green of a storm-tossed sea, and he was turning into a damned poet.

"Why are you chuckling?"

Was he? "I want you so bad it hurts."

"You think that's funny?"

"So much the opposite that one can't help but laugh." Holding her gaze, he pushed her T-shirt up over her bra. Christ, he was doomed. The bra was virginal white and little more than lace—innocence and naughty all in one package. How was he supposed to resist that? He simply couldn't. Lowering his face to a breast, he sucked lace and nipple into his mouth.

"Oh," she murmured, drawing the word out.

His cock strained against his jeans and he rubbed it against her. He felt her hands fumbling with the snap on his jeans, and when he reached down to help, the phone and doorbell rang simultaneously.

They both froze.

"Let it ring," she said.

He didn't know which she meant, maybe both, but he stood and backed away. Fuck. He'd come too damned close this time, the thread on his control slipping knot by knot. "You get the phone, I'll get the door." Turning away, Logan was halfway across the room when he heard the voice on the speakerphone.

"Danielle, I'm coming for you."

CHAPTER NINE

Dani listened to the voice that sounded so much like Evan's. There had been a time when she'd loved that voice, but no longer. The man on the other end of the phone had taken something precious from her. She clicked off, unable to respond. Instantly, Logan was behind, wrapping her in the safety of his arms.

"What does he mean by he's coming for me?"

Logan tightened his hold on her. "I won't let him hurt you."

Leaning back, she rested her head against his chest and drew on his strength. "Who was at the door?"

"I don't know, I didn't make it that far."

She pulled away and went to the peephole. "It's the delivery truck with my window." When she started to unbolt the door, Logan stopped her.

"Let me." He signed for the packages and carried both in as if they weighed no more than a five-pound bag of potatoes.

"I'll get the box cutter."

The antique stained-glass window was as beautiful as she remembered and the mirror just as gaudy. She wasn't sure which she loved more. Seeing the silhouette of the naked woman, Dani remembered Logan's suggestion to write a story in which her heroine finds the hero making love to his mistress in front of the mirror.

Logan had a mysterious smile on his face as he looked at it. His lashes lifted and he focused on her.

The air crackled, sending shivers up her arms. Was he remembering the scene he'd painted for her? Was he imagining the two of them acting it out?

"Where do you want these?" he asked, breaking their connection.

"In my bedroom." She got some hooks, and after he hung the stained glass in front of her window and mounted the mirror on the wall, Dani stood back and admired her purchases.

"That has to be the ugliest mirror I've ever seen, but there's something about it."

There was. "I know. I think it probably once hung in a brothel. Imagine the stories it could tell. I can't get your idea out of my mind. May have to write it. I'll call it something like, *The Naked Earl and the Secrets of the Mirror*, or maybe, *The Naughty Earl and the Naked Lady.* The naked lady could refer to all three: the mirror silhouette, the mistress, and his betrothed."

"I thought only the earl and mistress were naked."

"Little do you know."

Something flashed in his eyes. "You have no idea."

What did that mean? Standing close to him, Dani felt his heat, inhaled his scent, and pushed her feet onto the floor to keep from crawling up his body and wrapping her legs around his hips.

"Well, I guess I'll call it a night."

"Dani, about earlier—"

"If you're going to apologize again, don't. I swear to God, Logan, don't you dare."

His cell rang. He took it from his pocket, glanced at the screen, and sighed. "Kincaid," he said.

She saw the caller ID said Suzanne, but Dani heard the irritation in his voice. So, Slinky Suzanne wasn't the wall between them.

Dani was glad to know it, but if not her, then who? She thought he would leave so he could speak in private, but he didn't.

While he listened, he walked to the mirror and traced the naked lady's outline. Transfixed, she watched his finger as it tracked the curve of the silhouette's breast, down her belly, and then lower. Dani shivered. As if he knew what he was doing to her, he turned his gaze on her while his finger lazily retraced its path. By some kind of osmosis, she felt his touch glide over the same places on her body. Holy moly, she had bought a magic mirror.

"I don't know when I'll be home," he said, breaking the spell. He turned his back and Dani shamelessly listened to his conversation. "How many ways do I need to say there is no us, Suzanne?"

Dani grinned and decided to paint her toenails.

Logan stared at the phone. "Guess she didn't like that."

"Mmm? Why's that?" Sitting on her bed, Dani painted her big toe, then stopped to admire the color.

"She hung up on me." He sat in the chair, stretched out his legs, and crossed his ankles.

"Does that upset you?"

"Do I look upset?"

Dani tilted her head and studied him. "No, can't say as you do."

"What color is that?"

She held a foot up. "Glittering Sunshine. Like it?"

"Not sure I've ever seen yellow polish before, but since it means you're happy, yeah, I do."

"Why do you say that?"

"What?"

"That it means I'm happy."

"I finally figured it out, but if I tell you, you'll stop."

He seemed right at home lounging in her bedroom. She liked the intimacy of a man sitting in her room, watching her paint her toes. And this one was fascinating. Without doubt, he had demons. His childhood had much to do with his hang-ups, she was sure, and she wanted to know more. Not wanting to spoil his amiable mood, however, she held in her questions.

Finished, she capped the polish, leaned back on her elbows, and wiggled her toes. "So, tell me what you think you've figured out."

"No."

"I'll tickle it out of you."

His eyes glittered with mischief. "You can try."

She swung her feet over the bed. "You are ticklish, aren't you?"

"I don't know."

"How can you not know?"

He shrugged. "No one's ever tried."

The man just kept breaking her heart. Didn't all mothers tickle their babies? "Well, we'll have to rectify that." She stood, but before she could approach him, she heard Regan.

"I'll get her," he said, and left.

Dani thought he seemed to welcome the excuse to leave. He obviously resented the chemistry between them, and she was determined to find out why. It wasn't because of another woman, unless there was someone she didn't know about. No, if he loved another, he wouldn't be eyeing her with longing. Logan wasn't the kind of man who played around. The only explanation he'd given was that it was a matter of honor, but honor to whom? Evan? Whatever his thinking, he held it close. Well, except for the desire he couldn't hide, which was more obvious than he probably wished.

She was a romance writer, after all, and had trained herself to watch lovers' eyes. When she and Evan had gone out, sometimes he would tease her about being more interested in the undercurrents of those around them than him. Not true, she'd protested while feeling guilty that sometimes it was true, especially if she was in the middle of a work-in-progress.

What she saw in Logan's eyes made her want to run to her computer and find the words to capture that hot, I-want-to-devour-you look he turned her way. God, she wanted to explore the possibilities his heated glances promised. For sure, if—no, *when*—it happened, they would burn the sheets to ashes.

As soon as her stalker was caught, Logan would leave. He would always be only a phone call away if she needed him, which was a comfort, but each day she was with him, he grew more captivating. She wanted to learn his secrets, soothe his hurts, but most of all she wanted to make love with him.

Oh yes, Doxy Dani, that was her. She gave one last admiring look at her sparkling yellow toenails and then went to find Logan and her daughter.

The next morning, after dropping Dani off at Jared and Scott's, Logan made another round of the nearby motels. Although he kept an eye out for the black Ford truck, he thought it likely the man had changed vehicles. After the seventh stop, he decided to give up for the day. A few miles down the road, however, he noticed a seedy motel set back from the road, almost hidden by a secondhand clothing store. What the hell, might as well check it out.

"I'm looking for my brother," he told the man behind the counter.

Bloodshot eyes distorted by the thickest pair of glasses Logan had ever seen peered back at him. "And I'm Santa Claus."

Logan ignored the sarcasm and described a bald Evan. Recognition flared in the man's eyes before he hid it. Logan slid a twenty halfway across the counter, but kept his hand over it. "You have a name for him?"

The man eyed the money. "Would you believe John Smith?"

"I believe that's the name he registered under, yes. Is he still checked in?"

"Left yesterday."

Shit. "What kind of car did he drive?"

"Never saw him driving one."

Logan pulled the twenty back his way.

"Never said I didn't see a car parked in front of his room."

He pushed the bill back toward the clerk. "What kind?"

"A white one."

Tired of the game, Logan pocketed the twenty and turned to leave.

"Ford Taurus. Late model."

"Anything else you can tell me about him?"

"Would think you'd know him better 'n me, you being his brother and all."

"Humor me."

"Didya hear the one about the three ducks that went in—"

Logan grabbed the man's collar and pulled him halfway across the counter. "I don't think you're as stupid as you want me to believe. You know something, and I want to know what."

"Could be I have a thing for numbers. Let go, and I'll tell ya."

Logan left with the license plate number. He considered going to the police department and giving it to Detective Langley, but decided against it. It would be better to have a heads-up on who this character was before involving the police any further.

Seeing a McDonald's ahead, he pulled into the drive-through, got a hamburger and coffee, and then called Buchanan. After relaying the plate numbers, he asked for an update.

"Turner's in Dallas, but hasn't had much luck yet finding anyone who remembers the family before Prescott's mother supposedly died."

Logan frowned. "Why do you say 'supposedly'?"

"So far, we haven't found a death certificate. When did you say she died?"

"Evan said he was two, so that would be what, twenty-six years ago?"

"Well, we've looked for one from the time Prescott was born to several years after and found nothing, but we'll keep searching."

"You got a copy of Evan's birth certificate?" Logan asked.

"Yeah, why?"

"Check the hospital records and see if there's another one."

"I'm confused. Another one for Prescott?"

Logan hesitated. The idea had been brewing, but he'd yet to put it into words. It sounded crazy, but the feeling was too strong to ignore. "No, for Evan's twin."

There was a long pause. "I didn't know he had one."

"I'm not sure he did, and if so, I don't think he knew. You said the fingerprint was very similar to Evan's, and I did some research. That's common with twins, and there are some other things that make me think it's possible. Call me when you know something."

Logan clicked off and scanned the area. There were two white Taurus cars in the parking lot. Why couldn't Dickhead drive a purple Caddy? Crumbling up the hamburger wrapper, he stuck it and his empty cup in the sack. He'd done as much as he could for the day, so he headed to Jared and Scott's.

Although he kept an eye on the rearview mirror, his thoughts turned to Dani. Christ, he'd almost taken her on the floor—on a bed of popcorn, no less. His intention to be honorable was seriously at risk. Next time it happened, he needed to think of Mrs. Jankowski, and how disappointed she would be if he broke her number-one rule and screwed his best friend's wife.

That damned mirror of Dani's—the way her eyes had darkened and her breath had hitched when he'd traced the nude woman's silhouette—had him wanting things. Things he'd managed to suppress for a very long time. And when she'd painted her toes the color of sunshine, unknowingly signaling she was happy, dangerous thoughts had crept into his mind. Dangerous to him anyway.

Claim Dani, make her his, and never let her go.

Yet, if he did, he'd have to face Mrs. Jankowski. From the day he'd received his first high mark in math and gotten a smothering hug from her—the first embrace of his memory—he'd begun to set goals. Get good grades, make Mrs. Jankowski happy. Work hard at the store, make Mrs. Jankowski happy. Be an honorable man, make Mrs. Jankowski happy and get a hug. Because of his self-appointed foster mother, he'd finally realized he could be more than Lovey Dovey had ever allowed him to believe.

His debt to Mrs. Jankowski was more than he could ever repay. If not for her, he would not be the man he was today, would likely be in prison. He had to decide between his love for Dani and failing the only woman who had been a steadying influence in his life. Mrs. Jankowski had, knowingly or unknowingly, set the bar high, and he suddenly had one question.

Was the bar fair?

Logan pulled over to the side of the road, his heart hammering so hard he feared he would blindly rear-end the car in front of him. He had to go see her. What if it didn't count if his best friend was dead? What if he didn't have to decide between love and honor? But he hadn't brought Evan safely home to Dani. Did that take away his right for a chance with her? He had questions only Mrs. Jankowski could answer.

There were times when the influences of the two women who'd raised him clashed and his reasoning suffered for it—a weakness that he recognized and with which he struggled. Although he had turned his back on his mother's lifestyle, he'd spent the first half of his existence living it, watching Lovey Dovey whore her way through life.

Then Mrs. Jankowski entered the picture. She'd been the light to his mother's darkness. Once she'd shown him what could be, there had been no middle ground, no shades of gray for a boy determined to make a better life for himself and his sister. She'd taught him to reach for the stars, that they could be his. Could Dani be his, or was she a star far out of his reach?

Logan leaned his head back and closed his eyes, shutting out the noise of the passing traffic. What to do about Dani? Was it wishful thinking that it wouldn't be wrong to pursue her? He could no more see the answer than he'd been able to see his hand in front of his face in a haboob, a massive sandstorm of the Middle East.

He had to talk to Mrs. Jankowski, and he didn't want to do it over the phone, so it seemed a trip home was necessary. Whether Dani liked it or not, she and Regan were coming with him. It would do Dani good to get away from this situation and spend a few days at the beach.

Logan took out his cell phone and called Mrs. Jankowski to tell her he was coming home and bringing guests. He then called Buchanan. It wouldn't hurt to meet with his team and have a strategy session to make sure they were all on the same page.

"Get anything on the license plate yet?" he asked as soon as Buchanan answered.

"Jesus, boss, you only gave me the numbers thirty minutes ago. Give a man a little time."

"And it shouldn't take more than five minutes to run it. Do you have anything?"

"Yes and no. The plate is registered to a company called Gateway, but it's a dummy corporation. Gateway is owned by The Way.

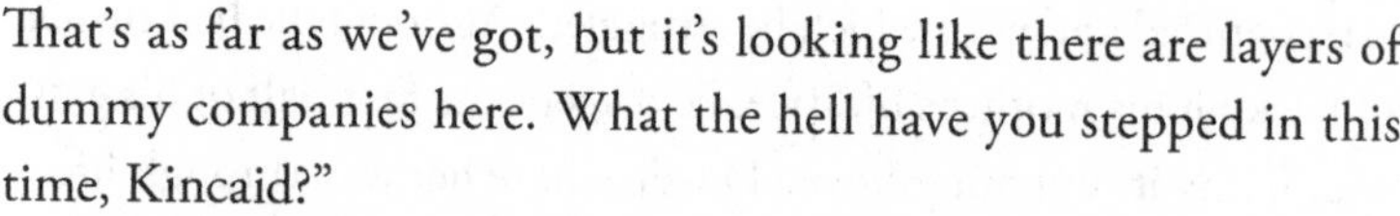

That's as far as we've got, but it's looking like there are layers of dummy companies here. What the hell have you stepped in this time, Kincaid?"

"I don't know, but I'm not liking what I'm thinking. Those names, especially The Way, have the sound of a religious group."

"Are you thinking cult, boss?"

"I don't know what to think yet. We need more information. Our man could have stolen the truck and this is nothing more than an obsession on his part. If there is some religious group involved, then what the hell could they possibly want with Dani? Get Maria on this. She has a few more weeks before fall classes start. She loves this kind of thing, and if anyone can make sense of it, she can."

"I was going to suggest that. She's been hanging out here begging for something to do."

Logan scowled at his cell. "Romeo, you get any ideas about Maria and you're a dead man." The hesitation on the other end raised the hair on Logan's neck. He hadn't missed the little glances recently occurring between Maria and Buchanan.

"Right, dead man. Got it loud and clear, boss."

Logan was about to hang up when he heard Maria's voice in the background.

"Is my brother threatening you again, Jake?"

Buchanan disconnected before Logan could hear his answer. Damn it all. It was a good thing he'd decided to go home. He needed to put a stop to whatever was starting between those two before it was too late. Romeo was . . . well, Romeo. There was no way he was going to let Buchanan sniff up Maria's skirts.

If Maria had a problem with that, he would lock her in her room until it was time for school to start. There were plenty of nice young men at the university. She needed to find one who wasn't nicknamed Romeo.

Logan started the Jeep, and as he drove, he planned how he would sneak Dani away without her stalker knowing. He also prepared for the argument he was sure she would give him about leaving Asheville, one she would lose. There was absolutely no way he was leaving her behind, unprotected. Especially if there was a cult involved. If he had to toss her over his shoulder and carry her away kicking and screaming, he would do so.

CHAPTER TEN

Dani unloaded the groceries, curious why Logan had insisted they buy food for just two days. He had something planned, but was staying closedmouthed about it. The frustrating man had also refused to tell her if he'd learned anything at any of the motels he'd stopped at, only saying they would talk later.

She sliced some strawberries and put them on the tray of Regan's highchair. "Want a strawberry?"

Regan held one up. "Wont?"

Dani opened her mouth and let Regan feed her. "Yummy."

Her daughter held out another one. "Wont?"

"No, you eat the rest. Yum, yum."

"Yummmm!" Regan screamed, and smashed the piece on the tray.

Leaving her to play with her food, Dani turned to start dinner. Logan stood in the doorway, his hair still damp from his shower. He wore jeans and a black T-shirt, and was barefoot. Unable to help herself, her gaze roamed over his body, across his broad chest, over his stomach, down to lean hips, the long legs, and his feet. She clenched her hands to keep from reaching out and running her fingers over his arms just to feel the ripple of his muscles.

She swallowed hard and lifted her gaze to his. He stared back at her, his eyes darkening to almost black, his look intense.

Remembering her resolve to rattle him, she licked her lips. One side of his mouth curved in a knowing smile—one that said he knew her game. What woman didn't love a smart man? *Whoa, where did that come from?*

Logan moved toward her in the way she thought a sleek panther would stalk something of interest, something it had caught the scent of and wanted. Her heart fluttered wildly as excitement raced through her. What was he going to do? He stopped in front of her and without saying a word, cradled her face with his hands, angled his head, and kissed her.

Her knees threatened to buckle, but she locked them in place. He didn't try to part her lips with his tongue, didn't do anything but frame her face with his warm hands and kiss her as if she were the most precious thing in the world. Something told her not to touch him, even though she ached to feel his skin under her palms, but she knew if she did, he would stop. She never wanted him to stop. Ever.

"Yummmm! Mama, yummmm."

He lifted his head, a smile playing on his mouth. "I agree. Yum."

Leaving her standing in the middle of the kitchen, dazed and unable to think, he moved to sit next to Regan. Dani touched her tingling lips. My God, the man sure knew how to kiss, but he confused her. One minute he was kissing her senseless, the next apologizing for doing it.

"You've made quite a mess here, Regan, my girl. You must be really proud of yourself," Logan said.

Dani turned to see her daughter holding out the only piece of strawberry not either in her hair, smeared over her face, or smashed on her tray.

"Wont?"

He leaned forward and let Regan put it in his mouth. "Yummmm!" Logan mimicked.

Regan laughed and slammed both hands on the tray, splattering strawberry juice. She then leaned down and licked the tray. Looking up at Logan, she grinned and said, "Mama."

"No, I'm Logan. Can you say 'Logan'?"

Regan waved at him.

"You're a smart little girl. I know you can say 'Logan.' Lo . . . gan."

She scrunched her eyebrows together. "Gan."

Logan's answering smile was one of the sweetest things Dani had ever seen.

"'Gan' will work." He slid his finger through the mess and licked it. "Yum." Turning to Dani, he grinned. "I'm not an expert on babies, but I didn't think they talked this early."

Dani shrugged. Secretly, she thought Regan was the smartest little girl in the world. "It varies. She's talking more than most at her age. Personally, I think she's going to be a jabber mouth, and there will come a day when I look fondly on the time before she could speak."

He chuckled when her daughter held out her arms the way she did when she wanted to be picked up and said, "Gan." Tears burned Dani's eyes, her hurt for the man who would never have his strawberry-smeared daughter reach for him. She'd always been sad that father and daughter would never know each other, but seeing Logan interact with Regan painted a vivid picture of how it could have been.

Logan tapped Regan's nose. "I'm not picking you up until we get you cleaned up." He glanced at Dani. "What's wrong?"

She shook her head. "Nothing."

"It's a mystery to all men why women always say 'nothing' when it is clearly something. You're about to cry. Why?"

"I was just thinking about Evan."

His face blanked. Why was that? Evan had been her husband and his best friend. Shouldn't they be able to talk about him without it causing tension? Logan was hiding something, or maybe just holding his feelings about Evan's death close.

His gaze returned to Regan, his words directed to Evan's daughter. "Your father was the most honorable man I've ever known. He was the brother I never had. As you grow older, I'll tell you stories of him so you'll know him as I did." He then leaned close to Regan's ear and whispered something.

Dani thought she heard the word "sorry," and would give anything to know what he'd said. Regan reached up and patted his face with her red-stained hands, almost as if she were absolving him of guilt. "Gan," she said.

"Jesus," he whispered just before he walked out of the room.

For the first time in her life, Dani truly understood what it meant when someone said the lightbulb went off, because it did for her in a brilliant, blinding radiance. He blamed himself for Evan's death. Of course he did. How had she not realized? He had been the team's commander, responsible for the success of their missions. If he didn't bring them home safely, Logan was the kind of man who would hold himself responsible whether warranted or not.

And of all the ones to lose, Evan had been like a brother to him. Was that why he hadn't come to see her when he got out of the hospital? Because he couldn't face her? Was that why he resisted giving in to his desire for her? What had he said a few nights ago? Something about it being a matter of honor.

Gah, men were the stupidest creatures on earth when it came to their honor. She needed to think about this and figure out how to get him to talk about it. Without doubt, he would resist—would have to be dragged by his toenails to her Dr. Phil session. Didn't matter. Whether he liked it or not, they were going to bring his demons out in the open and then blow them to smithereens.

Dani picked Regan up.

"No." She pushed away and looked at the doorway. "No, Mama. Wont Gan."

Dani froze, her heart turning over as her daughter reached another milestone. Oh my God, her first sentences and there was no one to share it with. It did no good to wish Evan were alive, though she did.

After bathing Regan and getting her to bed, Dani showered, and then took twenty minutes deciding what to wear. To go with her Mexican-themed dinner, she finally decided on a multicolored knee-length cotton skirt and a white off-the-shoulder blouse. She slipped on a pair of red-beaded earrings, along with her silver watch. She considered painting her toenails orange, but decided the yellow matched well enough. Besides, Logan said he liked the yellow.

Barefoot, she went to the kitchen to start dinner and stopped in the doorway. Wearing her apron, Logan stood at the counter, tears streaming down his face as he chopped onions.

"Logan, what are you doing?"

"Chopping the damn onions."

"I see that. Here, let me finish." Probably best she didn't tell him how adorable he looked in her lacey apron.

"No, no need for both of us to ruin our eyes. Sit. I've got dinner tonight."

"Do you know what you're doing?"

He rolled watery eyes. "I've been cooking since I was seven. If I didn't do it, we didn't eat. As we're pretty sure Maria's half-Latina, I learned to cook Mexican, Cuban, and anything remotely related to a Latin dish, thinking she should love the food of her heritage."

He chuckled. "Except for tacos and enchiladas, she hates it all. Turns out, she's a junk-food eater. Sit."

Sometimes he could break her heart. She saw a little boy, unloved and uncared for by his mother, desperately trying to learn how to make the foods he thought his sister should eat.

Although he wouldn't want her pity, she couldn't resist wrapping her arms around his waist and holding the boy that surely could have used a hug. Somehow he turned in her embrace, pulled her close, and rested his chin on her head.

"Logan?"

He kissed the top of her head. "Hush. Go sit and let me take care of you."

She could have stayed in his arms all night, but he'd offered to cook for her, something no woman could resist. "How about we take care of each other? I'll make us a pitcher of margaritas while you surprise me with your culinary skills."

Brown eyes warmed to the color of rich dark chocolate. "Works for me."

He kissed her then, in the same way he had earlier. God, she could do this with him forever. It was a soft, exploring kiss, one that said he had deep feelings for her. Was that what she wanted? She didn't know. She had thought they would have an affair as hot as a flashing fire and when it burned out, they'd return to their respective lives. He was changing the rules, but she wasn't sure she minded.

The slide of his palms down her arms sent little shivers through her. He entwined their hands, lifted his face, and stared at her as if he were searching for answers. What was the question?

She smiled and pulled her hands from his. "Right. I'll just go make the margaritas." The pitcher of margaritas made, she salted the rims and poured them each a glass. "Here you go. Can I do anything to help?"

"No, sit and relax."

As he'd already set the table, she relaxed and sipped her drink. Although she loved to cook, it was nice having him take over. He obviously knew what he was doing.

"So, did you find anything out today?" she asked.

"Yes, but we'll talk about it later, after dinner."

"All right. What would you like to talk about?"

He turned and speared her with that intense look of his. "You."

"I'm the most boring person in the world."

Leaning back, he braced his hands on the counter. "Are you? I hadn't noticed."

The way he stood accentuated the muscles in his chest and arms. How was she supposed to have a coherent thought when all she could think about was undressing him? "What do you want to know? I mean, you pretty much know everything about me. Great childhood, great parents, blah, blah, blah."

He chuckled. "All right. What about your writing? I haven't seen you doing any since I've been here."

"I'm between deadlines. I finished my children's book. It was something I really wanted to do, but I'm ready to get back to my romances. The mirror story is bubbling in my head, and I'm itching to get started on it."

"What made you want to write a children's book?"

Dani skimmed a finger around the rim of her glass and licked the salt. If she was right about Logan feeling guilty over Evan's death, the answer was going to spoil the mood, but she wanted to tell him. She gave a slight shrug.

"I did it for Regan and in a way, for Evan, too. The title's *My Daddy Book*. It's about a young girl whose father doesn't return from the war. She's sad and misses him terribly. She starts the fourth grade in a new school and doesn't know anyone, hasn't any friends. A bully makes fun of her every day and she thinks, if only her daddy were here he would make the mean boy stop." Logan's face had shuttered and she hesitated.

"Go on."

"You sure?"

He nodded.

"Well, another little girl finally befriends her, and they scheme to get back at the bully. On an overnight at her friend's house, the father overhears them talking about all the mean things they plan to do to the bully. He's a police officer and knows the boy, knows that he's being raised by a single mother and they're having a hard time.

"He convinces them to try and make friends with the mean boy, and so, eventually they do, and the three children become fast friends. Simplistic, I know, but that's the story part to keep a young reader interested. The theme of the book is how the little girl goes through the grieving process and learns to cherish memories of her father. The book's interactive with places where a child can write in their daddy's name, his favorite color, things like that. There's also a page in the front to insert a picture.

"I started it to give to Regan one day, and I didn't think of publishing it. I mentioned what I was doing to my agent, and she asked to see it when I finished. Without telling me, she sent it to an editor who handles children's books." Dani shrugged. "He liked it and there you have it."

The oven timer went off and he turned away. What was he thinking? She was afraid she'd added to his guilt, if that was his problem, and that was the last thing she wanted to do.

"Logan?"

"Do you have a copy here?"

Hoping he wasn't slipping into one of his dark moods, she wished he'd turn around so she could see his face. "I have an advance copy, why?"

"I want to read it."

"All right, I'll get it for you after dinner." Was it a good thing for him to read it? Would it help him understand that even when the worst happens, life does go on, or would it make his remorse worse?

Logan put the enchiladas on the plates, glad he had an excuse to keep his back to Dani. All the guilt he'd managed to smother the last few days came screaming back with the force of a ballistic missile. If he'd brought Evan safely home, she wouldn't have had to write their daughter a daddy book, and what about Regan? The little girl he was growing to love would never know Evan, never hear that deep laugh of his, never listen to him tell one of his stupid jokes. Earlier, when he'd whispered to Regan that he was sorry for not bringing her daddy home and she'd patted his face, it had felt like she was forgiving him. He'd almost lost it then.

He desperately wanted Evan's girls: He wanted Dani for his wife and longed to step into the role of father to Regan. Not an admirable thing to want another man's family, nor did he deserve them.

"Anything I can do?"

The question confused him. There was nothing she could do to make it right.

"You're staring at that plate as if you're not pleased with it. It looks good to me, actually so good, my mouth's watering."

She meant dinner, and he sighed in relief. The longing in her eyes when she spoke of Evan tore at his heart. If he tried to explain his guilt, she'd just blow him off again, tell him he mustn't think such things. She could never understand the bone-deep responsibility he'd felt for his team, how not keeping Evan safe for her was something for which he couldn't forgive himself.

If he didn't shake off his dark thoughts, though, she'd start to question him and he'd have to lie, so he leaned over and sniffed, catching the scent of flowers.

"You smell nice."

"Gardenia-scented shampoo. Are we going to eat this or just stand here and admire it?"

The way she changed her toenail colors and shampoos fascinated him. If she were his, he would spend half his time wondering how she would smell or what color her toes would be next. He shook off the thought and picked up the plates. Dani refilled his glass and brought it to the table.

"You've gone quiet. Did talking about the book upset you?"

"I'm fine. Eat your dinner," he said, and forced himself to take a bite. It was undoubtedly good, but to him it tasted like sawdust.

A drawn-out sigh followed her first bite. "My God, Logan, this is amazing." She glanced at the casserole dish. "Oh goody, there's enough left for lunch tomorrow."

"Thanks. It's one of the few dishes Maria will eat. Probably because it's got so much cheese in it."

"You said she eats junk food. What does she like?"

"Loaded chili dogs, fried bologna sandwiches, and corndogs are her favorites."

"Seriously?"

"I kid you not. I've put food from every country in the world in front of her, and all I hear is, 'Why can't you just fry me up some bologna?'"

"If that's all she wants, can't she make it herself?"

"Maria and fire don't mix. One night I made an elaborate meal, I don't remember what now, but when she turned up her nose, I gave up. Told her I was done and she could cook for herself. The next night when she finally realized I meant it, she tried to make dinner. Almost burned the damned place down."

Her eyes glittered in amusement. "I'd like to meet her."

Logan glanced at his empty plate. When had he finished it? He grinned at the woman who had the ability to make him forget he was eating sawdust. "That's good to know because you'll meet her Tuesday night."

"I will? She's coming here?"

He hadn't meant to bring this up yet. "Tell you what. I'll clean up while you make us a pot of coffee. Then grab the baby monitor and we'll sit on the deck and talk."

"Okay. Thanks for making dinner, by the way. It really was delicious."

"My pleasure," he said, and meant it. He enjoyed cooking for her. When they got to Pensacola, he would make her his specialty, seafood paella.

While she checked on Regan, Logan stacked the dishwasher and then went to his room to get his gun. He carried their coffee out back and put the cups and gun on the table. It was dark, and if Dickhead was out there, there was no way of knowing. Hopefully the man was holed up in his motel room for the night.

Settling in a chaise longue, Logan stretched out his legs. It was a beautiful night, and he leaned his head back and looked at the stars. Dani came out, and instead of taking the longue on the other side of the table, she sat between his legs and leaned back against his chest.

He tensed. "What are you doing?"

"Getting comfortable."

She arranged an afghan over her legs, her bottom wiggling against his crotch as she did so. Jesus. She was killing him, but his cock liked it. A lot. Logan gritted his teeth and waited for her to get settled. Her gardenia-scented shampoo was nice, but he liked the apple pie one best. It was probably a good thing she hadn't used that one, though. He'd probably be licking her by now.

When she reached for her coffee, she noticed the gun. "I keep forgetting."

"That's okay as long as you're with me, but if I'm not nearby, you need to remember to be on guard."

"It's funny, until you came, I didn't forget at all. You make me feel safe."

He gave up on not touching her. Wrapping his arms around her, he rested his chin on her head. "I will always keep you safe, Dani." Or die trying.

She put her hand over his. "I know. Now, tell me about Maria coming to visit."

So much trust she put in him. It was unnerving and scared the hell out of him. What if he failed? What if no matter his precautions, the man somehow managed to get to her? He had to make sure that didn't happen because it would destroy him.

"Logan? Hello."

She twisted and peered at him. Before coming out, he'd opened the curtains in the kitchen so they'd have some light. Green eyes gazed at him, and when her lips parted, he couldn't help himself. Putting his hand under her chin, he lowered his mouth to hers.

Her soft sigh undid him. He deepened the kiss, loving the taste of her, the feel of her lips against his. When he ran his tongue over her lips, she parted them, her tongue reaching for his.

For almost three years, he'd fantasized about kissing her, about touching her, making love to her. It had been his guilty secret. His imagination had been seriously inadequate.

The last thing he wanted to do was stop, but if he didn't now, he wouldn't be able to. If there came a time when they made love, he wanted to know it was the right thing to do. There would be no regrets for either of them. And if it did happen, it would be because she was his.

He reluctantly pulled away. "Your coffee's getting cold."

She gave him a cross look. "You're a tease, Logan Kincaid."

That startled a laugh out of him. He brushed a strand of hair away from her face. "Sorry, I don't mean to be, but we need to talk, and if we keep this up, I'm going to forget everything I need to tell you."

"All right," she grumbled, and picked up her cup. "I'm listening."

He took a deep breath and plunged in, fully expecting a battle. "Maria's not coming here. We're going to Pensacola. I have some things I need to take care of, and I'm not leaving you and Regan here by yourselves." He waited for the eruption.

She set down her coffee and turned around on her knees to face him, her eyes alight with excitement. "Cool, when do we leave?"

Would she ever stop surprising him? "Tuesday night. That'll give you two days to pack and get ready."

"Awesome. I'm going to start now. It'll take me two days to decide what to pack. Oh, this is so exciting." She smacked him on the lips and was off before he could blink.

Logan chuckled. That had gone better than expected. It was getting harder and harder to resist her, and he needed to talk some things over with Mrs. Jankowski. When he made love to Dani—if it happened—it would be at his house where a picture of Evan wasn't next to her bed.

Maybe he was being stupid. Maybe if he'd had a normal mother, he wouldn't be so afraid of turning out like her. Lovey Dovey had tried her best to drag him into the gutter with her. When he'd resisted, she had sneered and made fun of him for putting on airs, calling him Mr. Hoity-Toity. What was it she'd said more than once in a fit of anger—*blood will tell*? She hadn't seemed to grasp the irony that they shared the same blood.

There had come a time when he'd almost proved her right, a night he tried his best to forget. He did have bad blood in him, so he'd kept a tight leash on his urges.

It was the reason he was still a virgin.

CHAPTER ELEVEN

Logan returned to his room and found Dani's book for Regan on his pillow. He stared at it, wanting to snatch it up and devour every one of her words, yet couldn't bring himself to touch it. How long he stood there looking at it, he didn't know.

To put off reading the book, he showered, brushed his teeth, and shaved. He packed even though they weren't leaving for two days, called Buchanan, called Mrs. Jankowski, called Maria. When he could think of nothing else to do, he settled back on the pillows of his bed and picked up the book. As he held it in his hands, he feared Dani's words would revive the regret and guilt at the death of his friend. This was going to kill him, but he turned to the first page and began to read.

Reaching the last page, he read the words Dani had chosen to end the story, and then read them again.

> Every night before going to sleep, Regan went to her window and searched the night sky until she found the brightest star. "Good night, Daddy," she would whisper. That night, when she turned for bed, she stopped and looked back at the star. "I know you would have loved me. I know you are in heaven and watching out for me. Mommy has told me all

about you. I love you, Daddy, but your jokes were really silly."

Logan laughed. "No shit, Evan, your jokes really were bad."

He sucked in a breath, realizing he'd just laughed for the first time when thinking of Evan. Though written for a child, the story had drawn him in. Dani had dealt with the subject of death in a straightforward, poignant manner. It was a story of hope and love, one of acceptance. In a way he didn't understand, her words eased his heart. He flipped back until he found the page he wanted.

Regan's mommy tapped her heart. "Your daddy lives here, in your heart. He's with you every day and always will be. I'll tell you stories about him. I'll tell you all his silly jokes because I want you to know how wonderful and funny he was. I have a present for you."

She handed Regan a beautiful jeweled-top box. "This will be your Daddy Memory Box, and we'll write down all the things you don't want to forget and put them in it. They will be memories of your daddy you can treasure forever."

Regan took the box from her mother and opened it. "It's empty," she said.

Her mommy nodded. "Yes, that's because it's up to you to decide what to put in it."

"I want to put something in it right now. I want to put a silly daddy joke in it," Regan said.

"All right. How about this one. It was one of Daddy's favorites. Why isn't your nose twelve inches long?"

Regan shook her head. "I give up."
"Because it would be a foot!"

Logan smiled and traced the words of the joke with a finger. Treasured memories. He had his own Evan memories and bad Evan jokes, although the ones Evan delighted in telling the team were not printable in a children's book.

What was it she'd said? He searched for the page.

"Daddy wouldn't want us to be sad, Regan. He didn't want to leave us, but he did, and it would hurt him if he knew we didn't learn how to be happy again."

It was the honest-to-God truth. If Evan knew Logan blamed himself for his death—that the guilt was eating him alive—his friend would be royally pissed, would probably beat the shit out of him on general principle. Putting the book aside, he stood and went to the window, searching the sky until he found the brightest star.

Evan's last words had been to make Logan promise to take care of his wife and child. "I wish you'd been more specific about just how far I could take that promise, Cowboy."

Feeling silly talking to a star, he turned away, but like the girl in the story, he stopped and turned back. "I'll never let your daughter forget you, my friend."

Logan's plan to sneak Dani and Regan out of Asheville was simple. They invited Jared and Scott over for drinks and appetizers on the back deck. Throughout the next two hours, each of them made several trips in and out of the house.

If Dickhead was out there, Logan wanted to lull him into believing they were either going to the bathroom or refreshing drinks. Halfway through the evening, Scott left and snuck the suitcases out the front, putting them in his car.

At nine, Logan judged it was dark enough. "It's time, Dani. Get Regan and get in the car."

"I feel like I'm in a James Bond movie." She giggled and reached for her glass.

"No," he said, "leave it here, like you're coming back."

"Right, Double-O-Seven. Leave the glass." Giving another chuckle, she walked inside.

"I think your girl's a little nervous, Logan," Jared observed.

"Can't say I blame her," Scott said. "It's really spooky knowing some creep's watching you."

Logan's hands fisted. "And when I find him, he's going to wish he never heard her name. Listen, I've given you his description, so both of you be extra alert. I don't think he'll bother you, but once he realizes she's missing, I don't know how he'll react. You've got my cell number. If anything happens, no matter how insignificant you think it is, call me."

"When will you be back?" Scott asked.

Logan hadn't told them where they were going, and both seemed smart enough not to ask. He saw no reason not to answer Scott's question. "Not sure yet. Regan has an appointment with her pediatrician a week from Thursday, so we'll be back in time for that."

"I don't much like the idea of a cult involved in this," Jared said.

"That makes two of us." Logan stood. "You both know what to do." He picked up his empty glass, walked inside, and set it on the table. Grabbing the ball cap that matched the one Jared wore, he put it on, walked out of the house, and got into the passenger side of the car.

"You okay back there?" he asked.

"Yes, sir, Double-O-Seven, over and out," Dani answered from her prone position on the backseat.

He grinned. "You do know where all Bond's girls end up, don't you?"

"Oh yeah."

From the way she sighed her answer, Logan thought he just might lose his virginity in Pensacola. Long ago, he had made a promise to himself that he wouldn't sleep with a woman he didn't love. He'd been tempted to break the vow many times since then, but the boy who was determined to be a better man had stood fast.

Well, both he and the boy were in love with the woman he was taking home with him, so he prayed it was finally going to happen, please God. He still had to talk to Mrs. Jankowski, but he was beginning to believe that if he and Evan had thought to have a conversation about Dani's future should something happen, Evan would have slapped him on the back and said, "I trust you to do right by her."

Scott walked out of the cabin, and Logan ducked his head, keeping his eyes closed when the overhead light came on. As soon as the door closed and darkness descended again, he opened them and peered out into the night. No hairs on the back of his neck stood up, and he was confident they'd gotten away with their ruse.

Scott sat there a few seconds, then started the car. "Now what?"

Logan refrained from rolling his eyes. "Now you drive us to the airport."

Dani considered herself a world traveler. From as far back as she could remember, she'd flown here and there with her parents, always in first class on a commercial airliner. But as she looked around the lush interior of the Learjet Logan had chartered, she—used to what money could buy—was impressed.

How the hell could he afford it? Somehow, she would have to find a way to reimburse him without wounding his pride. Whatever the cost, it would be worth it to see Logan's home, to meet the people who mattered to him. She peered out the jet's window at the twinkling lights thousands of feet below.

The question she kept asking herself with no clear answer reared up again. What did she want from him? At first, it had been to keep her and Regan safe. She had no doubt he could do that.

But did she want to have an affair with him? Yes. God yes. Without her understanding how, she'd started thinking she wanted more. But what did that mean? Was she thinking long term?

She could almost see them growing old together. Deep in her heart, she knew Evan would approve. Her husband had always wanted nothing more than for her to be happy. She could have been happy with him forever, but he had left her—had gone and died.

Sometimes she resented him for that. He could have left the SEALs before that last mission, as his six years were up. Yet, because his team needed him, he'd reenlisted even after she'd told him she might be pregnant. Well, she'd needed him, too, but that hadn't seemed to matter.

"We're flying over Montgomery," Logan said.

"How do you know?" His mouth was inches from hers as he leaned forward to peer out the window. If she turned her head, their lips would meet. Her heart did a funny little flutter, the way it had when she was first falling in love with Evan. She resisted the urge to kiss him.

"By the position of the stars."

He sat back in his seat and she missed his warmth. "I don't believe you. Fess up, you're just guessing."

That earned her an amused chuckle. Opening his hand, he showed her the GPS. He slipped it into the magazine pouch in front of him and then gestured at Regan. "She travels well."

Dani glanced at her sleeping daughter. "I thought we'd be going commercial and was worried she would be one of those babies everyone wants to throw out of the plane because they won't stop crying."

He touched Regan's hand and she grasped his finger. "That was one reason I chartered a flight."

His eyes softened when Regan's little fingers wrapped around his. *He would make a good father.* Where did these thoughts keep coming from? Was she falling for him? It wasn't what she had thought she wanted. Even though he was no longer a SEAL, from what she understood, his company had government contracts. Did he go on secret missions? She had no wish to relive the agony of kissing a man good-bye and then sitting home praying he would return safely. She just couldn't do it again.

"You've gone away. What are you thinking?"

She jerked her gaze to his. "I was wondering exactly what your company does."

"This and that," he said with a shrug.

"Such as?"

Maybe he saw the determination in her eyes, because he sighed. "Mostly consulting with companies on security, everything from teaching a CEO's driver evasive tactics to how to protect their computers from hackers, both domestic and foreign."

She could live with that, but what wasn't he telling her? "And the government, what do you do for them? Are you involved in any black ops?"

His eyes shuttered. "I'll take you on a tour of K2 Special Services while we're in Pensacola."

Nothing like evading her question. She would let it go for now, but not for long. "I assume the K is for Kincaid, but why the 2?"

"Stands for two Kincaids. Maria's shown an interest, and I'm hoping she'll come on board after she graduates law school."

It was humbling to think of the two children who'd defied the odds and made something of themselves. Having been born into money and sheltered from the darker side of life, her childhood had been the polar opposite. Her parents donated large sums of money to their favorite charities, held and attended fund-raising events for the less fortunate. It now seemed ironic those occasions usually involved black ties and glittering gowns, champagne and caviar. Had any of those fat checks signed by diamond-clad fingers made a difference in someone's life the way Mrs. Jankowski had?

Dani couldn't wait to meet the woman who'd saved a thieving boy and his sister. What would Logan's future have been if he hadn't tried to steal from her? She peeked up at the man she liked more and more. He had his GPS out again, studying it. He did love his toys.

"Where do you think you would be today if not for Mrs. Jankowski?"

Black lashes lifted and deep brown eyes focused on her. "In prison or dead."

And what a gimongous waste that would have been. She reached over and squeezed his hand. "Then I thank God for your Mrs. Jankowski."

His gaze moved to her hand on his. He turned his palm up and slipped his fingers between hers. "So do I. Every day."

As they sat in a comfortable silence, Dani closed her eyes, concentrating on the feel of touching him, loving the way he made her feel safe and protected. Warmth flowed from his skin into hers, and when he began stroking his thumb over hers, tingles of pleasure floated up her arm, causing goose bumps. She shivered and opened her eyes to find Logan watching her, one side of his mouth curved in a curiously shy smile.

Her heart and stomach reacted as if she were on a roller-coaster ride. "Logan," she whispered.

"Dani," he answered, and lowered his mouth to hers.

"Mama," Regan cried.

Damn, her daughter had the worst timing in the world.

He raised his head, brought her hand to his lips, and kissed her knuckles. "My lady, you could make a man forget his name."

Dani narrowed her eyes. She had written those exact words. "Have you been reading my books?"

Grinning, he reached down and pulled a paperback out of his tote. Dani read the title. *The Countess Takes a Lover.* Well, crap, the book in which she'd used him as the model for her hero. Did he realize?

"Is it my imagination or does your hero look a little like me?"

Okay, he did. She didn't need a mirror to know her face glowed bright red. His amused laughter irritated the hell out of her. Regan cried again and Dani turned her attention to her daughter, glad to have a reason to ignore him.

He picked up the GPS and studied it. "You have about twenty minutes to feed her before we land."

"I need to change her diaper first."

The look on his face was comical. "Uh . . . I need to speak to the pilot."

Holy moly, the man could move fast. "Wimp," she called after him.

"And not ashamed of it," he replied before disappearing into the cockpit.

When they deplaned at the executive hanger, Jake Buchanan was there to meet them. Dani grinned when she saw him. She'd met all the guys on Evan's team, and he was one of her favorites. The man was an unabashed flirt and apparently hadn't changed.

He wrapped his arms around her. "Hello, beautiful, have you missed me?" he asked, and gave her a smack on the lips.

Laughing, she hugged him back. "Never doubt it." She glanced over his shoulder at Logan. He was scowling at Jake, but the baby he held in the crook of his arm diminished the effect.

"Kincaid's glaring at the back of my head, isn't he?" Jake whispered.

She grinned and nodded.

He winked and then put his mouth close to her ear. "He needs a good woman to turn his life upside down. Are you up to the task?"

"Maybe," she murmured.

Jake stepped back and turned to Logan. "Hey, boss man, what you got there?"

"That's my daughter, Regan," Dani said.

"She's got her daddy's eyes," Jake said softly. He stepped up and clucked Regan under her chin. "Hey, gorgeous."

Regan giggled and hid her face in Logan's neck, one little hand clutching his ear. Logan leaned his cheek against Regan's head, and when he closed his eyes and inhaled her daughter's scent, Dani's heartbeat stuttered. Why wasn't there a chair nearby she could sink her bottom onto?

"Boss man's a goner all right," Jake murmured from next to her.

"Make yourself useful, Buchanan, and load our suitcases."

Dani walked to the car with Logan and helped him buckle in Regan. "You think of everything, don't you?"

"Most of the time, but Buchanan gets the credit for thinking of bringing a car seat."

She climbed into the backseat with Regan and watched the passing scenery as they drove to Logan's house, eager to see where he lived. When she'd asked on the plane, he had shrugged and would only say, "You'll see," which made her all the more curious. Would his home give her clues about the man?

After a twenty-minute ride, part of which took them over a causeway, Jake turned onto a cobblestone driveway. Though it was dark out, she thought she'd glimpsed the ocean between two houses a few minutes before. She wished it were day so she could get a good look at the house, but landscape lighting illuminated the place well enough to get the impression it was big. They pulled into a garage under the house and Logan got out, opening her door. She took the hand he offered and stepped out of the car.

Surprising her, he lifted her chin with his finger and kissed her. "Welcome to my home, Dani."

The words were soft, as if they came from his heart, as if it was important to him that she was there. She placed her palm on his chest and felt the beat of his heart. "Thank you for bringing me."

As soon as they unbuckled Regan, her daughter reached for Logan. "Wont Gan."

Jeez, the silly girl was head over heels in love with the man. Amused, Dani let him take Regan. When this was over—for her daughter's sake—she was going to make him promise to visit often. She snorted. For Regan's sake? Who was she kidding?

"Did you say something?" he asked.

"Nope, not a thing."

His eyes searched hers before he finally turned away and she could breathe again. Whatever this thing was that was building between them, it couldn't stay contained much longer. If something didn't happen soon—the sooner, the better—she just might combust.

Dani didn't doubt he would be the most experienced lover with whom she'd ever slept. Just look at him. With that body and face, all he had to do was crook a finger and women would fall at his feet.

"Are you coming? Buchanan will get our bags."

Logan stood halfway up the stairs to the house, staring back at her. Everything about him appealed to her, and she was determined that by the time she returned home she would know how it felt to be possessed by a man as intensely focused as him.

"Beware, Logan Kincaid," she murmured, "I've got you in my sights."

CHAPTER TWELVE

Logan had gone into life-threatening firefights with nerves as cool as steel, but as Dani followed him up the stairs, his fingers tingled in anticipation, and he thought maybe butterflies had decided to nest in his stomach.

Would she like his home and his family? He didn't want to acknowledge how important her opinion was to him, tried not to set his hopes too high. Permanency in his life was what he wanted from her, but what if she never wanted more than an affair? Could he give her that and then walk away? Maybe, but could he do it and remain unscathed?

No way.

Regan grabbed his ear and he smiled down at her. He hadn't spent any time with Maria when she was born because he'd been twelve and finding excuses to stay away from home. Between Lovey Dovey, her johns, and a screaming baby, home was the last place he had wanted to be. It wasn't until he'd realized his baby sister was neglected and half-starved that he took an interest.

Now, looking at the precious girl in his arms, he wished he could turn back time and appoint himself Maria's protector from the day she was born. And as long as he was at it, he could wish for a different mother and even a loving dad, or at least the name of his father.

"I'm gonna gobble you up." He lifted her tummy to his mouth and blew raspberries.

She screamed in delight and pushed her stomach against his mouth. "Wont."

Obliging her, he blew on her belly as he opened the door. She banged on his head, bouncing up and down. Logan laughed and swung her up in the air, while at the same time noticing Maria and Mrs. Jankowski standing in the middle of the kitchen staring at him as if he'd just stepped off a spaceship from Mars.

"Hello," he said, reaching behind him and taking Dani's hand, pulling her next to him. "This is Dani Prescott, and this little imp is her daughter, Regan."

Mrs. Jankowski eyed him, then Regan and Dani, and he would swear there was a calculated gleam in her eyes. Not surprising, as he'd never brought another woman home with him, and she'd understand the significance of Dani now standing in his kitchen.

She walked up to Dani and hugged her. "Welcome, my dear."

Dani grinned and gave herself over to Mrs. Jankowski's motherly embrace. Logan glanced at his sister in time to see her lips thin before she smiled. He recognized that look. What was her problem?

Mrs. Jankowski turned her attention to Regan and charmed her out of his arms. Ignoring the fuss being made over the baby, Maria came and hugged him.

"What's wrong, brat?" he whispered.

"Nothing. I just missed you, and I'm so glad you're home." She took his hand and pulled him a few feet away. "Are you back for good?"

Something was bugging her, and he would find out what when they had some private time. "No, just here for a few days, why?"

Her gaze fell on Dani. "So you're going back with *her*?"

"Yes." The emphasis Maria put on the word "her" gave him his first hint. He'd been the only anchor in his sister's life, the only thing she could depend on in their house of horrors. She was acting like a territorial cat. He dated now and then, and it had never seemed to bother her. Why now?

Dani came to his side. "Hi, Maria. I've looked forward to meeting you. Logan tells me you're going to study law. I'm impressed."

"Then you know more about me than I know about you. Logan hasn't told me anything."

He was going to strangle his sister. Opening his mouth to apologize for her behavior, Dani stopped him from speaking by putting her hand on his back and pressing her fingers against his spine.

"No problem, anything you want to know, just ask," she said to Maria. Her gaze swept the room. "You and Logan have a beautiful home, and I'd love it if you'd take me on a tour. If the rest of it is anything like this amazing kitchen, then I'm dying to see it."

Maria was going to refuse; he could see it in her expression. He narrowed his eyes. Her chest rose in an annoyed sigh. "Sure, why not?" She walked out, not waiting for Dani.

Not trusting Maria to play nice, he started to follow.

Dani shook her head. "No, stay here. Give me a few minutes alone with her."

"I'm sorry, I don't know what her problem is."

"She's afraid I'm going to take you away from her."

"Well, that's just stupid," he muttered as Dani left the room to join Maria.

"It's the way you look at her."

He'd forgotten Mrs. Jankowski was in the room. "How's that?" he asked, joining her at the table.

Regan had fallen asleep and Mrs. Jankowski gently rocked the baby. "Like—"

Buchanan entered with their suitcases. "Where you want these, boss?"

Damn, Logan wanted to know how he looked at Dani. "Just put them in the hall, and we'll sort them out later."

"Sure, just call me a mule."

"I like jackass better."

Buchanan snorted and disappeared. Logan turned back to Mrs. Jankowski. "What did you think of her?"

"From the few minutes I spent with her, she seems nice." She peered down at Regan. "And this little one is a cutie pie. You're in love with her, aren't you?"

"Which one?"

"Both, I imagine."

"Maybe, but I don't know if I deserve them."

"Logan Kincaid, I'm fixing to slap you upside your head. Maybe that'll put some sense in that mind of yours."

His foster mother had always been able to read him like an open book. He studied the woman he respected above all others. In her late sixties, she was showing her age, and the few extra pounds she'd put on since coming to live with him and Maria gave her the look of a sweet, gentle grandmother. Nothing could be further from the truth. The woman was tough as nails and ran his household with the precision of a five-star general.

He owed her more than he could ever repay—had tried to get her to retire and enjoy the life he offered. Sitting on her butt and eating chocolates was not for her, she'd declared, and had appointed herself the role of housekeeper and sometimes cook. Logan secretly believed she loved bossing the day maid around.

"I have some questions I need to ask you later," Logan said.

"And I have some answers for you."

That, he didn't doubt. Dani and Maria walked in, Buchanan trailing behind them. Maria held up one of Dani's books. "You didn't tell me she writes romance novels."

Dani leaned close to Maria and whispered in her ear. His sister's eyes widened. "I don't believe it. You're actually reading this?" She turned the book so he could see the cover.

Mrs. Jankowski squinted and read aloud the title. "*The Countess Takes a Lover.*"

Buchanan laughed, and Logan feared he might be blushing. "What of it? It's a damn good book."

Compared to the pleased smile Dani gave him, Logan decided his embarrassment didn't amount to jack beans. "Don't you have some place to go, Buchanan?"

His gaze slid to Maria. "No, boss."

Logan gritted his teeth when Maria inched closer to Romeo. "It's almost midnight. Go home."

"Thanks for picking us up, Jake," Dani said. "It's great seeing you again. You'll be around, right?"

"You bet. You coming by the office tomorrow, boss?"

"Yeah, I'm bringing Dani by for a tour."

Buchanan gave Dani a hug. "See you tomorrow, then." He glanced at Maria before leaving.

Logan was at a loss as to how to handle what was an obvious attraction between Maria and Jake. He made a mental note to talk to Dani about it.

Mrs. Jankowski stood and gently placed Regan in Dani's arms. "Let's get this baby put to bed. We've set up a crib in your room. Is that okay?"

"That's great," Dani answered.

"I'm off to bed, too," Maria said, following them out.

Logan picked up the suitcases and took Dani hers. "Would you like to join me for a glass of wine after you get settled?"

"I'm tempted, but it's been a long day. I think I'll shower and call it a night."

Disappointed, he left her in Mrs. Jankowski's care and went to his room. After showering and changing into sweats, he made his way to the kitchen to scrounge up something to eat. Not surprisingly, Mrs. Jankowski had anticipated his needs, and he took a seat across from her at the table.

"Thanks," he said, and dug into the ham and cheese sandwich. "You get Dani settled in?"

She put her cup down. "Yes. Other than telling us you'd be in North Carolina, you were pretty closedmouthed about why. Is she in trouble?"

"Someone's stalking her."

Her eyes widened and she put her hand over her heart. "Dear Lord, why? Who?"

"I don't know yet, but I'm sure as hell going to find out." He finished the last bite of his sandwich and pushed his plate aside. Getting up, he went to the refrigerator, got a beer, and twisted the cap off.

"You said her last name's Prescott, so I assume she was your friend Evan's wife?"

Leaning back against the counter, he nodded. Trust her to get right to the problem.

She looked at him with knowing eyes. "And how long have you been in love with her?"

Yeah, let's dig right in. He could never lie to her; she always knew when he did. He told her the truth. "Since the first time I saw her." So she would understand, he told her how he and Evan had

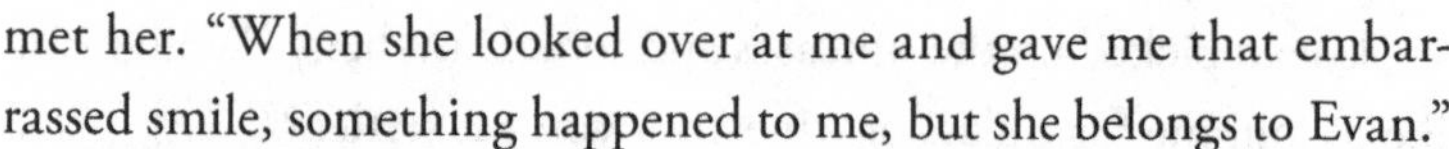

met her. "When she looked over at me and gave me that embarrassed smile, something happened to me, but she belongs to Evan."

"Belonged, past tense."

"But I was responsible for bringing him home safely, and I failed her. Failed them both." He brought the bottle to his mouth and took a deep drink.

She raised her eyes to the ceiling. "Lord, please deliver me from stupid men. It was war, Logan, and one sad fact of war is men die. Good ones along with the bad. Did you make a mistake that caused his death?"

"No, but our intel was wrong. We all had a bad feeling about the mission. I should have refused the orders."

"Sure, and that's easy to say with hindsight. Every one of you knew and accepted that your next mission might be your last. Think about it this way: if you had refused, you would have been taken off the team and they would have gone in without you, right?"

He nodded.

"Who knows what would have happened then. You might have lost them all."

Well hell, he'd never thought of it that way. Because he'd carried the guilt of loving Dani for so long, he gave it one last try. "But you taught me not to covet another man's wife. I tried not to. God, I tried."

"I'm not going to tell you it was all right to feel that way about her when your friend was alive, but hearts have a way of doing as they please no matter how much we might wish otherwise. The thing is, you never acted on it, and for that, I'm proud of you. Did she love him?"

"Very much, I think. She never gave me any encouragement when Evan was alive."

"And now?"

"Now I think she's interested, but I have my mother's bad blood in me, and I don't want to hurt her."

"Logan Kincaid, I really am going to smack you upside the head. You are not in any way like your mother. Maria grew up in the same house, has your mother's blood in her. Do you fear she's going to be like Lovey Dovey?"

Never. He wouldn't allow it. "No, of course not."

"Then stop talking stupid. Find whoever's stalking our Dani, put an end to it, and then marry the girl."

Thankfully, he hadn't taken a swallow of beer or he would've spewed it. "You make it sound so easy."

"I have faith in you." She stood and picked up his plate, carrying it to the sink. "You can wash this. I'm off to bed."

"One day, you're going to accept the fact that the dishwasher does actually clean the dishes," he said, opening the door and putting the plate in it.

On an impulse, he hugged her. "Thank you, Mrs. Jankowski."

"For what?"

"For everything." For saving him and Maria, for always being there for them, for being so wise. She wasn't a demonstrative woman and she gave his back an awkward pat, but he could see the pleasure in her eyes.

At the doorway, she stopped and asked him one last question. "If Evan knew he was going to die, who would you say he would want to take care of his wife and child?"

Remembering Evan's last words, Logan's eyes burned. "Me."

"And if you were the one married to her and you knew you were going to die, would you want her to spend the rest of her life alone?"

"No."

"Then if you could pick who she would fall in love with after you, who would it be?"

"Evan."

She nodded in obvious satisfaction and left.

Logan took his beer and walked out to the back deck. The moon would be full in a few nights and it reflected across the sea in ribbons of shimmering light. The gulf was calm, and he listened to the gentle lapping of the waves as he thought about their conversation.

He'd known Mrs. Jankowski would help him put everything in perspective. If wanting to develop a relationship with Dani had been wrong, she would have set him straight on that, too. More than anything, her last question had vanquished his guilt.

In everyday life, in his missions, he never had a problem with knowing right from wrong. It was only in relationships—and then his love for Dani—that he didn't trust himself to get it right. He blamed his mother for that. He'd always feared he would use women the way she used men, and almost had once.

The only way he'd known how to keep that from happening was not to be intimate with them. He'd done his share of kissing and a little fondling, but every time he had come close to breaking his vow, he had ended the relationship.

Funny how it had never occurred to him to think Maria would turn out like their mother. If he hadn't fallen into whoring his way through life by now, the odds were high it wasn't going to happen.

Mrs. Jankowski's words had sunk in, and as he stared out over the ocean, he accepted the truth that he didn't have it in him to be like Lovey Dovey. He gave a humorless chuckle. Too bad he hadn't understood that years ago, because he wouldn't be a thirty-year-old virgin. Yet he didn't regret Dani would be his first. At least, he fervently hoped so.

He still wasn't sure he was good enough for her. She was a princess and he was trailer trash. His lips curved in a smile. Mrs. Jankowski would box his ears for thinking that way. "You have nothing to be ashamed of. Just look at what you've done with your life," she would say.

Logan turned and stared at the house he had bought two years earlier. He'd long dreamed of having a beautiful home on the gulf, one where he could walk out his back door and feel the sand warm on his bare feet or stand under the night moon and feel the breeze on his face.

Except for necessities and what he gave Mrs. Jankowski and Maria, he had saved every penny of his Navy pay. When he left the military after twelve years, he'd had enough for the down payment. The first thing he did was start looking for a house.

The minute he walked in the door, he knew it was the one. It was the one time in his life he'd been selfish. Because he didn't want Maria, whose taste ran to craftsman style, or Mrs. Jankowski, who preferred traditional, to try and influence his decision, he hadn't told them he'd bought a house until the final papers were signed. It was his house and he wanted a contemporary with clean lines and no clutter. As different from his past life as possible.

Looking up, he admired the tall windows reaching from the ground floor to the second. In daylight, the views from inside were spectacular, and sometimes he stood in a room overlooking the ocean and pinched himself to make sure he wasn't dreaming.

What had Dani thought of it? Maybe his ego needed to show her what he'd made of himself, because he had wanted to be the one to take her on a tour, wanted to watch her face, to hear her comments.

Did she like it enough to consider living in it? She was a writer and could live anywhere, whereas his company was in Pensacola, and as much as he loved the mountains, he didn't think he could bear giving up his ocean.

Getting ahead of yourself, here, Kincaid. She's given no indication she wants your ring on her finger. He finished the last of his beer, warm now, and went inside. Tomorrow, he would take her on a tour of K2.

Unable to sleep, Logan got out his copy of *The Countess Takes a Lover* and turned to the page he'd marked. A few chapters later, he stopped reading and stared out the French doors, for once not noticing the view. In the book, the heroine, Elena, wanted to be courted.

Did Dani? Was that a clue to winning her heart? Didn't a writer, especially one who wrote romance, put their own desires into their stories, consciously or even unconsciously? Wouldn't her hero act in a way Dani would want a man in her life to?

Believing he had stumbled on a way to learn her fantasies, he went back to reading, mentally noting all the things Jonathan did to make Elena fall in love with him. Because of his lack of experience with women, he could use all the help he could get. He stayed up half the night, and when he finished the book, fell asleep to ideas forming in his mind.

The next morning, he made a quick trip to the grocery store and then settled down at his desk, a cup of coffee in hand. At his best when he had a well-thought-out plan, Logan outlined a schedule for their time in Pensacola, along with notes on how to act and the things he needed to do. One thing that had caught his attention in Dani's book was how much Elena loved Jonathan's scent. Logan gave that a lot of thought.

For years, because of what he did, he had strived to have no scent at all. No one on his team was allowed to smoke, as the smell or the glow of a cigarette could result in being dead. They had also never used cologne, aftershave, or scented deodorant. But Elena loved Jonathan's scent, so Logan made a list of some things to buy. Maria had given him a bottle of cologne one Christmas, and he could give that a try.

When he finished, he read over his notes and grunted his satisfaction. If his team knew he was planning a courtship with the precision and detail of a SEAL mission, he would be the butt of their jokes for years to come. He didn't give a damn. Already he was having the time of his life and couldn't wait to start.

Inclining his head, he listened to Regan cry. He smiled and shoved his courtship plan into a desk drawer. "Let the games begin."

CHAPTER THIRTEEN

Dani pulled a chair to the picture window and settled in to nurse Regan. "Enjoy, my little stinker, because starting tomorrow your breakfast is coming in a bottle."

Regan gurgled her answer. Dani looked down and experienced a bittersweet moment. This was the last time she would nurse her daughter. "You're growing up, sweetheart, and I'm not sure how I feel about that."

Regan grinned back at her without letting go of the nipple.

"You're rotten, you know that, right?"

Someone knocked on the door. "Come in," she said, expecting Mrs. Jankowski. Logan walked in with a cup of coffee in one hand and a yellow rose in the other.

Regan's gaze shifted to Logan, and she let go of Dani and gave him a flirty grin. Dani lifted Regan and whispered in her ear. "You're a little tease, but I really don't blame you."

"Gan," Regan said, and reached for him.

Logan handed Dani the flower, and accompanied it with a gentle kiss on her lips. "Good morning."

Oh, my. She smiled at him. "Good morning to you."

"Trade you." He pulled a table next to her, put the cup on it, and took Regan from her.

Dani swirled the rose, pleased by the gesture. For sure, the man was worming his way into her heart, and the silly thing was letting him in despite her mind arguing against it. She sipped her coffee. "Hazelnut," she sighed, savoring the rich flavor of the coffee. "I was going to ask you to stop by the store today to pick some up."

His gaze settled on her, his look curling her toes. "I know it's your favorite, so I went out this morning and got some."

"Oh. Well, thanks." How sweet was that? Coffee and a flower delivered by a hot man. Great way to start the day.

"How's my favorite girl?" He lifted Regan in the air and blew on her stomach, making her giggle.

"Are you asking me or her?"

He set Regan on the floor and came to Dani's chair. Putting his hands on the back, enclosing her in, he stared at her lips. They tingled in anticipation. Slowly, so achingly slowly, he lowered his mouth to hers. She wrapped her fingers on the arm of the chair to keep from putting her hands behind his neck and yanking him to her. It wasn't a passionate kiss, but soft and tender, one promising there was more to come.

Lifting away, he brushed his finger over her bottom lip. "I was asking the baby. I'll get to you later."

The air swished out of her lungs. God, she wanted to jump his bones. She'd always liked sex in the mornings, and if Regan hadn't been playing at their feet, she would have probably dragged him to the bed.

Then she noticed something else. Other than when he'd showered using her bay soap, she'd never smelled a scent on him. "You smell nice."

His smile was secretive, as if he knew something she didn't. He picked up Regan. "I'll entertain this one while you get dressed. If you like, I'll show you around K2 this morning."

"I would like that."

"Good. Mrs. Jankowski will have breakfast ready in about thirty minutes."

Dani finished her coffee and worked to get her breathing back to normal. When she thought her legs could support her again, she stood and glanced around the room. Spying a small vase on the dresser, she filled it with water in the bathroom and put the rose in it, setting it on the night table.

She dressed and headed downstairs. Logan's house was amazing, and when she'd toured it the night before with Maria, she hadn't been able to appreciate the incredible views from each room. It must be totally awesome to live right on the beach.

The first floor was open, with no walls between the great room, dining room, and kitchen. The furniture was classically simple; the off-white walls and accent colors of teal and peach were perfect for a beach house. Her favorite feature was the floor-to-ceiling windows.

The house and furnishings were obviously very expensive and not what she'd expected. Logan was full of surprises. She turned to the kitchen to see him watching her from a bar stool at the granite-topped island. Regan sat in front of him on the counter, banging a wooden spoon on it.

Lord help her. He was stealing his way into her heart, and she still didn't know if she was ready for more than a romp between the sheets. Before she could allow their relationship to go past a hot affair, she needed to know if he involved himself in dangerous missions. She hoped to learn the answer when they toured his company. Taking a deep breath, she joined him at the counter.

Dani studied the nondescript brick building devoid of any signage. "I'm guessing the company name's not on the building because you prefer to keep a low profile."

"Correct. It's not that someone can't find us if they want to, but no need for the locals to wonder what K2 does."

It was the same for the black Chevy Malibu with tinted windows they were in—not a car anyone would pay attention to. But she'd seen the classic Mustang and another Harley-Davidson in his garage.

How many women had he taken for rides in the convertible sports car or on the bike? For sure, she'd been way off base in her assumption of his financial status. Although she didn't care if he had money, it eased her mind to know that they were on more equal footing than she'd thought.

When she reached for the door handle, he touched her arm.

"Wait." Exiting, he came around the car, opened her door, and offered his hand. When she was standing in front of him, he twirled a lock of her hair around his finger and brought it to his nose. "You smell like flowers today."

"Gardenias again." He was behaving so courtly all of a sudden.

"It's very nice, but I still like the apple pie one best. When you wear it, all I can think about is tasting you."

Well then. Certain her leg bones had melted, she put her hand on his waist to steady herself. If he kept doing things like this, she just might decide to keep him.

Clasping her hand, he laced their fingers and led her to the entrance of K2. At the door, he stopped, and with his free hand he took his cell from his pocket and glanced at the caller ID. "Mrs. Jankowski," he said. He answered and listened, then looked at Dani. "She wants to know if you would mind if she takes Regan with her to the grocery store."

"That's fine."

After hanging up, he grinned. "Mrs. Jankowski doesn't need a damn thing from the store. She just wants to show Regan off to her friend who works there."

"Regan will love the attention."

They entered the building, and it struck her that no one driving by would ever guess at the interior. Groupings of black leather couches and chairs and glass-and-chrome coffee tables sat on white, thick shag area rugs in the lobby. A receptionist sat behind a tall, red-tiled counter. The artwork on the walls was ultra modern, slashes of black, red, and yellow paint. Yellow and white orchids in chrome pots were scattered about the room.

"Wow, you have a great decorator." The pleasure in his eyes at her comment caught her attention. "You?"

He nodded.

Another thought occurred to her. "And your house was also you?"

His cheeks turned beautifully pink. "Yes, but if you tell a soul, I'll have to kill you."

Oh, how marvelous, he was embarrassed. She let go of his hand and turned to face him. "My God, Logan, why not take the credit? Do you have any idea what it would have cost to pay a decorator to do this and your house?" Out of the corner of her eye, she noticed the receptionist watching them with rapt fascination.

"Because . . ." He glanced at the woman before pulling Dani to a far corner. "Because the guys would never let me live it down. And I didn't just come up with the ideas on my own. I pored over every decorating magazine in the fucking world and tore out the pages of the rooms I liked. Everything you see is an idea stolen from someone else. What the hell would I know of good taste considering where I came from?"

Dani's heart turned to liquid, and though she longed to cup his face with her palm, she was aware of their audience. This dangerous, intelligent, self-taught man still carried deep inside him the little boy unsure of his place in the world.

She leaned forward and whispered, "Even under threat of having my fingernails pulled off by a pair of pliers, your secret's safe with me."

The tightness at the corners of his eyes eased and his gaze lowered to her toes, which today were a bright red. "Toenails, too?"

She gave a slow, sad shake of her head. "Sorry, but those get threatened and I'm a blabbermouth."

When he laughed, the receptionist stared at him as if she'd never seen him before. Good Lord, had the woman never seen the boss laugh? Come to think of it, Dani hadn't seen him laugh much—even before Evan died. Sometimes he broke her heart. She could easily sink to the floor and cry a thousand tears for him and that little boy.

He took her hand. "Come on."

At the counter, he took the pink message slips the receptionist handed him and put them in his pocket. "Barbie, this is Dani Prescott. If she ever stops by asking for me, notify me immediately."

"Absolutely, boss," the girl replied.

He leaned close to Dani, and in a stage whisper said, "You want to be nice to Barbie. She's always got a gun on her and can shoot an acorn out of an oak tree from a hundred paces."

Seriously, a gun-packing, blond bombshell named Barbie? There was definitely no gun hidden inside the silk blouse, and Dani didn't see any bulge in the pencil skirt. Barbie must have seen her doubtful look because she grinned and lifted the skirt to show a gun strapped to the inside of her thigh.

Dani leaned over the counter to get a better look. "Wow, I want to be you."

"Honey, there can only be one me in this world."

Dani could believe that. She considered whether she should be jealous. The woman was drop-dead gorgeous with curves that would drive a man wild, but she sensed no sexual chemistry between Barbie and Logan. She was also pleased to see a wedding ring on the woman's finger.

Logan's cell phone vibrated and he pulled it out of his pocket. "Kincaid."

While he talked, Barbie scrutinized Dani. "You're the first woman he's brought here, and from the way he looks at you, you must be special. You even got him to laugh, and for that, I like you. But if you hurt him, honey, I'm gonna kill you."

Holy moly. "You know what, Barbie?"

The Barbie-doll assassin raised a finely arched brow. "What?"

"You scare the hell out of me."

That was apparently the right thing to say because the woman gave a hearty laugh. "Then we understand each other?"

"Oh yeah. Under no circumstance hurt the boss."

Logan finished his call, walked to the door, and put his index finger on a pad. A green light flickered on, and he punched in some numbers. "Welcome to K2," he said.

As she took in the inner room, she saw it was totally different from the lobby. It was what she imagined a government situation room would look like. Maps covered one whole wall—some with different-colored stickpins in them. Were those places he had operations going on? Opposite the map wall were offices, all with glass windows, though some had the blinds closed.

Several men wearing headsets sat in the back, watching what looked like a team of soldiers in some kind of jungle on a huge screen. One of the men looked behind him and did a double take at seeing her. He leaned over and said something to the man next to him. The screen went blank, and they got up and went into one of the offices, closing the door and blinds.

"I didn't mean to disrupt whatever it is they're doing," she said.

Logan put his hand on her lower back. "No problem, they have a smaller screen in the office."

She liked the feel of his hand there. "What were they watching?"

He hesitated as if deciding what to tell her. "Here, I'll show you."

He led her to a large table in the middle of the room, to a digital map of South America, and pointed to an area near Ecuador. "Some missionaries were kidnapped and are being held for ransom. The team you just saw on the screen is going to try and rescue them."

"I didn't know you did things like that. Who kidnapped them?" She wished they hadn't turned off the feed in the main room, as she would've liked to watch the rescue.

"Drug lords. They want ten million to release them, and their church doesn't have that kind of money."

A shudder went through her. Drug lords were ruthless killers, and it was highly probable the team she'd just seen were former SEALs. This was the kind of danger Logan put himself in when he went on a mission, and what would keep her from committing to a permanent relationship with him. She refused to bury another man she loved.

His hand caressed her back. "Are you cold?"

"No, I was just thinking about the danger those guys are walking into."

He tilted his head and studied her. She didn't try to hide the emotions roiling inside her. If she hadn't asked him to come to Asheville, would he now be in that jungle with his men? Would this be the day he died? Tears burned her eyes and she turned away. She had already shown him too much, and she didn't have the right to ask anything of him.

From behind her, he sighed. "Come with me," he said, and took her hand.

He led her to the back corner of the room, stopping in front of a tapestry hanging on the wall. Woven with gold, burgundy, and brown threads, it featured a scene of a desert in full moonlight. An oasis was visible in the far distance, the obvious destination of the man and woman dressed in flowing robes. Between them, holding each of their hands, was a child of about six, and following them were two camels. There was a loving smile on the woman's face as she looked down at the child. Knowing Logan's background, she understood why the tapestry had appealed to him.

"This is beautiful," she said. "Did you bring it back from Afghanistan?"

"Yes." He put his palm on the wall next to it and it started to move.

Startled, Dani squeaked. He chuckled and pulled her into the room. She looked around. "Oh my, did you decorate this, too?"

"Yes."

The room, obviously his office as there was a massive desk of what she thought to be mahogany, was understated elegance. Mahogany bookcases lined one wall, and a deep-brown leather couch sat along another. Sand-colored Berber carpet covered the floor, and the coffee table looked like a large piece of driftwood, highly varnished. She went to it and slid her fingers over the glossy surface. "This is awesome."

"It's my favorite and cheapest piece. I found it on the beach one day, and all it cost was the varnish and base."

"It's incredible."

"Come and sit."

Dani sank onto one of the soft leather chairs in front of his desk. Logan turned the other chair to face her and sat. Steepling his fingers under his chin, he regarded her as though her thoughts were stamped on her forehead for him to read. She resisted the urge to squirm.

"The men you saw on the screen are facing a dangerous situation and that upsets you, especially because of what happened to Evan. Now I think you've decided to worry about me."

All right, so he was a mind reader. She scrubbed at her forehead as if she could wipe away the words written there. "Yes," she whispered.

"Listen, this is important. Before we go on a mission, we research, plan, research some more, and plan some more. I have men who do nothing all day but sit at their computers and dig for information. We talk to anyone and everyone who might have the slightest scrap of knowledge that could help us, and then we plan some more. We practice and train until we're performing the operation in our dreams."

He gestured behind him. "Beyond this wall is a warehouse big enough to set up mock villages. In a remote area not far from here, I own over a hundred acres where we also train. And all of that happens even before we get the intel from my government contacts."

"Like the CIA? Because I have to tell you, those three letters scare the hell out of me, Logan. Their games are deadly, and they don't give a damn about you when all's said and done. Rescuing missionaries is admirable, and I'll even admit going after terrorists is necessary, but I wish it was someone besides you doing it. All your planning and training is impressive, but it didn't save Evan, did it?"

Hurt flashed in his eyes before his face blanked. Oh God, she shouldn't have brought that up. It sounded as if she blamed him and she didn't. But maybe she did, a little, along with Evan for staying in the SEALs, and the military for sending him on the mission, and herself for not being enough to keep her husband at home.

She wiped away a tear that fell down her cheek. "I'm sorry, I shouldn't have said that."

The last time Logan's heart ached this badly was when Evan lay dying in his arms. Of course she was right to blame him for failing her and Evan. He choked down his regret. Later he would try to answer the two questions crowding his mind, the same ones he thought he'd put behind him. Did he deserve her, and could she ever love him after he'd failed her so spectacularly?

"No, never be afraid to speak freely with me, Dani. And to answer your question, no, to my deepest sorrow, it didn't save Evan. I'm not sure it's the right thing to do, but I'm going to tell you something you don't know. That mission was doomed from the start and we all knew it. The intel was bad, the vibes were worse. None of us wanted to go, but we had orders. It was a setup by the Taliban in retaliation for killing bin Laden. That part we didn't know until we rescued the army captain, but every one of us thought the mission smelled rotten. I . . ." He hesitated. No one outside of his team knew he'd offered them an out.

"Tell me. If anyone has a right to hear what you were about to say, it's me."

"After the briefing, I sat down with each team member privately and told them they didn't have to go, that I would cover for them."

"And, of course, not one of them accepted."

He met the gaze of the only woman he would ever love. "No," he said softly.

"Evan called me that morning before you guys left on the mission, and I gave him the news that I was pregnant. That should've been reason enough to stay behind if he believed the operation was doomed."

Logan understood her bitterness and didn't blame her for thinking so, but she could never understand a SEAL team's bond.

Evan would never have turned his back on his brothers. And if any one of them had agreed, Logan would have found a way to transfer them without hurting their career.

"I didn't tell you this to hurt you. I probably shouldn't have told you at all. We had orders and it didn't matter that we didn't want to go. What I want you to understand is this. I give the orders now, and if any mission smells bad, I call it off. I won't send my men into a situation I don't believe we can win."

"I wish you'd had that power in Afghanistan."

The tears pooling in her eyes tore at his heart. "And I wish I had it to do over again. I would refuse the orders as I should have then, court martial be damned."

She swiped at the tears rolling down her cheeks. "And if you had? What would your superiors have done? Would they have found another team?"

"No, they would have removed me and put someone else in my place."

"Evan."

She wasn't asking. She would have known Evan was in line for a promotion. How had the conversation veered in this direction? Maybe it was something she needed to talk about and face.

"Don't you need to be out there in the situation room, or whatever you call it, giving orders?"

"No, my people know what to do."

"How often do you go yourself?"

"Go where?" He knew damned well what she was asking, and the answer could erect a brick wall between them, or an even bigger wall than what already existed. Her eye roll implied he was stupid. Likely so, considering he'd fallen in love with his best friend's wife.

Her lips turned down in a frown. "Never mind. I don't think I want to know."

"You know, I could walk out the door and get run over by a bus. Life is full of uncertainties."

Her glare left no doubt of what she thought of his reasoning. "Yeah, you go do that." She took a deep breath and let out a puff of air. "I'm sorry. I didn't mean that. I don't want to lose my heart to you, Logan. If I did and something happened to you, I couldn't bear it."

Did that mean she had feelings for him even if it wasn't love? "What do you want?"

Her eyes shifted away, and when she turned back, the sadness was gone. "I don't know. I won't deny I'm attracted to you, extremely so. I think we should spend the time I'm here just enjoying each other's company, see what happens. I refuse to allow myself to fall in love with you, though, so no need to worry there'll be any tears or begging when all this is over."

Did she have any idea how much her words hurt? He could have her on her terms or not at all. Could he live with that? It was very possible there would be tears and begging, but they would be from him, not her.

He shot up from the chair. Going to his desk phone, he picked it up and punched in Buchanan's extension. "Be in my office in five with what you've found out so far."

CHAPTER FOURTEEN

Logan scowled when Jake walked in with Maria at his side. "I don't recall asking for anyone other than you, *Romeo*."

"Oh, shut up, Logan," his sister said.

He turned his glare on her. "Exactly when do you need to return to Tallahassee, because I gotta tell you, I can't wait." If for no other reason than to put distance between her and Buchanan.

Her smile was sugary sweet. "I can only guess what has you tied in knots." She sent Dani a significant look. "I'll be out of your hair in two weeks, dearest brother. Now, do you want to know what I've found? If not, then I'm outta here and off for an afternoon at the beach."

"Brat," he growled. He was antsy, might just crawl out of his skin, couldn't get Dani's words out of his head. *I refuse to allow myself to fall in love with you.* She'd suggested they just spend time together and see what happened. They were both single and there was nothing wrong with an affair. It was what men and women did, right?

At least it was what normal people did if the talk among his men was any indication. To hide the fact he'd never been with a woman, he'd learned to joke with them, sometimes claiming he had a hot date, then checking into a motel room—alone—where he'd spend the night. Not something he was proud of looking back on.

Why hadn't he manned up and just told them his personal life was none of their fucking business?

Now the opportunity to rid himself of his cherry sat next to him, and he was hesitating because he wanted love to figure into his first time. Was he being honorable or just plain stupid? He drummed his fingers on the arm of the chair, hating his indecisiveness.

Dani rested her hand over his. How did her touch calm him, and how did she know he needed calming? "What do you have, Buchanan?" he asked.

"Not much. I talked to Turner a few minutes ago, and he's going to see a woman who used to live across the street from the Prescotts. He'll call as soon as he meets with her. She did tell him on the phone there were twin boys."

Dani jerked her gaze to Logan. "Evan had a twin and he's stalking me?"

He shifted his chair to face her. "That's what it looks like, but it appears there's more to it."

"Like what?"

"That's what I'm hoping we're about to learn. Anything else?" he asked Buchanan.

"Whoever set up the dummy companies is very clever, but we're—no, *Maria's* getting there." He glanced at Dani. "Put Maria in front of a computer and there's nothing she can't find."

Logan turned to Maria. "Talk to me."

"Wait, what do you mean, dummy companies?" Dani asked.

Buchanan answered her. "When we ran our guy's license plate number, it came back as owned by a company called Gateway, which is owned by The Way."

"Which led me to more dummy companies: The Light and from there, Good Shepherd," Maria inserted. "They've layered them one on top of the other." She drew a square on the bottom of a page, then two squares above the one and three squares across the top, then turned the page toward Dani. "Look at it this way. The bottom square is the real thing, but they want to fly under the radar, so they created these first two companies to hide the real one. They might buy their automobiles, supplies, whatever, through these companies. But these people are paranoid, and they've got at least three other corporations that these first two phony ones own."

Dani's brows furrowed as she stared at the squares. "Those names, they feel . . . I don't know, religious?" At Maria's nod, the color drained from her face. "I don't like the sound of this."

Christ, he was an idiot. He should have told her this privately. "Neither do we, but I promise, we'll get to the bottom of this."

She grabbed his hand. "Why me?"

He gently squeezed her fingers. "Are you all right? Do you want some water?"

Buchanan hurried over to the mini-fridge and grabbed a bottle of Evian. Logan took it from him, twisted off the cap, and handed it to Dani. She drank about half of it down, and he was pleased to see some of the color return to her face.

"Let's move to the conference room so everyone can sit." Once they were settled, he asked if anyone wanted coffee.

"I could use something stronger. Got any Baileys to put in it?" Dani asked.

"Me, too," Maria said.

Logan rolled his eyes. "Not happening, sis."

"Black for me," Buchanan added.

Maria turned to Dani. "Do me a favor and see if you can teach my brother how to let loose."

"I know how," he protested. But did he, really? He pressed the intercom. "Barbie, two coffees with Baileys, one black." He glanced at Maria. "And one grape Kool-Aid."

Maria threw a pencil at him. "I want a root beer, Barbie. Closest thing I'll get to a beer until I get away from my jailer."

"Big brother no fun?" Dani said.

Maria sent him a glare. "Not in my experience."

Just what did she get up to at school? While the others made small talk as they waited for Barbie, Logan tried to recall a time in his life when he had played just because. There certainly hadn't been any fun times as a child, and then he'd joined the military as soon as he was of age and most definitely there was no play there. Then he'd spent a few months recovering from being shot in the head by a faceless Taliban sniper before dedicating his time to setting up a house and business.

In a much shorter time than he'd projected, K2 was a success beyond his wildest dreams. The money was pouring in to the point where he could afford to rescue missionaries at no charge to their church. When the pastor, an ex-SEAL, had contacted him, Logan had quickly determined money was an issue when he was asked if K2 had payment plans. It had given him enormous satisfaction to be able to accept the mission at no charge to the church.

His goals had been to escape his mother, become a SEAL, own his own business, put Maria through college, and find a woman who would love only him. He'd achieved everything on his list but one thing. His gaze shifted to Dani. Until recently, she'd been off-limits—his love for her a guilty secret—and he'd accepted she would never be his. Now the unexpected had happened and there she was, something he'd never dared to dream. Where they were headed was the question, one he'd like a damn answer to.

The door opened, Ken holding it for Barbie as she entered carrying a tray. "Need anything else, boss?" Barbie asked.

"No thanks, but bring your husband in and introduce him to Dani."

She crooked her finger, and the besotted man holding the door came to her as if pulled by an invisible string. Logan supposed he couldn't blame Ken—every man in the building drooled over Barbie. He was the only one who didn't understand the appeal. There was no disputing she was beautiful, but her looks reminded him of his mother.

Barbie, a head taller than her husband, draped her arm around his shoulders. "Baby doll, this is the boss's special friend, Dani Prescott. I like her because . . . well, because we have an understanding."

What the hell was that about?

Dani's eyes sparkled in amusement. "That we do, Barbie," she agreed. "It's a pleasure to meet you, Ken."

Ken slipped out from under Barbie's arm and came around the table. He took Dani's hand and bowed over it, air-kissing her knuckles. "You're entirely wrong, Mrs. Prescott, the pleasure is all mine."

Dani grinned. "You should probably let go of my hand now. Your wife packs a gun, and I don't want her to shoot me."

He gave a theatrical shudder. "Guns. Horrid things, but you needn't worry. My Barbie knows my heart is hers."

Christ, he was watching a farce. "Back to work, Ken, and take your Amazon with you."

After the door closed behind them, Dani laughed. "Ken and Barbie?"

"It's actually Kent, but the guys, who all have the mind of a twelve-year-old, couldn't resist renaming him," Maria said.

"I resemble that remark," Buchanan declared.

A quick smile was exchanged between the two that seemed way too intimate for Logan's liking.

"What does he do here?" Dani asked.

"He's the best analyst I've ever met," Logan said. "I'm lucky to have him. The CIA keeps trying to steal him, but fortunately for me, he'll never leave Barbie and she swears she'll never live anywhere she can't wear a bikini year-round."

He reached over and picked up one of the spiked coffees. "Now let's get down to business so Dani and I can get out of here." Suddenly, and more than anything, he wanted to play. With Dani. "What do you have, Maria?"

"I've told you the names of the companies we've unearthed so far, all with PO boxes for addresses and all based in Delaware. There are a lot of walls erected around each of them, but nothing I can't get past with enough time."

"We don't have time," Logan said.

"I did find a name associated with Good Shepherd, and I think they made a mistake there. It looked like they tried to remove it, but they didn't go deep enough."

Logan sat up. "What name?"

She rifled through some pages. "Herbert Ballard."

Dani put her cup down. "Once, the guy who calls me, he started to say something and then stopped. He said 'Papa Herb' . . . but cut himself off. He even said he wasn't supposed to say it."

"Sounds like you hit pay dirt, Maria," Jake said.

His sister's eyes softened. Logan was sorry for it, but it was becoming clear he was going to have to kill Romeo. "Keep digging on the companies, Maria. And you start seeing how many Herbert Ballards you can find," he told Buchanan. "If our bad guy is calling him Papa, it's likely he's older than Evan. I want both of you to copy Ken on whatever you find and let him start doing his magic. He has a way of seeing the bigger picture."

Buchanan took his phone out and looked at it. "It's Turner."

Good, maybe he had some news for them. "Put him on speaker."

"You're on speaker, Turner," Jake said. "The boss is here along with Maria and Dani Prescott. Learn anything new?"

There was a pause and Logan wondered if Turner was hesitant to speak while Dani was listening. He glanced at Dani and could tell she was thinking the same thing.

She leaned forward. "Hi, Jamie, long time."

"Hey, Dani, too long. Sorry I'm not there. Would've loved to see you."

"Same here, but I promise to come back sometime. Listen, they've been filling me in and I know Evan had a twin, so don't worry about upsetting me with whatever you have to say."

"Okay, I wasn't sure how much you knew. Yeah, Evan had a twin. His name's Eli. The old lady I talked to couldn't remember much, but she said when the boys were about two, their father told her there had been a terrible accident, and his wife and one of the twins were killed. She didn't know which one. He and the remaining son moved almost immediately after that. I called to check for the death certificates, and there's no record for either one. Next, I checked the microfilm from local newspapers at that time, and there's nothing about an accident involving them."

Damn, he hated mysteries.

"What if . . ."

"What if?" he asked when Dani paused, her gaze distant.

"I was just thinking, what if the parents split and each took one of the boys? I could cry to think of Evan and his twin separated by a divorce." Her eyes misted, and she blinked as she cleared her throat.

"That's another puzzle, boss," Jamie said. "There's no divorce on record."

"I think Evan truly believed his mother was dead, and he didn't remember he had a twin," Dani said. "He had dreams about playing with another little boy, but he just thought it was some kid he went to kindergarten with. I find it really sad that he had a brother and neither knew of the other."

"I think Evan didn't know, but this Eli, he knows," Logan said.

Dani's eyes widened. "Oh, you're right. Does he think he's Evan? Is that why he left Regan a teddy bear with a note that it was from Daddy? That's just creepy."

And fucking alarming. If they were dealing with a man not in his right mind, then there was no predicting what he would do next. Was Eli acting on his own, or was the cult involved somehow? Getting the answer was a priority.

"Anything else?" Logan asked.

"That's all I have for now, boss, but Evan and his father moved to Austin after the supposed tragedy, so I'm figuring you want me to head there next."

"What time's your flight?" Logan said.

Turner chuckled. "That's what I thought. Later, Dani. Nice hearing your voice."

"Yours, too, Jamie. Like I said, it's been too long."

"Wait," Logan said before Turner could hang up. "What did Evan's father do for a living?"

"He was an evangelist," Turner said.

"He was an insurance salesman," Dani said.

Dani eyed the bikini she'd bought a year before and never worn. Logan was waiting for her, and it was the only bathing suit she'd brought. She seriously considered putting on a pair of shorts and a T-shirt, but then she'd be a coward. Sighing, she stripped and put it on, and then went into the bathroom and studied the stretch marks on her stomach. Well, that's what happened when one had a baby. If they turned Logan off, then he was an ass.

She grabbed the matching cover-up off the bed, slipped it on, and skipped down the stairs. What she had learned earlier that day about Evan's family disturbed her. There was some bad business going on, so bad she didn't want to deal with it until she could think about it without feeling sick.

If Logan had allowed it, she would've holed up in her room and worked herself into a depression. "This afternoon is for us," he'd told her when they left K2 and then added, "All this shit, we'll think about tomorrow."

That worked for her.

Logan stood at the bottom of the stairs wearing board shorts and nothing else, Regan cradled in his arm. Her heartbeat sputtered. Good God, he was too damn sexy. A smoking-hot man holding a baby? Who knew that would start a fire in her belly that spread to areas no man had touched since Evan?

His gaze slid over her, from her face and then slowly down to her breasts, which peaked under the hot look in his eyes. From there, his eyes lowered to take in her belly, then to her upper thigh area, where he paused. The bathing suit cover-up was a see-through, and oh boy, was he ever looking.

She felt herself dampen under his stare and marveled that he could do that to her with only a look. Her legs were next to come under his scrutiny, and unable to help herself, she let out a long sigh. The man was making love to her without touching her body. If he could do that, how fantastic was it going to feel when they actually touched?

She put her foot on the next step, narrowing the distance between them. "Hello," she said, hearing the breathiness in her voice.

"Hello to you." His soft voice was like an intimate caress over her skin. He held out his hand. "Come with me. Today is for fun and games, but first I have to tell you something. I look at you and think I've died and gone to heaven. God help you if you smell like apple pie."

"Then God help me," she answered, and put her hand in his. "In case you didn't realize, I ache for you." His pupils dilated and his nostrils flared. Oh yeah, God help her. Her legs gave out, and she sank down onto a stair.

Brown eyes deepened to a dark chocolate as he sat next to her, her daughter still cradled in his arm. He leaned toward her and inhaled. "Did you do that on purpose because you want to be licked? From head to toe?"

Well, yes. "Maybe." His hot breath against her ear sent heat as searing as molten lava to the area between her legs. She squeezed them together in a futile attempt to squash the ache. It had been so long since she'd been with a man, and now that she wanted to, she wanted it now. Immediately.

"I'm going to kiss you."

"I'm going to let you," she said.

He chuckled and lowered his lips to hers. It started as a soft kiss as he explored the corners of her mouth, and then he sucked on her bottom lip. His kiss grew demanding, his tongue seeking hers. Was she the one moaning, or him? Both, she decided. His mouth was hot and minty tasting, and oh God, she loved kissing him.

He stilled, and they looked at each other just before they both burst out laughing. There were three of them kissing. Dani tapped Regan's nose. "Were you feeling left out? Do you want a kiss, too? Can you say 'kiss'?"

Regan giggled and clapped her hands. "Iss!" She puckered her lips.

Dani gave her daughter a smack on the lips. "There, are you happy?"

"Gan, iss!"

Logan tapped his cheek. "Lay one on me, pumpkin."

Regan obliged him with three kisses, screaming "Gan, iss!" between each one.

"I think we've created a kiss monster," Dani observed. He was so good with her daughter, and she almost wished he wasn't. She meant it when she'd told him she didn't want to fall in love with him, but it didn't seem her heart was listening.

Standing, he held out his hand. "Let's go play."

Dani sank into the bath until her chin floated just above the bubbles. She had sand in places she didn't even want to think about, but oh, what an afternoon. A smile lifted her lips. It was a coin toss who had played harder, her daughter or Logan. Regan had gone out like a light after a bath and dinner and would no doubt sleep until morning.

She reached for her shampoo, the one that matched the peaches-and-cream scent of the bubble bath. The apple pie one was tempting, but she didn't want Logan to get bored. Maybe he would want to lick this one off her as well.

Deciding what to wear took a few minutes, but she finally chose a little cotton sheath with spaghetti straps. She painted her toenails glittery yellow because it matched the flowers on her dress, and Logan had seemed to like the color. After blow-drying her hair and letting it curl naturally, she decided to keep the cosmetics to a minimum, putting on nothing more than mascara, a little blush on her cheeks, and lip gloss.

Now, what shoes? None of the ones she brought appealed to her. "Barefoot it is, then." Hopefully she wouldn't scandalize Mrs. Jankowski too much by appearing for dinner shoeless and in a dress about five inches above her knees.

Since Evan had died, she'd dressed for herself, preferring jeans or shorts and T-shirts, or bulky sweaters if it was cold. Tonight she dressed for Logan. She checked herself in the mirror and chuckled.

Well, she should probably say, barely dressed for him. Anticipation hummed through her.

She skipped down the stairs to the kitchen. "Oh, hello," she said, disappointed to find Mrs. Jankowski the only occupant.

"Don't you look pretty," Mrs. Jankowski answered, eyeing her up and down. An amused smile appeared. "Our boy's going to have trouble thinking straight tonight, I think."

Heat crept up Dani's neck to her cheeks. She felt half-naked. She *was* half-naked. "I should go change."

"Don't you dare. Do him good to pant after a woman. He never has, you know." Mrs. Jankowski grinned mischievously. "I probably shouldn't have told you that."

No, she didn't know. "Surely he's had girlfriends. I mean, just look at him. He could have any woman he wanted." It was a strange conversation to be having with a woman she hardly knew, especially with the one who'd practically raised him.

"No one he's cared about. Why you're different, I don't know, but I'm glad for it." She poured wine into two glasses and set one on the counter in front of Dani. "Have a seat. He'll be down shortly."

"Thanks," Dani said, climbing onto a bar stool. This woman had known Logan since he was fifteen, and curiosity got the best of her. "What was he like when you first met him?"

Mrs. Jankowski took a sip of wine, her eyes turning distant. "Angry. Half-starved. On a one-way road to prison, and that was if he was lucky and didn't get himself killed first. Has he told you about his mother?"

Dani nodded. "As a mother myself, I have a lot of trouble understanding how you could treat your child like that."

Although Mrs. Jankowski busied herself wiping off an already sparkling counter, Dani caught the surprise in her eyes. "It's interesting he's told you anything, but I doubt he's told you the worst of living with Lovey Dovey. Maria experienced a little of it, but he protected her as best he could. When they tumbled into my life, I like to think I played a small part in helping them. I couldn't love either one more if they were my own children."

"They were very lucky to have found you," Dani said softly. "Why did you decide to help them?"

"It was the boy's eyes. They were the saddest eyes I had ever seen, but there was so much intelligence in them. When I caught him stealing, he lifted his chin, all pride and fierce determination on his face. 'My sister needs this more than you' were the first words he said to me. Here he'd just been caught red-handed, and most kids would be crying or begging me not to tell their parents. Not Logan. I only thought to take him home and have a word with his mother or father, but when I saw where and how he lived, I did the only thing I could to help and not destroy his spirit. I put him to work."

Dani stood and moved around the counter, giving a big hug to the woman who had saved a lost boy and his sister. "You're amazing, Mrs. Jankowski."

"Believe me, I've gained more from knowing those two than they'll ever understand," she answered with a catch in her voice. "I had no one until a belligerent boy stepped foot in my store."

Dani understood—she felt like crying herself. Lifting her eyes, she saw Logan leaning in the doorway, watching them. How much had he heard? Would he be angry with Mrs. Jankowski for talking about his childhood? His expression was blank, giving her no clue as to what he was thinking.

"I'm trying to decide if I want to know why the two of you are hanging on to each other for dear life," he said.

Mrs. Jankowski winked at Dani before turning around. "None of your business, young man. Where is that girl? If we don't leave now, we're going to miss our dinner reservations."

"You're not staying and eating with us?" Dani asked.

"No, for some reason I can only guess at, Maria and I were gifted with a girls' night out. Dinner, movie, a suite at the Palms, and all the works at their spa in the morning, and then lunch at their five-star restaurant. Seems you two will have the house all to yourselves until tomorrow afternoon."

She untied her apron and handed it to Dani. "Put this on him or he'll ruin his shirt." Leaving, she waved her hand. "You two have fun and don't do anything I wouldn't. Better yet, do something I wouldn't." Laughter trailed behind her as she walked to the stairs. "Maria, girl, let's go!" she yelled.

Dani stood where Mrs. Jankowski had left her, her gaze centered on Logan. Would there ever come a time when he didn't steal her breath away? He wore a pair of loose white trousers that looked Middle Eastern and a V-neck white silk shirt, rolled up at the sleeves. Like her, he was barefoot.

Well, someone needed to bring her oxygen right now. She didn't know what to do. Apparently he'd arranged for them to be alone, but she feared she had ruined everything by asking questions about him.

"Hi," she stupidly said.

"Come here, Dani."

There had been no change in his demeanor, no welcoming smile. Just "Come here," the words spoken roughly. She went. Stopping in front of him, she waited to see what he would do. He inclined his head, listening to the sounds behind him.

Mrs. Jankowski's voice floated to her as she ushered Maria out the front door, and then all was quiet except for their breathing. She was sure hers was coming faster, maybe his, too. There was heat in his eyes—hot, burning fire.

"I want to kiss you."

Dani exhaled. "I wish you would."

There was no answering smile, no words of agreement, just his lips crashing down on hers. Having experienced how easily he could steal the strength from her bones, she grabbed his waist with both hands.

Minutes, hours, maybe days passed before he raised his head. "Are you hungry?"

"I'm starving," she whispered.

CHAPTER FIFTEEN

I'm starving. Logan understood that she didn't mean for food, but as tempted as he was to pick her up and carry her upstairs, he had a courtship agenda. He'd made a decision earlier not to do any thinking tonight. If they made love, he wouldn't be breaking his vow. At no time had he thought to include a rule that the woman had to be in love with him. If this turned out to be a brief affair, at least he would have memories of being with her. The pain of losing her, he would deal with when the time came.

She was always beautiful, but tonight she was so damned sexy that he grew hard just looking at her. Sometimes she straightened her hair, but now it was a mass of curls he wanted to comb his fingers through. He liked it. A lot. This afternoon, in the sunlight, her hair seemed to have streaks of fire in it, but tonight in the dim light, it was the color of a rich burgundy. Winding a lock around his finger, he brought it to his nose and inhaled.

"I was hoping for apple pie, but I think I've just discovered another one of your scents that makes me want to taste you. What is it?"

"Peaches and cream."

"Another lickable dessert. Nice." He leaned back so he could see her toes, grinning when he saw she had painted them her happy yellow. His gaze traveled up long, sleek legs, over the little sundress, and back up to her face. It was a damn good thing he was a disciplined man; otherwise their first time would happen right now on the floor of the kitchen.

Taking her hand, he led her to the bar stool. "Sit here and talk to me while I finish our dinner." He topped off her wine and took the wrap off the plate of grapes, cheese, and crackers.

"What are you making?"

"My specialty, paella. I hope you like it."

"I've never had it before. I love trying new things."

When she picked up a grape and sucked on it, his cock jerked its agreement. *Dinner. Concentrate on dinner.*

Since he'd prepped as much as possible earlier, he only had to cook. He put the paella pan on the gas burner and tried to think of something to talk to her about other than sex, or Evan's twin, or sex.

"It was nice of you to give Maria and Mrs. Jankowski a night out," she said.

He snorted. Getting them out of the house had been purely selfish. It reminded him, however, that he wanted her opinion on what to do about Maria.

"I'm worried my sister is starting to like Buchanan a little too much." He gently shook the pan to even out the rice. "I'm not sure what to do about it, though."

"Why should you do anything? Don't you like Jake?"

"Sure I do. I just don't want Maria to like him, at least not like that." He picked up his glass and turned around, leaning back against the counter just in time to see her sucking on the end of another grape. The wine he'd just started to swallow went down his throat the wrong way and he choked.

"Are you all right?"

No, he wasn't. "I'm fine, just swallowed wrong," he answered when he could speak again. "Why do you eat grapes like that?"

"I don't know, just something I've always done. When I was a little girl, I liked to suck the juice out of them." She grinned. "Didn't really realize I still did it."

Christ, he couldn't think straight. He shifted, glad he'd decided to wear the loose trousers instead of tight jeans. He had to stop thinking about sex, or dinner was going to end up burned.

What were they talking about? Oh, yeah. "I don't think Jake would be good for Maria. His nickname's Romeo for a reason."

"Reformed rakes make the best husbands."

He frowned. "What the hell does that mean?"

"Just a Regency saying. Means he pretty much got his screwing around out of his system, and when he falls in love, it's forever. Or something like that."

"That's bullshit. If it walks like a duck, then it's a duck."

She shrugged. "Possibly, but if you try to interfere, you're just going to drive her right into his arms. Let it play out, Logan. She's young, and tomorrow it'll be the cute guy in her English class that makes her heart go pitter-patter."

That was probably true, but he didn't like it. He also didn't like the cute guy in her English class. "What if Jake hurts her?"

"If he does, it won't be the end of the world. She'll get over it eventually, and she'll learn from the experience. You can't control another person's heart, so don't try."

And there was a truth he didn't like. When she picked up another grape, he turned back to the paella.

"What all's in that?"

Hanging onto his control by a thread, he didn't dare turn around. One more sucked grape and he would decide the kitchen floor really was the perfect place to lose his virginity. "Lobster, shrimp, chorizo, chicken, clams, and Spanish rice."

"Sounds awesome. Can I help?"

"Yeah, you can stop filling up on grapes." *Please stop.* "Top off our glasses and take them out on the deck, then grab the salads out of the fridge. The table's set." He opened a drawer and grabbed the butane lighter, handing it to her. "If you'll light the candles. I'll be right behind you." *Behind you* conjured up an image of her bottom. "Damn," he muttered, and sucked on the finger he'd just put in the fire.

Dinner was apparently a great success if the moans accompanying Dani's every bite were any indication. He barely touched his food. Would she moan like that for him? What if she didn't? What if he didn't please her? He suddenly regretted he wasn't experienced, that he didn't know how to pleasure a woman.

Would she compare him to Evan? Logan didn't know if he could bear it if she did. He didn't necessarily want to be a better lover than Evan, just different. Well, he was going to be different, all right.

"Not another bite." She pushed her plate away. "That was one of the best things I've ever eaten. You have to give me the recipe."

"Sure." If she would marry him, she wouldn't need the damn recipe. He'd make it for her—every night if she wanted. Restless, he stood and walked to the railing. She followed, standing close, her arm brushing his.

"It's so beautiful here. If I didn't love my mountains so much, I think this is where I'd want to live."

Logan angled his body to face her. "Or, you could live here half the year and the mountains the other half." He could make that work.

"Summer in Asheville, winter in Pensacola? Sounds a little like Camelot."

The breeze ruffled her hair, the moonlight making it shimmer. He burned with wanting her. If he let the fear take over that his inexperience would ruin tonight, then that's exactly what would happen.

He'd survived brutal firefights, camel spiders as big as his hand, and friendly fire. How hard could it be to figure out how to please a woman? It seemed the best thing to do was just worship her body and the rest would follow.

Moving behind her, he wrapped his arms around her chest and pulled her against him, something he'd been longing to do all night. "Would you like living in Camelot?"

She lifted her hands and rested them on his arms. "Who wouldn't?"

"Dani?"

"Hmmm?"

"All I can think about is kissing you." To start with anyway.

"Yes, please."

She twisted around in his arms. Eyes darkened to the color of forest moss stared back at him. A man could fall into those green pools and never leave. God help him, he was a goner. He brushed his lips across hers, marveling at their softness.

Though he tried to keep it a teasing kiss, when she parted her lips, he gave in and stroked his tongue over hers. She tasted of spices and wine, and he couldn't get enough. He rubbed his groin against her, and when she pressed back, he squeezed his eyes shut. Damn, he was too close to the edge.

"Let's go upstairs," he said. Maybe he could cool down between the deck and his bedroom. Or, maybe not.

"Let's stay here. I want to feel the breeze on my body when you make love to me."

A racehorse's heart couldn't possibly beat faster than his did at that moment. "You will, I promise." Logan took her hand and pulled her—probably too roughly—along behind him.

"What about the dishes?"

"To hell with them." He was going to make love to a woman for the first time in his life and she was worried about the fucking dishes?

Opening the door to his bedroom, he pulled her inside. She stopped and looked around.

"Wow."

"I thought Maria took you on a tour."

"She did, but she said your room was off-limits. I think she was still feeling a little jealous of me at the time and didn't want me to see it."

He didn't want to talk about his sister. Didn't want to talk about anything. Words weren't his priority right now.

"I've always wanted a fireplace in my bedroom," she said.

Marry me and you will have one. "When I first saw the house, I knew I wanted it, but it wasn't until I saw this room that I decided I had to have it no matter the cost." He'd left the French doors open and the wind blew the sheer white curtains, making them look as if they were doing a kind of slow dance.

"I want your bed."

They were in agreement, then—he wanted her to want his bed. He looked at the four-poster and imagined her in it. Later. They'd get to the bed later.

Taking her hand again, Logan led her out to the deck. "This is my favorite part of the room."

She turned in a slow circle, taking everything in. He looked around, trying to see it through her eyes. On the back wall was a sink and counter, a mini-fridge underneath.

Half the deck was under cover, and he'd spent many hours under it watching storms stir up the sea, something that, for reasons he didn't understand, calmed him. A chiminea sat near a chaise longue on the part of the deck with no roof. That was his destination.

"I hate to keep repeating myself, but wow," Dani said. "If you're ever looking for me, try here."

More pleased by her words than she could ever know, he smiled. He steered her to the chaise. "Make yourself comfortable. I'll join you in a minute."

"I need to check on Regan. As hard as she played today, there's no doubt she's in never-never land, but I need to make sure."

"There are baby monitors in every room, but go ahead."

"Really, where?"

"There." He pointed to the monitor next to the sink. Why that earned him a look that appeared to be amazement, he didn't know. It almost pissed him off. Did she have no idea he would do whatever necessary to ensure Regan's safety?

"Go check on her." His command was more abrupt than he'd meant it to be.

An eyebrow rose at his tone, but she left without commenting.

Don't be an ass, Kincaid. She didn't know he'd called Mrs. Jankowski and told her to buy ten monitors, one for every room of his home. He'd never known there was such a thing until he'd seen Dani's.

His mother had certainly never used one, not that she would've spent her booze money on one. Besides, who needed a monitor in a one-room shack?

Hell. He was working his way to places he didn't want to go. Logan lifted his face and breathed in the salty air. Soon he would hold the woman he loved close and finally know the secrets every man but him knew. Nothing else mattered.

Though it was a warm night, he started a fire in the chiminea and lit the candles on the table next to the chaise. Next, he pushed the button on the coffee machine and then flipped the outside lights off. He turned in a circle, surveying the scene. Had he forgotten anything? Christ, he was as nervous as a kid on his first date.

Condoms! Hurrying into his bedroom, he took one out of his night table and then, deciding to be optimistic, grabbed another. He hoped he'd bought the right size. When the girl had asked, he'd felt his cheeks heat. Hell if he knew. Wanting to pay for them and get out of the store, he'd said extra large, his shirt size. Why hadn't he thought to test one? Practicing putting one on would've also been a good idea. The Navy had passed them out, but his had never left his wallet.

Returning to the deck, he put the condoms on the table. Too obvious? He tucked them behind one of the candles. Better. What was keeping her? The coffee machine gurgled, and he made two cups with Baileys in them, adding whipped cream to hers. He took a minute to mentally run down his checklist to make sure he had remembered everything.

The only thing that seemed to be missing was the woman. Too tense to sit, he walked to the railing and looked out over the gulf. The wind was picking up, and there were dark clouds in the distance. Rain was headed their way, but he estimated it was at least an hour away.

Warm hands slipped under his shirt and he stilled. They slid over his sides, up his ribcage, and then over his back. She tugged on his shirt. "Take this off."

Logan turned. "Well, look at you." She'd changed into a short silk robe. He didn't think she wore anything under it, fervently hoped not. The robe barely covered her bottom and was so thin he could see the outline of her nipples. Any minute now he was going to embarrass himself and start drooling.

She tugged on the hem of his shirt. "Off."

"Yes, ma'am." Logan pulled it over his head and, forgetting he was standing at the railing, tossed it over his shoulder. He leaned back and glanced down. It had caught on the umbrella stand, waving in the wind like a flag.

"I surrender," he said.

Her eyes gleamed with amusement. "I wonder what Mrs. Jankowski will think about that."

"That I was struck stupid by the most beautiful woman in the world?"

"I don't know, are you?"

"Yes." It was the simple truth. The wind blew the bottom of her robe open and he had a brief glimpse of dark, springy curls. His cock must have a direct line to his eyes because it immediately sprang to attention. Shit, he was going to last all of sixty seconds when it finally happened. He should have jacked off when she was checking on Regan.

Her gaze roamed over his chest, which did nothing to help his condition. "You're beautiful, too."

"Men aren't beautiful."

"I beg to differ." She reached up and with one finger traced the dark arrow of hair on his belly, stopping at his waistband and pulling on it. His erection was obvious even with the loose trousers.

She glanced down and smiled. "I think he's happy to see me."

Too damned happy. For sure, every drop of blood in his body was now crammed into his cock. If they didn't slow things down, he really was going to embarrass himself. Glancing over her shoulder, he eyed the coffee.

"Coffee!"

She jumped and he realized he'd yelled it. "I made us a cup with Baileys. Yours is the one with the whipped cream. Why don't you have a seat, and I'll be right back."

Logan walked past her, straight to the bathroom, closing and locking the door. Hell, she probably thought he'd lost his mind. He stripped and did what he should have done earlier. Afterward—for extra insurance—he took a quick cold shower. Slipping his trousers back on, he leaned his forehead on the door and took a deep breath. "You can do this, Kincaid. Just muddle your way through it."

"Are you sick?" she asked when he returned.

"Scoot up." He slipped onto the chaise and pulled her back against him. "No, why would you think that?"

"You looked pale before you ran off."

That was because of where all his blood had gone. "I just had to take care of something," he said, and almost snorted.

She ran her hand over his arms, then reached behind her and touched his hair. "Your arms are damp and you hair's wet. Did you just shower?"

There was no way he could explain. "I meant to tell you at dinner that the rescue mission was a success."

"That's wonderful. All your men came back safely?"

"They're on the plane now, heading back to the States."

"I'm so glad, but you're trying to change the subject. Why are you wet?"

He rested his chin on the top of her head and tried to think of a plausible answer.

"Tell me," she said softly.

Maybe it was the gentle tone in her voice, maybe because he thought she'd half-guessed the answer, or that he didn't want to lie to her, so he told her the truth. "I took a cold shower."

She pressed her head against his shoulder and peered up at him. "There's only one reason a man does that. I thought . . ."

He waited for her to finish, but she remained quiet, her eyes searching his. "What did you think?"

"I thought you wanted me, that we would make love tonight."

"I do, and we will if you're sure that's what you want." He kissed the top of her head.

The wheels were turning; he could see it in her eyes. She was puzzling out why else he would jump in a cold shower. He knew the instant the answer came to her.

"You rushed off because you thought—oh, my." Her grin stretched from ear to ear. "Has it been a long time since you've been with a woman?"

His burst of laughter sounded harsh to his ears. "You could say that." Damn, she wasn't stupid. He shouldn't have said it like that.

"How else could I say it? What aren't you telling me?"

In an attempt to distract her, he brushed her hair aside and nuzzled the skin below her ear. She put her hand on his chin and pushed him away. Turning halfway around, she leaned back on his leg and shook her head. "I want to know what you meant."

The little wrap she wore rode up, almost revealing the part of a woman he'd never touched, and, God above, he wanted to touch it more than he'd ever wanted anything in his life. He grew hard again, but thankfully his hand and the cold shower had taken the edge off.

Tearing his gaze away from the secret he wanted to discover, he picked up his cup. The coffee was lukewarm, but he didn't care. As he gulped it down, he wished he'd made it all Baileys with only a splash of coffee.

"Talk to me, Logan."

He put the cup down and leveled his gaze on her. The stubborn set of her mouth said she wouldn't rest until he spilled his guts. Could he trust her with his secret? Would she laugh if he told her? If she did, he would get up and walk out of her life forever.

"Trust me," she said, as if she could read his mind.

Did she understand what she was asking? No, how could she? But she was like a starved dog with a bone and wasn't going to give it up without a fight. And he wanted to tell her his secrets. Either he was a glutton for punishment, or it was the right thing to do. The words spilled from his mouth.

"I've never been with a woman before."

CHAPTER SIXTEEN

"You've never had sex?"

"Define having sex."

This was not a conversation she could have prepared for, and Dani had trouble believing him. The look in his eyes grew wary. *My God, he's telling the truth.* "I don't understand what you mean."

He held up his hand. "This has been very intimate with a certain part of me, so I can't say I've never had sex."

"You have any wine up here?" She needed a minute.

His face blanked. "Red or white?"

"Red, a Cabernet if you have it."

Easing away from her, he went to the outdoor kitchen. Her gaze followed him, noting how the white silk trousers rode low on his waist. Shirtless, he was a sight any female would sigh over. Tall and muscled, with those lean hips and that face, a woman passing him on the street would think, *I want him.* She sure as hell wanted him.

How was it possible he'd never been with a woman? She'd almost said, yeah, sure, when he made his surprise confession, but his guarded expression stopped her. What had it cost him to admit such a thing? There had to be a reason, but she couldn't imagine what it could be. She was going to find out, though.

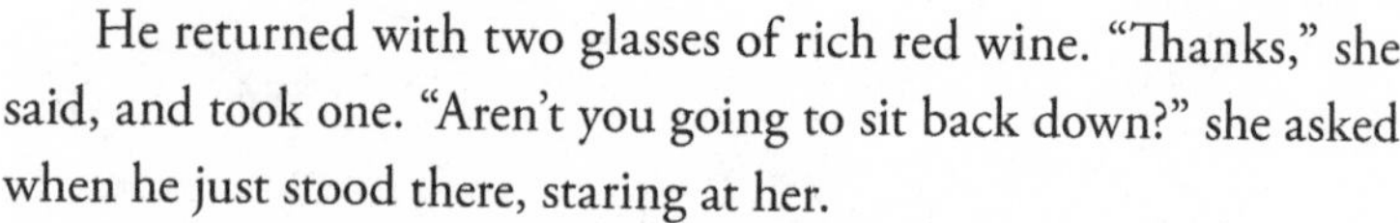

He returned with two glasses of rich red wine. "Thanks," she said, and took one. "Aren't you going to sit back down?" she asked when he just stood there, staring at her.

"I don't think so. It was a mistake to tell you. I don't know why I did. Let's just call it a night."

"Oh, no you don't." She scooted up. "Sit, Logan."

If she let him escape now, the subject would be closed forever. He would go back to being nothing more than her bodyguard, and she wanted more than that from him. How much more remained to be seen, but he was already putting up a barrier between them, and she wasn't going to allow it.

"I'm not leaving, so you may as well sit down."

He grumbled something under his breath but did as she asked. When he was situated, she leaned back against him. God, his chest was hard. She couldn't wait to explore his body—something she fully intended to do before the night was over. First, however, she had to get to the bottom of his claim. What was he? Thirty? Wow, a thirty-year-old male virgin and one of the hottest men she'd ever seen. It boggled the mind.

"Why?"

"Let it go, Dani."

Was he kidding? There was no way she could let it go, and she had the feeling he needed to talk about it. Why else would he have told her in the first place? She took a sip of the wine she hadn't really wanted and put it aside. The stubborn man wasn't touching her like he had been earlier.

Hoping he would start talking, she stayed quiet for a few minutes and listened to the sound of the waves hitting the shore. When he remained silent, she took his free hand, brought his arm around her waist, and entwined their fingers.

She twisted her body a little and leaned against his arm. "Tell me why. Please."

He stared at her for what seemed like a long time, his eyes unreadable. His mouth thinned into a firm line and her heart sank. He wasn't going to talk. Her mind sorted through what she knew of him.

From what she knew of boys and young men, all they thought about was sex and how to get it. So, if he'd never been with a woman, the reason had to go back to his teen years. Had he been sexually abused? No, he said he'd never been with a woman. Had a man abused him? That had to be it.

"You're trying so hard to guess the reason, smoke's coming out of your ears. Whatever you're thinking is probably wrong."

"Then tell me."

He took a deep drink of his wine and set it on the table. His chest rose as he blew out a sigh that sounded like surrender. "Turn around. I don't want you to look at me. I don't want to see the disgust in your eyes."

"All right." She settled back against him, keeping hold of his hand. The wind had picked up and she smelled rain. Sending a little prayer to the heavens that it would hold off and not interrupt him, she waited for him to start talking.

"I made a vow when I was fifteen not to have sex with a woman until . . ."

He shifted behind her and she wondered what it was he didn't want to say, almost asked, but her instincts told her not to speak.

"Until it was with the right woman," he said softly.

Oh God, he'd decided she was the right woman? After fifteen years of waiting? It almost seemed like a burden. Should she feel honored, or run in the opposite direction like there was no tomorrow? He started speaking again, so she shelved her thoughts. She would examine how she felt about being *the one* later. Right now, he needed her to listen.

"Two things happened within days of each other that caused me to make that decision. The first, I won't talk about. Ever. The second one—"

His hand tightened on hers and she understood he was having trouble getting the words out. She pressed her lips together to keep from saying he didn't have to tell her. Whatever this secret was, he'd carried it inside him for years and she thought it was slowly crushing him.

"I almost raped a girl."

The confession was rapid-fire, as if he couldn't get the bitter taste of the words out of his mouth fast enough. Dear God, if this was the secret he was willing to talk about, then the one he refused to ever speak of had to be really bad. Dani tried to think of the right thing to say.

He pulled his hand from hers. "Obviously, I've shocked you. Go to bed. I'll send you home tomorrow with Buchanan. He'll protect you until this is over."

Tears burned her eyes, but she willed them away. Out of all the tortured heroes she'd written about, this flesh-and-blood man held the place of honor. There was more to the story—she just knew it—but he was willing to play the martyr and let her walk out of his life without a fight. That didn't settle well. She tried to turn around, but he grabbed her waist, holding her in place.

"Go, Dani. I mean it."

She slapped at his hands. "Let go of me and I will." As soon as he freed her, she twisted around and sat back on her legs. There was so much pain in his eyes that it made her heart hurt. And then, it was gone, blanked out so fast she wondered if she'd imagined it. No, she had seen it. The ice-cold look in them now was a defense mechanism—daring her to give a damn. Poor baby. Maybe he'd defeated enemies in battle, but he had no clue what he was up against when dealing with her.

"Go away." He picked up his wine, draining the glass. His sights settled on the horizon.

"Logan, look at me."

A muscle twitched in his jaw, but he turned back and focused his gaze on the vicinity of her left ear. Okay, so he couldn't meet her eyes, but she would at least make him listen. "You said you almost raped a girl, but you didn't. Why not? What stopped you?"

Troubled eyes flickered to hers before returning to the study of her ear. "Her hair reminded me of Maria's and I thought . . . I thought, what if some guys were doing this to my sister?"

"Guys, as in there was more than one of you?"

His eyelids closed and he sighed. "I don't want to talk about this."

Liar. He wanted to, but more important, he needed to. If he didn't, he would've left by now. Once again, she found herself searching for the right words. If she'd known she would be having this conversation, she would've studied psychology. There were no magic words, so she decided to worm the story out of him with questions.

"How many boys were involved in the almost-rape?"

"Three."

"How old were you?"

"Fifteen."

Where would a fifteen-year-old most likely be for something like a gang rape to happen? "Were you at a party where there was drinking?"

"Yes."

If she was going to have to guess and get only one-word answers in response, they might be there all night. So be it. He was about to find out how stubborn she could be.

She wished he would open his eyes so she could gauge his reactions to the questions. "I imagine everyone was drunk or near to it and there was some making out going on?"

"You could say that."

"Where were you?"

"On the beach."

"With a bonfire and a boom box blasting out music?"

"Don't forget the hotdogs and beer."

Well, at least she was getting more than one-word answers now. She took it as a sign of progress. Teens with too much to drink at a party did stupid things, things they'd never do otherwise. An image of Regan, fifteen and at a drinking party, flashed through her mind. No way. The kid was staying locked in her room until she was at least thirty.

Dani took a guess. "Things got out of hand, maybe? A line got crossed and one of you convinced the others she wanted it, so the three of you took her away from the party."

He nodded.

Now for the big one. "Was it your idea?"

His eyes opened and focused on her. "No."

Careful not to let her relief show, Dani nodded as if she had fully expected that answer. "But you stopped it. Peer pressure at that age is a parent's nightmare, but you stood up to your friends when it would have been easier to go along."

"Only because her hair reminded me of Maria's."

"Stop it. I don't believe that for one second. Maria was what, four or five when it happened? Although that may have been the excuse you gave yourself at the time because you were looking for a reason to put an end to something that had gotten out of hand, you didn't look at that girl and think of your sister.

"What happened to the girl?"

"I got her out of there and walked her home."

An insight came to her then. "As much as you might not want to hear this, you should probably thank your mother you're not a rapist."

The warmth that had been slowly returning to his eyes vanished. "Like hell. If anything, she would've been the reason I would have taken a girl against her will. I have her blood in me."

"Bullshit." Dani lowered her face toward his, could almost feel the fire flashing from her glare. "Bullshit, Logan Kincaid. Blood keeps your heart beating, keeps you alive, nothing more. You are everything she wasn't and never, God damn it—" She paused and took a deep breath. "You could never bring yourself to use a woman like that because you never wanted to be like her."

"You don't have to yell, I'm right here," he said just before his mouth crashed down on hers.

Logan couldn't believe she stayed after his confession. Why wasn't she disgusted? She should've run away as fast as her legs could carry her. But she'd stayed, asked him questions he didn't want to answer, yet found himself doing so, and the only thing he could think to do now was kiss her. "I love you" almost tumbled out of his mouth when she'd dismissed his bad blood so easily, but he managed to bite back the words.

If he told her the other thing, how would she react? He pushed the thought away. Never, ever would he tell her about that. He wasn't a religious man, but he couldn't help thanking Jesus she was snuggling against him and not in her room packing so she could leave tomorrow with Buchanan. Offering to send her home with Romeo had been the hardest thing he'd ever done.

She curled up on his lap and wrapped an arm around his neck, holding his mouth to hers. Logan stopped thinking. Her bottom settled over his cock, the material of his trousers so thin it was almost as if there was nothing between them. He ground against her, gritting his teeth when she moaned.

If he wasn't buried deep inside her soon, he was going to die. "Dani."

"Hmmm?" She lifted her head and put a finger against his lips. "Shhhh. I know what you need." Her lips were wet from his kiss, her eyes dilated. "Take my wrap off."

God, yes. He'd seen naked women in movies, knew what they looked like, but this was Dani. This was real. His fingers fumbled with the knot. Christ, his hands were shaking. He finally got it untied, and she held out her arms for him to remove it.

"Jesus, you're beautiful," he whispered when her body was bared to him.

"Touch me."

"Where?" A sudden fear struck him that he wouldn't be able to please her, that he wouldn't measure up to the lovers she'd known before him.

She took his hand and brought it to a breast. "Here." Taking his other hand, she put it on her thigh. "And here. Wherever you want. Just explore."

That sounded easy enough. He tested the weight of her breast, molded it, traced the curve of it, flicked his thumb over the nipple, making it peak. His grunt was pure male satisfaction that he could make it do that. With his other hand, he stroked her leg down to her knee, amazed at how silky and soft her skin was.

Her gaze never wavered from his, and when he moved his hand to her curls and slid a finger along her folds, her eyes turned dark. His heart pounded, sending a roaring into his ears. She was so wet, and it was for him.

He'd tried thousands of times, but never in his wildest fantasies had he come close to imagining how it would feel to touch her, to feel her slick heat on his fingers. It was possible he wouldn't survive being inside her, but he didn't care. He found her clit and rubbed it with his thumb as he pushed his finger inside her.

"Oh," she murmured. Her eyes closed and she pressed down on his erection.

"I need to be inside you, Dani. Now." Her lips curved up in a dreamy smile, one he hoped to see often.

"Soon. I promise." She opened her eyes and leaned forward until a breast was at his mouth. "Taste me."

"I swear to God, you're going to be the death of me," he said, and sucked the nipple into his mouth. Cradling her breast with one hand, he stroked her back and bottom with the other while he licked her nipple.

Christ, maybe he should've added ice to his shower. He wanted his hands everywhere on her, wanted his mouth everywhere, wanted to learn her body, to memorize it, to love it. Would she make sounds when she came? Maybe call out his name?

She pulled away and he started to protest, but she moved her other breast to his mouth. "It was feeling neglected."

"Can't have that." He lightly pinched the nipple with his thumb and index finger. "Your breasts are perfect, so beautiful."

"Which do you like better, dark nipples or lighter ones?"

"These. I like these best." Not that he had anything to compare hers with, but if he'd seen a thousand, hers would still be the most beautiful.

"That's too bad. They're darker and larger now because I'm nursing. Normally, they're smaller and pinker."

"When that happens, then those will be my favorite." He thought he would very much like pink, pert little nipples.

She chuckled. "You have a glib tongue."

"Yeah? Let me show you my tongue's other talents."

So far, he seemed to be pleasing her. Maybe men were born knowing how to love a woman, or perhaps it was because his first time was with this particular woman. She was subtly guiding him without making him feel like a bumbling teen, and he loved her all the more for it.

When she reached between them, slipped her hand under his waistband, and wrapped her warm fingers around his cock, he let go of the nipple in his mouth and hissed. He closed his eyes and tried to freeze the moment in his mind. The first time a woman was touching him like this was as momentous to him as man's first steps on the moon. Christ, if the mere touch of her hands could make him feel like this, what was it going to do to him when he slid inside her?

"Time for these to come off," she said, tugging on his trousers.

Logan couldn't agree more. With her help, they got him naked. "Now what?" he asked, trusting her enough to voice the question. She was on her knees, maybe a foot between the parts of them he desperately wanted joined. "What now, Dani?"

Lowering her mouth to his, she licked her tongue over his. He tried to capture her, but she reared up and shook her head. "Now, a little foreplay."

Wasn't that what they'd been doing? Apparently not, because when she took him in hand again and rubbed the tip of his erection through her wet folds and over her clit, he understood she was teaching him a new lesson.

At thirty, he'd led a full life, or so he'd thought. He'd raised a sister, led men into battle, had faced death. Never in all his sorry years had he understood what he'd been missing until now. If he'd known, he might have turned his back on the vow he'd made at fifteen. Dani made him glad he hadn't.

I love you, he said in his mind when she sank down on him. *I love you.* The intense pleasure of having her wrapped all tight and hot around him was beyond description. Energy coursed between them, heating his blood. He raised his eyes to the stars, amazed at how bright they had turned.

Logan lifted his ass, trying to go deeper inside her. "Fuck me, Dani," he growled, gritting the words out.

"That's the plan." She began a rhythm he had no problem recognizing.

"Damn, I'm sorry," he said when his seed shot out like machine-gun fire. Embarrassed and unable to bear the disappointment he knew he would see in her eyes, he pulled her against him so her face was buried in his neck. "I'm sorry."

She pushed away and sat up, still straddling him. Her smile was soft and sweet. "This time was all for you, babe. After you're rested up, I expect reciprocation."

He liked her calling him babe. Cupping her face with his hands, he leaned forward and kissed her. "Thank you."

"Better than your hand?" she asked after snuggling against his chest.

Jesus, was she kidding? Logan trailed his fingers through her hair. "Yes. Good God, yes. It was amazing, better than my fantasies. It was . . ." He tried to think of a word to describe the feeling but didn't think such a word existed. "Powerful," he finally said.

"It is that."

Still nestled inside her, he stroked his hand down her back to her bottom. He was still semihard, and when he slid a finger along the crevasse of her ass, she shuddered and began to move. He was instantly full-blown hard again. She lifted up and he moved his hand to the front and found her clit.

"Yes, like that," she said when he rubbed it in a circular motion with his thumb.

The rhythm of their dance began again, and her breathing grew heavy. As did his. The sky opened and rain poured down on them, but it didn't seem she cared any more than he did. Water trickled down her skin. Unable to resist, he leaned forward and licked the droplets from her breasts. Suddenly her muscles clenched around him and she leaned her head back, closing her eyes.

"Oh God. Now, Logan. Now."

He put his hands around her waist and thrust hard into her, watching her face as she came, imprinting it in his mind. The pressure built in his cock again and he climaxed with her.

"Jesus," he rasped. "Jesus, Dani."

She fell against him and he felt the pounding of her heart. Or maybe it was his. When they'd recovered their breath, he stood, wrapped her legs around his waist, and turned to carry her inside. He glanced at the table. "Hell."

"What?"

"The condom. I forgot it." Had pretty much forgotten his name.

"It's all right," she said, and nuzzled his neck. "The reason I had you take me to my doctor before we left was to get an IUD fitted, and I don't think we have to worry about diseases. I've not been with anyone since Evan died."

That information was music to his heart. "So you were already planning to seduce me?" he teased.

"I admit I had high hopes, and I don't trust condoms, though I would've made sure you wore one if I hadn't learned tonight would be your first time." She gave him a mischievous grin. "Wanna do it again?"

"Now there's a stupid question. What do you think?"

He walked them inside and straight into the bathroom. Lowering her down, he reached into the shower and turned the water on. Another first was about to happen. He'd never bathed with a woman before.

"Your bathroom is fantastic. Two of mine would fit in here," she said, looking around. "What's that?" She walked to the decorative shelves filled with mementos of his travels.

Logan watched her pick up the frame. Crushed between two pieces of glass was the rose she'd given him before his last deployment. Would she remember? She had met them at the base with two roses, a red one for Evan and a yellow one for him.

"In the time period I write about, the colors had meaning. Yellow is for friendship," she'd said, and handed it to him, following the gesture up with a sisterly hug and a kiss on the cheek. "Keep Evan safe for me," she'd whispered.

He had held his yellow rose of friendship, standing awkwardly by when she told Evan that red signified love before throwing herself in his arms. That night he'd pressed the flower between the pages of a book and carried it to Afghanistan and back.

Maybe if she'd given her husband the yellow one and whispered in his ear, it would have been Evan who returned to her. Logan wished to God it had been so, because he loved both of them with every fiber of his being and every beat of his sorry heart.

What would Evan say about her standing naked in Logan's bathroom after being thoroughly fucked by his best friend? Because she was magnificent, every single part of her, and she'd never been meant for the likes of him.

The guilt he thought he'd banished returned with the force of a desert storm. What right did he have to love Evan's wife? He turned off the shower and walked out of the room, through his bedroom, and onto the deck. A hard rain battered him and he welcomed the beating. It was no less than he deserved.

CHAPTER SEVENTEEN

Dani stared at the space where Logan had stood only seconds before. What had just happened? Jeez, he was one moody, difficult man. She looked at the rose in the picture frame. Was it the one she'd given him? If so, why had he saved it, and why had it upset him that she'd seen it?

She remembered the first flowers a boy had given her. Thinking herself in love, she'd wanted to save the corsage forever and had pressed it between the pages of a book. Where it was now, she didn't know. Chad Mitchell, as it turned out, wasn't her forever love.

Had Logan thought he loved her back then? If so, the guilt of being in love with his best friend's wife would have been a heavy burden for a man striving to be noble. Then, when he didn't bring that man safely home . . . She gave her head a little shake. That was without even touching on his belief he was defective because his mother's blood streamed through his veins.

What did all this mean for her? She might be figuring him out, but she was more confused than ever as to what she wanted from him. Why did she keep falling for these alpha males who thrived on danger? Why not a nice man whose closest brush with death was driving his car to and from his nine-to-five office job?

She set the picture frame back on the shelf, wrapped a towel around her, and then went in search of the man who kept breaking her heart. Walking through the dark bedroom and not seeing him, she stepped up to the French doors and looked out.

Logan stood at the railing, wearing not a stitch of clothing, staring into the night. She imagined she was one of the privileged few to see a Greek god in person, and a naked one at that—and what a fine ass her hero had. She dropped the towel, walked out into the rain, and stood next to him.

"Logan?" His gaze stayed on the gulf; his lips stayed pressed together. Rain poured down around them and lightning flashed every few seconds in the distance. Thunder rumbled long and low, but she barely noticed.

"Logan," she said louder, more insistent. "Damn it, look at me."

"You shouldn't be out here. You're going to get chilled and then get sick." He kept his eyes focused on the water.

Stubborn man. "Then it appears we'll be sick together. Besides, it's warm and the rain feels good." No response. "Please, Logan, talk to me."

He turned to her then, anger radiating from him. "You want me to talk? Fine. I made a mistake and I don't like making mistakes. I should never have touched you. You can rest easy it won't happen again. Now go away."

She touched his arm, and his muscles tensed under her fingers. "Why? What if I want it to happen again?"

"You're Evan's wife!" he practically shouted, jerking his arm away.

That might be a part of his problem, but there was more going on in his mind than just the idea she'd once belonged to Evan. "I *was* Evan's wife, past tense. I loved him, you know that better than anyone, but he's gone and he's never coming back. Would you have me spend the rest of my life alone because I was once his?"

Instead of answering, he went and picked up his wet trousers, putting them on. He grabbed her wrap and handed it to her. "Put this on. I can't think straight when you're naked."

Hiding her smile, she slipped the garment on, although as soaked as it was, she was still nearly naked. A bolt of lightning struck nearby, and she shrieked at the loud boom of thunder that immediately followed.

"Christ, first I take advantage of you, and now I'm going to get you killed," he said, and grabbed her hand, dragging her under the overhang. "Sit," he ordered, and pushed her toward a deck chair.

There was something sexy about an alpha male bossing her around. Not that she would stand for it when it mattered, but at the moment she rather enjoyed it. He left, returning shortly with two bath towels; he handed her one and then lit the candle on the table between them. She rubbed the towel over her hair and then wrapped it around her shoulders.

Logan stared moodily out at the rain, not speaking. There was still another secret he kept close—the one he'd said he wouldn't talk about ever—but she sensed it was the one at the root of all his issues.

No matter what happened between them, even if they didn't have a future together, she at least wanted to part company knowing he had put all his demons to rest. He would never be at peace otherwise, and this beautiful man deserved to be happy.

Dani stole a peek at him. He stared off into the distance, his body taut, his jaws rigid, his lips pressed firmly together. Apparently it was going to be up to her to get the conversation going again. She leaned her head back against the chaise and sighed. Men.

"You should know, I take issue with your claim that you took advantage of me. I'm a single, consenting adult, and I assure you, I was eager to consent. But back to my question, are you going to answer?"

He finally looked at her, but his expression was blank. "What question was that?"

She tried to decide whether to sigh again or roll her eyes, but maybe it would be more effective if she just bashed him on the head. "You're not stupid, Logan, so don't act like it. You don't want to answer, do you? You know it's unreasonable to expect me to remain celibate for the rest of my life, and you think you should tell me I deserve someone better than you, but you can't bring yourself to say it." His eyes flared. Well, she'd hit the nail on the head.

"You can and should find someone better than me."

"Why? What makes you so bad? From what I know of you, you're an amazing man. You made something of yourself when the odds were against you, you raised a lovely sister, you're one of our country's heroes, and you created a company that appears to be highly successful. Best of all, you make an awesome paella. Where's the bad in all that? And if you say it's in your blood, I'm going to go find one of those guns I know you've got hidden all over the house and shoot you just to put you out of your misery."

Logan was self-destructing and he knew it, but like a cruise missile locked on its target, he couldn't seem to keep it from happening. All the things she'd just praised him with might be true, but it was all a facade, a false front he'd erected to fool anyone who looked at him too closely. She wanted to know the bad in him? Fine, he'd enlighten her. See how amazing she thought him then.

"That other thing, the one I said I would never talk about—"

"You don't have to tell me," she interrupted, but her eyes said different. She wanted to know his dirtiest secret.

He leaned forward and glared at her. "Oh, but I do. You've got it in your mind I'm some kind of hero. What would you say if I told you . . ." He couldn't say it. Couldn't tell her about that damned, godforsaken morning.

The woman he would willingly die for, the one who'd given him his first taste of the pleasures he'd listened to other men talk about, sometimes joke about, lifted her leg and stroked her toes over the top of his foot.

"If you told me what?"

Her toes found their way to his knee, and he stupidly wondered how far they might travel. His cock responded to her touch the way it had since the day he'd walked in the door of her cabin. Pavlov's dog—that was him and it fucking pissed him off.

"Little girl," he growled, "you're playing with fire. I may be new at this, but I promise, I pay close attention."

"Fire can be a beautiful thing." Her foot crept up a few more inches. "If you told me what, Logan? Come on, I dare you to say it."

"You dare me? Fine then. I shared a bed with my mother. Satisfied?" That should have the desired effect of sending her back to Asheville, so far away he might be able to find some kind of peace of mind and forget all that happened that night. In about a hundred years.

Between anger and intense arousal, she'd somehow managed to suck the confession out of him, the one he'd sworn would never be spoken of to anyone, especially her. And even then, he tempered his words, made them less crude than he'd intended.

Her foot stilled. "While I understand what you mean, and it may well be true, I don't think that's the whole story. Start from the beginning. Something like, once upon a time, this is what happened."

How could she be so blasé about what he'd just said? Apparently she wanted it spelled out. Logan pushed her foot off his leg. Although he wanted to look away, he kept his gaze on her, waiting to see her disgust, waiting for the moment when he would know he'd lost her forever.

"Once upon a time, this is what happened. I woke up to find my mother's mouth on me."

"I don't want to hurt your feelings, but I'm liking your mother less and less."

What the hell was wrong with her? "Do you not understand what I'm saying?"

"Yes, I do, and that was a horrible thing for her to do."

She didn't get it. "I had a hard-on," he snarled. "I was turned on by my mother's mouth wrapped around my cock." He couldn't put it any plainer than that.

She would get up and leave now, and letting her go would be the best thing he could do for her. Drained and embarrassed, Logan exhaled and fell back against his chair. Unable to bear watching her walk out, he closed his eyes.

Tomorrow, he would send her home with Buchanan after all. Making love to her should never have happened, but he couldn't bring himself to regret the night. It was everything he'd imagined, and everything beyond imaginable. Because of his training, his memory was highly developed, and every touch, every sigh, the very moment she'd shattered in his arms were imprinted in his mind forever. At least he had that.

"How old were you?" she asked softly.

He opened his eyes. She hadn't left? "I'm done talking about it."

"How old were you, Logan?"

A sigh escaped him. The woman could be relentless when she made up her mind to be. "Fifteen."

"And you awoke to someone giving you a blow job?"

"Didn't you hear what I said? It wasn't just someone, it was my fucking mother."

"But you didn't know that at first. There isn't a fifteen-year-old boy on this planet who wouldn't wake up with a hard-on under those circumstances. What did you do when you realized what was happening?"

Jeez? That was the extent of her reaction? "You're not going to let this go, are you?" Why she hadn't fled to her room and locked her door, he didn't know, but when she held out her hand, he grasped it, holding on for dear life.

"No, I'm not. What did you do?"

"In my haste to get away, I fell out of the bed and broke my nose on the nightstand."

"So other than a bump on your nose, what's your problem?"

He couldn't help it, he laughed. With it came an easing of the two-ton weight on his chest. "I think you're daft. Why doesn't this disgust you?"

The look she turned on him was fierce. "Oh, trust me, it does, but my revulsion is directed at your mother. What she did was sexual abuse of her son. That is in all ways despicable and inexcusable, but Logan, listen well because this is the most important thing I can say and what you need to believe. A child is never to blame." She squeezed his hand. "Not ever. You did nothing wrong, so stop thinking you're some kind of sordid monster."

"I can still hear her words as I crawled toward the door, trying to get away. She . . . she said, 'I'm sorry, baby. I wasn't trying to kill you. I just need a good fuck.' I always thought I'd done something to deserve her attention turning on me. I just couldn't figure out what." He sank back against the chaise, wondering if he was having a heart attack. He'd never thought to, wanted to, or planned to confess his dirtiest secret.

"Oh God. I said almost the same words to you. No wonder you were so upset. I'm sorry, I didn't know." Dani reached across the small table and placed her hand over his heart. "This heart of yours is pure, and you did nothing to deserve what she did to you. But, Logan, my words were the kind of play that happens between a man and woman attracted to each other. There's a damned big difference in me saying them and your mother saying them. You get that, right?"

Not until now, he hadn't. He'd lived with his shame for so long, he didn't think it would be that easy to let it go. It wouldn't go away overnight, he knew that, but for the first time, he thought there was enough light for him to find his way out of the tunnel. What could he possibly say that would tell her how much her words meant?

"I'm curious about something. How soon after that happened did the beach party take place?" she asked.

"Two nights later, why?"

Letting go of his hand, she stood and came to him, curling herself onto his lap. "No wonder you made your vow. It all makes sense now. Between erroneously thinking you were some kind of sexual deviant with tainted blood pumping through your heart and only days later, taking on the belief you had it in you to be a rapist, you did the only thing that made sense to you, the one thing you could think of to protect any woman crossing your path. Do you see how strong and honorable you actually were?"

No, he didn't see it, but he would start trying. He would do it for her and because of her. And maybe he would do it a little for himself. The tears burning in his eyes surprised him. Not wanting her to see him cry, he stood and carried her back out into the rain.

"Just when I was starting to dry off, I'm going to get all wet again," she said and giggled. She curved her hand around his neck, bringing his lips to hers.

"Sweetheart," he whispered against her mouth. *Sweetheart.* Another first. He'd never before called a woman by an endearment. What an incredible night this had turned out to be.

Logan stood on the upper deck of the home he'd once only dreamed of owning, heard his beloved gulf pounding its waves against the sand, held the woman he'd secretly loved for so long, and kissed her while crying in the rain.

Tonight he was going to hold her close, and without saying the words, show her how much he loved her. Dropping her legs, he let her slide down his body. He pushed the wrap down her arms, letting it fall to the floor. The wind had died down and the rain had slowed to a drizzle. Stepping back, he looked at her body, glistening with droplets of water.

"Beautiful," he whispered.

"Thank you. You're not so bad yourself, but I'd be much happier if you'd lose the trousers." She leaned back against the rail, and her lips curved into a teasing smile. "I want to see you, all of you."

"Done," he replied, and pushed them past his hips, stepping out of them. He kept his eyes on hers as he put his hands on the railing, caging her in. How could he be so hard and aching for her already after making love to her twice? Logan nuzzled her neck, lightly nipping her soft skin and then soothing it with his tongue.

She put her hands on his ass and tried to pull him closer. "You know, it occurs to me that you've taken to this sex thing like a duck to water."

"Quack, quack," he said, and dropped to his knees, wanting to make another fantasy come true. Tonight might be all he had with her, and he wasn't going to waste any chances. He buried his face against her curls and deeply inhaled the musky scent of her arousal. It was earthy and intoxicating. How would she taste? She spread her legs and put her hands on his head. It was all the invitation he needed.

Mine. No other word existed in Logan's mind but that. He feasted on her until she cried out his name and her knees buckled. Scooping her into his arms, he carried her to his bed and stretched out next to her. Her breasts beckoned and he touched a nipple with his finger.

She took his hand and stopped him. "I think you deserve a treat." Pushing his hand to the side, she kissed her way down his body.

Logan tensed. She was about to do something he'd often dreamed about, yet dreaded. The last person who'd had her mouth on him had been his mother, and that vision disgusted him. His erection wilted just thinking of it. He grabbed her arm.

"Dani, don't."

Lifting her head, her eyes searched his, and then her gaze traveled down to his soft cock. Understanding entered her eyes.

"Logan," she said softly, "you're wide awake, so you know it's me, Dani. This is something lovers do, and it will pleasure me just as much as you." She chuckled then. "Well, maybe not quite as much pleasure for me as you, but don't deny yourself knowing how this is supposed to feel when it's with the right person. If you haven't figured it out yet, that would be me."

She grinned up at him like a little spoiled brat who knew she'd get her way. Whether it was her humor, the bottomless green eyes wanting something he could give her, or because she so easily saw and understood why he'd tried to stop her, Logan closed his eyes and put his hand on her cheek.

"Then show me what I've been missing, Dani." He'd said her name so his brain would know whose mouth was lowering onto his cock. And, Christ, did she ever show him.

Much later, he rested his head on his hand and watched her sleep. He didn't know what tomorrow held, didn't know if he would ever have her in his bed again. Not willing to waste one second of his time with her by sleeping, he listened to her little, soft snore. Smiling, he put his arm around her waist and pulled her closer, spooning her.

So, his girl snored. Should he tell her? He thought he should because he didn't doubt she would deny it with fire flashing from those Irish eyes. She would glare at him all hot and defiant. The thought made him hard.

He rolled over on his back and put an arm over his eyes. How was he to go on without her? Who would scowl at him and tell him he was being stupid? No one else in his life would dare. Well, maybe Mrs. Jankowski might, but it didn't have the same effect. And then there was his hand. It no longer held the appeal it had before Dani.

The red numbers on the clock said it was four in the morning. Quietly slipping out of bed, he went out on the deck and collected their wet garments, the coffee cups, and wineglasses. Downstairs, he went outside, removed his shirt from the umbrella pole, and threw all their clothes into the dryer. Their dinner dishes were filled with leftover food and rainwater. Balancing them carefully, he took them inside, rinsed off the plates, and loaded everything in the dishwasher.

All the while, his thoughts centered on the woman asleep in his bed. Would she look at him tomorrow with those soft eyes? A SEAL motto filtered through his mind: *The only easy day was yesterday.*

If, in the morning, she acted as if their time together meant nothing to her, then tomorrow was going to be a bitch. Yesterday he could have moved forward in a life without her. Today, he didn't think it possible. If he'd truly understood how much he needed her, he doubted he would have straddled his bike and turned the wheels in the direction of Asheville. Buchanan could have protected her just as well, and Logan wouldn't have hesitated to send Romeo to her. Now, no one got near her but him, and that was likely going to be his downfall.

He no longer gave a damn. She was his.

Checking around, he saw no sign of their sexual romp through the house. Satisfied Mrs. Jankowski could find no reason to look at him with eyes too knowing, Logan returned to his bedroom and eased between the sheets.

Dani murmured and turned, snuggling into his body. He wrapped an arm around her waist and flattened his palm on her lower back. She quieted and her breathing evened. The idea that he had that kind of effect on her, even in her sleep, soothed him.

"Mine," he whispered, his mouth near her ear. "You're mine, Dani, and I'm keeping you."

All he had to do now was make his words come true.

CHAPTER EIGHTEEN

I didn't want to like you."

Dani smiled and zipped her suitcase closed before glancing at Maria, leaning against the door frame. "I know. Have a seat and keep me company for a few minutes."

Logan's sister sauntered in and sat on the bed. "I didn't like the way he looked at you, and I guess I had the silly idea you were going to take my brother away. From as far back as I can remember, he's been there for me. Kind of like he's always been mine, and then he brings you home, something he's never done before. Has Logan told you about our mother?"

"He's talked about her some," Dani said, cautiously. She was positive she knew things about their mother that Logan had never shared with Maria.

Curiosity lit Maria's eyes. "He never talks about her to anyone, even me."

"Well, you have to admit it's not a pretty subject."

Maria snorted. "Now there's an understatement. I shudder to think where I'd be today if not for my brother." She glanced away. "Probably headed down the same path as Lovey Dovey."

Dani thought there was no "probably" about it. "I'm very glad you had him, then."

"The thing is, I've never seen him this happy before, and it's because of you. He's barely growled at me since he brought you home, so I guess I'm going to have to like you for that, if nothing else."

"Dani, Maria, let's go," Logan's voice sounded from the hallway.

Maria jumped up and gave Dani a fierce hug. "He deserves to be happy, so thank you. I'm going to miss you. You have to promise to come back and see me."

"I promise, and you have an open invitation to visit me any time you want."

"Cool."

Since his confessions their first night, Logan had started smiling more, even laughing more, as each day passed. No matter what happened between them when everything was over, Dani hoped it was a permanent change for him. It felt good to know she'd played a role in helping him slay his demons.

Maria's claim that his happiness was because of her made Dani uneasy, though. Where their relationship went from here, she didn't know. She still had a big issue with the danger he put himself in.

Leaving Regan in the care of Mrs. Jankowski, Dani rode with Logan and Maria to K2. In the conference room, she sat down with them, Jake, and Jamie Turner, who'd returned from Texas the night before.

"We'll start with you, Turner," Logan said. "Your text said you found a source who knew the details of what happened between Prescott's parents."

Dani leaned forward. It seemed strange she was about to hear details of Evan's life that he'd never known.

Jamie read from the screen of the open laptop in front of him. "The man's name is Roger Milton. He, his wife Patti, and Prescott's parents, Tom and Ruth, were best friends. Tom Prescott was an evangelist, going to different churches for revival services, usually staying for a week. Milton was his music man."

"Music man?" Logan asked.

Jamie nodded. "Yeah, according to Milton, he had the voice of an angel, and after Prescott preached his fire-and-brimstone sermons, he would end the revival by singing 'Amazing Grace.' He said there wasn't a soul standing under the tent that could resist the two of them. He must have sensed my skepticism because he started to sing. I gotta tell you, I've never been so moved in my life. If Prescott's preaching was on a level with Milton's voice, they were a hell of a team."

"While that's interesting," Logan said, "how does it relate to Evan and Eli?"

Dani glanced at Logan. He winked and her heart did its pitter-patter thing. Forgetting where she was and the seriousness of the discussion, and because she was sitting to his right and within easy reach, she slipped her foot out of her flip-flop and danced her toes up his leg under the conference table.

"You okay, boss?" Buchanan asked when Logan choked.

"Swallowed wrong," Logan gasped, and reached for the water in front of him.

Smoldering brown eyes focused on her over the rim of the glass, their message promising delicious retribution. She lifted an eyebrow.

"Excuse us a minute," he said, standing and grabbing her hand. He towed her out of the conference room, closing the door behind him.

"Was there something you wanted, Dani?"

She lifted her eyes to the ceiling and thought about it. "Nope, can't think of anything."

"Little liar," he growled right before his mouth crashed down on hers.

God, the man could kiss.

He pulled away and stared down at her, his eyes dancing with amusement. "Behave and pay attention." With that order given, he put his hand under her elbow and escorted her back inside. The others gave them curious looks when she and Logan walked back in.

"Sorry," Logan said. "I needed to talk to Dani about something."

Buchanan smirked. "If you say so, boss."

Dani blushed. Even without looking in a mirror, she knew her lips were pink and swollen. Maria grinned, puckered her lips, and made a smacking noise, causing everyone to laugh. Dani felt her cheeks grow even hotter, but decided to fall back on the old adage that if you can't beat them, then join them.

"Busted," she said.

That set them off even more. Sneaking a peek at Logan, she thought he looked rather proud of himself. Well, who could blame him? For the first time in his life, he had a girlfriend, and it was probably the first time he truly felt like one of the guys. She took a satisfied breath knowing she'd played a part in putting that gleam of pride in his eyes.

"Let's get back to business," Logan said gruffly. "Give us what you have, Turner."

"Right. Enter Herbert Ballard. When the twins were two, Prescott and Milton were invited to lead a revival at Ballard's Christ's Gospel Church. They were scheduled to be there for a week, and according to Milton, that's when it all went wrong. He said sometimes they took their wives and kids, sometimes not, and this was one of the times they did. Milton said if he could go back and change one thing in his life, they would have left the women at home that time."

"I don't think Evan was aware his dad had once been an evangelist.

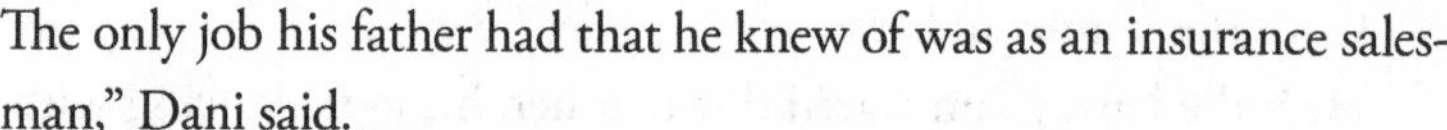

The only job his father had that he knew of was as an insurance salesman," Dani said.

"Were they close?" Buchanan asked.

Dani shrugged. "His father died before I met Evan, but he always spoke fondly of his dad, so I suppose they were."

"What happened then?" Logan asked Turner.

"Prescott caught his wife in bed with Ballard. Milton said a nasty scene ensued, with Ruth refusing to leave Ballard."

By the thinning of Logan's lips, Dani was sure he'd just put Ruth Prescott into the same league as his mother. Not caring about their audience, she rested her hand on his arm. He was tense under her palm, his muscles tight, but amazingly, she felt him calm under her touch.

"Continue," Logan said, his gaze on Dani.

Turner opened a folder, removed some pages, and handed them to Logan. "These are over twenty-five years old, but I managed to get copies of the Prescotts' and Ballard's driver's licenses."

While the group studied the photos, he continued. "The end result was Prescott returning home minus one wife and one child. Milton said Ruth wanted both of the boys, as did Prescott. After a lot of yelling and angry words, Ruth and Tom somehow came to the agreement that they would each get one, so they flipped a coin to decide."

Dani gasped and glanced at the others around the table, seeing that they were as horrified as she. "Poor Eli."

"How can you say that, considering he's out to harm you?" Logan demanded.

She turned to him. His eyes had turned to ice, his expression hard and unrelenting. This must be how he looked on a mission, dangerous and deadly. Strangely, it turned her on. She would like to go to bed with him when he was in his Iceman persona. Talk about playing with fire.

"Dani?"

Shaking her head to clear it, she shrugged. "It's obvious Evan won that coin toss. He grew up okay and apparently his twin didn't. I just feel sorry for him."

Logan glared at her. "Don't get it in your head to invite him in for tea and crumpets."

"Damn, there went that plan." If he thought he was intimidating her with that look, she wondered how he would feel if he knew it just made her want to jump his bones.

Realizing everyone watched her and Logan with rapt fascination, she waved a hand at Jamie. "Continue, please."

His lips twitched and then he slid a questioning glance to Logan, who gave a terse nod.

"Right. Milton said Prescott returned home, told everyone his wife and Eli had been killed in a car wreck, packed up his belongings, and moved to Austin. Nowadays, I doubt you could get away with something like that, but no one thought to question it. Milton said he and his wife only wanted to stay out of it, so they kept silent."

"So Ruth's still alive?" Dani asked. All these years Evan had believed his mother dead. This story was getting sadder by the minute.

Jamie shook his head. "No, she died ten years ago. The details are murky, but Maria found a death certificate filed in the state of Arkansas, which made it easier to follow Ballard's trail. He left Christ's Gospel, moved Ruth and Eli to Arkansas, settled on some land in the Ozarks, and founded The Temple of God's Divine Children. They have a website you'll want to look at. Ballard claims he's God's son reborn."

"Wow," Dani breathed.

"Jamie sent me a text with the name of the cult before he boarded his return flight," Maria said. "Jake and I have been researching them. There's not much on them, or at least we haven't found it yet. One disturbing thing did turn up, though."

She flicked through some pages and pulled one out. "Five years ago there was a complaint filed against The Temple of God's Children by a Mr. Gerald Scanlon. He claimed his wife cleaned out their savings and joined the cult. Since there was nothing else on the report, I called Mr. Scanlon. According to him, his wife, Amy, met Herbert Ballard and his son, Eli, at a local music festival. Next thing he knew, she was attending their church. Four months later, he came home from work and she was gone."

"What made him think she'd joined the cult?" Dani asked.

"She left him a note apologizing for taking the money but explaining that Herbert needed it for his ministry. She said, 'God told Herbert you would forgive me.' Mr. Scanlon went to the sheriff and filed his complaint. Said he didn't give a damn about his wife by then, that she'd turned into a woman he didn't recognize since meeting Ballard, but he did want"—she made air quotes—"his damn money back."

This was getting downright creepy. Dani glanced at Logan, but his face gave nothing away. "What did the sheriff say?"

"That Mrs. Scanlon's name was on the savings account and she had as much right to the money as he did. I got the impression he doesn't have a high opinion of the sheriff. One other thing, Mr. Scanlon told me he's found two other men in the area whose wives joined the cult after meeting Herbert Ballard. Both of them cleaned out their bank accounts before leaving their husbands."

"Do you know if Eli was involved with the other two?" Dani

understood Logan's opinion that she shouldn't feel sorry for Eli, but he was Evan's twin, shared Evan's DNA. For the life of her, she couldn't rubber-stamp evil over Eli's face.

Maria nodded. "Yeah, according to Mr. Scanlon, Eli was there each time the women first met Ballard."

"Maybe he wasn't given a choice."

A throaty growl sounded from the man sitting next to her, and she turned to Logan.

"Dani, you can't—"

"I know what you're going to say, but I can't help feeling sorry for him. Doesn't mean I'm going to invite him in for *tea and crumpets*." His fingers drummed hard on the tabletop, and she covered his hand with hers. "I understand how serious this is. I do. Just because my heart goes out to a little boy separated from his twin doesn't mean I'm going to welcome him with open arms."

"That relieves my mind." He held her gaze for a few more seconds before turning to Jake. "Do we know how many members there are in the cult?"

"As far as we can tell, fifty, give or take. The closest person I could think of to do some recon was Andre Decourdeau. He called this morning to report back. The compound is fenced in and heavily guarded. Dogs, regular patrols with rifles slung over their backs walking the fence line, that kind of thing. This is no little church on the corner your grandma goes to, boss."

"Decourdeau's a good man to have watching them," Logan said. "Can he get vacation time and hang out there? Tell him he'll be well compensated."

"Already done. Andre said he was getting bored anyway, wrestling alligators and catching water moccasins for dinner."

"Wrestling alligators, eating snakes?" Dani asked.

Logan grinned. "He's not bullshitting. Dude lives in some swamp in the bayou somewhere. Served on Team Three. Man was spooky the way he could disappear right in front of your eyes."

"Sounds like you should hire him," she said.

"Believe me, I've tried. Said he's had enough of being ordered around, but if I ever needed him for something special, he was my man."

"Ken's getting us satellite pictures. Should have them before you leave," Maria said.

"Good," Logan replied. "It seems we have you to thank for getting us this far."

Logan's sister blushed, making Dani glad he had complimented her. The girl adored her brother, but unlike in most families, he'd been not only her handsome big brother, but her father and mother, too.

"Really?" Dani asked, wanting to keep the spotlight on Maria for a few more minutes. "How did you do it?"

"It wasn't hard." She held up her fingers and wriggled them. "Just these and this," she said, pointing to her head.

"Impressive," Dani said, returning Maria's pleased smile.

"We needed to follow the trail of the dummy companies. The fastest way to do that was to put her in front of a computer, put her fingers on the keys, and then get out of her way," Jake said in obvious admiration.

Dani noted three things happening at once. Maria gave Jake a pleased smile, Jake's eyes softened, and Logan's eyes narrowed. She put her hand over Logan's and squeezed. He looked up at the ceiling and sighed. The poor man still struggled with the idea of Maria and Jake together, but he'd get over it. Eventually.

"Anything else?" Logan asked. "Dani and I have a plane to catch."

"Just this," Jake said. "I talked to a buddy of mine, an FBI profiler. If it turns out Eli's not acting alone—that if the cult is involved—it's possible Eli's been brainwashed by this Ballard dude. He said since Eli's been with him since the age of two, it would be an easy thing for Ballard to have done."

"If so, that changes everything," Dani said. She couldn't help but think that Evan had avoided a life with Herbert Ballard by a simple toss of a coin. Poor Eli.

"It changes nothing," Logan replied, glaring at her. "Go see if those satellite pictures are ready, Buchanan. I want to take a copy of them with me."

Dani carried Regan onto the chartered Learjet, every bone in her body wanting to grab Logan's hand and drag him back to the car, demanding that Jake take them back to Logan's house. It was safe there. Logan had worshipped her body and loved her there.

Her time in Pensacola had been the best days she'd had since Evan died. She and Logan had played in the gulf with Regan, had taken long walks on the beach, and one night, roasted marshmallows and smashed them between graham crackers and bars of chocolate.

Amazed he'd never had s'mores, she'd insisted he couldn't go through life without tasting the decadent treats. They'd eaten the damn things until they were sick, and then made love on the cool sand next to the fire. Like everything else he took a mind to, Logan was becoming quite an expert at the business of making love.

She watched the buildings below grow small beneath them as the Lear lifted. What was awaiting them back home? She couldn't rid herself of the unsettling feeling that they'd angered Eli by leaving like they had. What Evan's twin wanted and why he was focused on her, she couldn't imagine.

If Eli had been brainwashed, however, it meant Herbert Ballard pulled the strings—something worse than watching a Freddy Krueger movie, number one on her list of things that scared the living hell out of her, until now.

"What do you think's going to happen when we get back?"

His chest lifted as he took in a deep breath, and he wrapped his hand around hers. "I don't know but my gut tells me whatever it is, it's going to happen soon." He twisted toward her. "I'm sorry, Dani. I shouldn't have let things go on this long."

That didn't make any sense. "Don't be silly, you're doing everything you can."

"Now I am, but I wasn't before. I could have caught Eli if I'd really wanted to."

She pulled her hand away and frowned. "What are you saying?"

His head fell back on the seat, and he closed his eyes. "I could have caught him the first day, but if I had, there wouldn't have been a reason for me to stay."

Oh. Dani examined how she felt about his admission. With the advantage of hindsight, she realized she was glad he was still with her. Although, if he'd caught Eli and ended the threat, she would have never known what she was missing. She had no regrets. If given a choice, she would not give up these past days spent with Logan.

"Logan?"

"Yes?"

"There's something I've been wondering."

"What would that be?"

"For a man who's never made love before me, you're an amazing kisser. Why is that?"

His eyes opened, the grin on his face so purely wicked, her toes curled. "I never said I was a virgin kisser."

How many had he kissed to get this good? She wanted him to forget all those other women. "Kiss me, Logan."

"That I can do."

Her heart beat faster when his lips touched hers, something it had been doing more and more when he touched her. And he did like touching her.

Logan prayed that the last thing he did on earth was kiss Dani. If that wish came true, it would mean there would be a lot of kissing until then because he planned to spend years loving her.

"Dani?"

"Hmm?"

"Are you a member of the Mile High Club?"

Her eyes sparkled with interest. "No, but I've always wished to be."

"Let's make your wish come true, then. Wait here." In the cockpit, the two pilots gave him identical raised eyebrows. "No strolling back through the cabin until I say otherwise," he said, and left.

Logan returned to his seat, reached over, and pulled Dani onto his lap. He glanced across the aisle to make sure Regan still peacefully slept in her carrier.

"Hello, soldier. You looking for a good time?"

Straddled over him, she peered down at him with eyes that made him think of a green forest right after a soft rain. "Oh, yeah. Think you're up to the task?"

Her fingers were on the top button of her blouse. "I'm not sure. I guess you'll have to be the judge of that."

She undid the button and moved to the next one, his gaze hungrily following her movements. Another button undone, and then another. The plane hit a little turbulence and Logan put his hands on her waist, steadying her.

"I assume we're not going to get any unexpected visits from the pilots?" she asked.

"Taken care of." He traced a finger across her skin just above the lace of her bra, fascinated by the goose bumps that appeared. Sliding his hand under the flimsy material, he stroked his thumb over her nipple, feeling it harden. The bra was a front snap and he flicked it open.

"You're getting good at that."

"When you do a thing, do it well," he said, and lowered his mouth to a breast.

For the past four nights and early mornings, he'd made love to her, yet the newness of it hadn't worn off, and he didn't think it ever would. Each time had been better than the last as he learned what pleased her. One of the things she liked was for him to fondle and suck on her breasts. He was more than happy to accommodate her.

"My turn," she said, and slid off him, kneeling on the floor. She unsnapped his jeans and pulled the zipper down.

Logan's breath hitched. This was one of his new favorite things, and he'd decided to think positively when he dressed this morning, forgoing underwear. He lifted his ass when she tugged on his jeans, dragging them past his knees. She wrapped her hand around the base of his shaft and started licking him as if he were a popsicle. Her tongue was hot and wet, and he grasped the armrests when her mouth covered his cock. Watching her take him deep in her throat was incredibly erotic, bringing him to the edge.

"Enough," he said when the pressure started to build too much. "Come here." She gave him one last, slow lick and then stood, slipping her panties off.

"Do you know why I wore a skirt?" she asked after she straddled him again.

"So we could do this, thus making me a happy man?"

"You're so smart." Wrapping her arms around his neck, she eased down on him and made him a deliriously happy man.

Later, as Dani dozed against his shoulder, Logan wound a strand of her hair around his finger and wished he could read her mind. Was she still only looking to have an affair for however long it lasted, or was she maybe starting to consider a future with him?

That she liked him, he knew, but could she ever love him?

CHAPTER NINETEEN

Logan showered and then wandered into the kitchen. Dani stood at the counter whipping eggs, Regan balanced on her hip.

"Gan!" Regan yelled, and held out her arms.

Unable to resist, he walked up behind Dani, brushed the hair away from her neck, and pressed his lips to the soft skin behind her ear. "Hello."

She rested her head against his shoulder. "Hey, you. Hungry?"

"Oh yeah."

Her chuckle was soft and throaty. "No, silly, I mean for food."

"That, too," he said, his stomach growling, putting truth to his words.

"I heard that. I think there are only two things men care about, sex and food."

"I think you're right." He gently bit her neck, feeling a shudder pass through her. Regan grabbed ahold of his ear and tried to twist out of Dani's arm. He could imagine a lifetime of nights like this, the three of them in the kitchen, talking, playing, touching. Desperately wanted it.

"Come here, little girl," he said, and took Regan from her. "We'll be in the living room. Why don't you fix our plates and bring them in there, unless you need me to help."

"No, go entertain my little stinker," she said, and gave Regan a smack on the lips. "That's what you can do to help. Cheese omelets okay? That's about all we have until I can get to the grocery store tomorrow."

"Have I ever told you how much I love . . . cheese omelets?" he asked, and left before she could answer.

Apparently he had tickled Regan to sleep. He'd have to remember that little ploy. Glancing at his watch to see fifteen minutes had passed since he'd left Dani in the kitchen, he started to get up and check on her when she walked in with one plate and a cup of coffee.

"Here's yours. Be right back."

She returned and settled down on the floor near him, putting her plate on the coffee table next to his. "After hearing your stomach growl, I thought you'd be done eating by the time I got back."

The aroma of the omelet filled with cheese, mushrooms, and jalapeño peppers wafted up to him. "I do have some manners, though I'll admit it wasn't easy to wait." He scooped a forkful of the eggs into his mouth and sighed. She made a mean omelet. "Good," he mumbled around another bite. "Sorry." He chewed and swallowed. "Hungry."

"When a woman's meal reduces her man to one-word sentences, then she's doing something right."

Her man? His heart did an agreeable flip. The scene was so domestic and so foreign to him that his throat hurt. Was this how it was for most families? The father and mother laughing and joking over dinner while their child slept peacefully and safely nearby? Growing up, his perception of domestic bliss had been scrounging enough food to keep Maria healthy and successfully hiding her from their mother's johns.

His first real family had been his SEAL brothers. The basic underwater-demolition training had been a bitch, but it had been the first time in his life he'd made a true friend. In BUD/S training, he'd tried to maintain his distance from the others, knowing most of them would give up and ring the bell. From the first day, he'd sworn he wouldn't pull the rope that would toil his failure to endure the agony it took to call himself a SEAL.

He'd never had a close friend and didn't know how to go about making one. Enter Evan. Logan smiled thinking of his friend.

"Why are you smiling?"

Logan hesitated. A week ago, he would've shut down before talking about Evan, the guilt too much to bear. His heart no longer hurt, however, when the memories came. They were good ones and he wanted to share them.

He didn't want to make her sad, yet he wanted them to be able to talk about his friend, her husband, and Regan's father. Hoping she would like hearing his Evan story, he plunged ahead.

"I was just remembering when I first met Evan."

She put her fork down and sat back. "Tell me, please."

"I was thinking of BUD/S training. He was struggling a little, not as much as most of the others, but enough to worry him apparently. For some reason, he made up his mind I was going to make it through and attached himself to me like a damned leech. Annoyed the hell out of me."

He smiled as he remembered Evan's words. "I can't speak with his Texas twang, but when I tried to discourage him, he said something close to this: 'Not going nowhere, Kincaid, not gonna ring that bell. You got a look in your eyes that says you're gonna barrel your way through this, and I reckon I'm just gonna hang on to your shirttail and let you drag my sorry ass along.' I don't know how he managed it, but he got himself assigned as my swim buddy. Do you know what that means?"

Her lips curved in a fond smile. “Yeah, it means you couldn’t go anywhere without him, not even to the can. He probably drove you crazy at first, but then you couldn’t help yourself, you started to like him, right?”

“That I did. I’ll admit there were times I thought about killing him.” He loved the way she laughed at that, understanding how Evan could make him crazy even when he’d loved the man. “I loved him like a brother, Dani, and I miss the hell out of him.”

Tears pooled in her eyes. Why had he brought this up? They were both going to be bawling in a minute.

She placed her hand over his, something he’d noticed she did each time he wanted to climb out of his skin. “I know,” she said. “Thank you for sharing your memories of him. It means the world to me. I wasn’t going to tell you this, but I was mad at you when you didn’t come see me after you got out of the hospital. I had this idea we’d go out, have a few beers, and trade Evan stories. But you never came.”

Logan exhaled a long breath. Christ, how many ways had he failed her? “I couldn’t. I tried, but I just couldn’t.”

“I don’t understand.”

Although he’d been one at the time, he refused to act the coward now. He met her eyes. “I didn’t keep him safe for you, and I just couldn’t face you. I was wrong not to come.”

“Oh, Logan.” Surprising him, she crawled onto his lap, rested her head on his shoulder, and laced her fingers through his. “I should have realized that was why. If I had, I would’ve come to you. You have nothing to feel guilty about. It was war, nothing more, nothing less.”

She’d said that before, said it to absolve him. Over and over again, she kept turning his world upside down. The feel of her, the scent of her, the warmth of her hand in his, her words that she

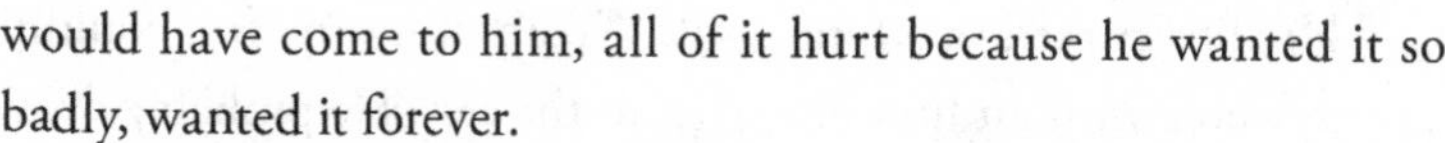

would have come to him, all of it hurt because he wanted it so badly, wanted it forever.

"Before we left for Pensacola, you said something I didn't understand, but now I think I'm beginning to," she said.

He rubbed his cheek over her hair. It seemed this was another night for confessions, but he was almost afraid to ask to what she referred. In the last week, he'd bared his soul to her and wasn't sure he could stand much more. He asked anyway. "What's that?"

"When you said it was a matter of honor. You think I belong to Evan and that you don't have the right to be with me. Am I right?"

"That's a part of it. It was all mixed up with all that other stuff I told you about."

She sat up and straddled his thighs. "So how is it different if I'm with someone else?"

A low rumble left his throat. There was only one man he would step aside for now, and that was Evan, if he rose from the dead. Unable to answer her question without giving himself away, he slipped his hand behind her neck and brought her mouth to his.

Sliding his hand down her back to the curve of her waist, Logan groaned when she pushed her tongue into his mouth. When she rubbed herself across his erection, he pressed his fingers into her skin. It wasn't until she pulled away that he realized Regan was crying.

She put her hands on his shoulders and pushed herself up. "Sorry."

No more sorry than he was. He leaned his head back on the couch and watched her through half-closed eyes. Her love and care for her daughter never ceased to fascinate him. Until now, he'd never quite understood just how much he and Maria had missed. If he somehow got very lucky and Dani fell in love with him, agreed to marry him, he thought he might want at least a half-dozen kids so he could spend his days watching her love them.

"She's hungry and needs a bath," Dani said, bouncing a teary Regan on her hip.

"Need help?"

"No, why don't you find something on TV, and I'll be back soon."

A little disappointed not to be included, he shrugged. "I need to study those satellite photos and do a little research on the computer."

After she left, he picked up the dishes, loading them in the dishwasher, and then retrieved his computer and the photos. Pouring two glasses of wine, he returned to the living room and spread the satellite images out on the coffee table.

Ever since the briefing from his team, he'd had the unsettling feeling this wasn't just Eli acting alone. Ballard had a history of going after women with money. Not only was Dani a successful novelist, but she was Evan's wife.

The last part bothered him the most. Would the lure of possessing the wife of the twin he'd not been able to take away from Ruth's husband be too tempting to resist?

The more he considered all he'd learned about the man, the more he wondered if Ballard hadn't resented not taking everything away from Evan's father. Wouldn't that spur the man to keep an eye on Evan? If so, he'd know Evan had been killed in battle, leaving a wife. Even better, leaving a wife with money. If Ballard could get Dani in his clutches, along with her money . . .

The Iceman saw things others didn't, and he just fucking knew Ballard wanted Dani and would come after her. When and how? He snatched up his phone and called Buchanan.

"Yo, boss."

"Listen, I've got a bad feeling about this cult business."

"Not surprised, but was wishing like hell your hair wasn't going to start standing on end. Gives me the heebee-jeebies when that happens."

"Right now, my hair feels like I stuck my finger in an electrical outlet."

"Fuck."

"Yeah," Logan agreed. "I want you to put Bravo team on alert and Delta on standby. In the meantime, send Turner and Watkins to keep Decourdeau company. Andre won't like it, but I don't give a damn. If something happens, I want them already in place."

"Boots on the ground, got it. Anything else, boss?"

"Have you studied the satellite photos?"

"Every inch and then again. The dogs are going to be a problem."

"Put Decourdeau on figuring out how to neutralize them. What else did you see?"

"Are you asking about the house with armed guards at the front and back doors, or the razor wire across the top of the fence?"

It was encouraging he could still count on Buchanan being as sharp as he'd always been in the field. "Both."

"I'd bet my mama the fence is either electrified or has an alarm of some kind, and you know how much I love my mama. I never bet her unless it's a sure thing."

"I love your mama, too, and would never let you lose her. If the unthinkable happens, you're in charge of getting us over the fence without getting torn to shreds or setting off any warning bells. Now, I'm going to borrow your mama and bet the house is Ballard's headquarters. If we end up in that compound, that'll be our target."

"Hoping it doesn't come to that, but if so, already got our way to it mapped. What else?"

"Just pray we don't have a reason to need these precautions."

"Doing it on my knees every night, boss. You're keeping our girl close, right? I mean, like, superglued to your side."

"So close I might have to steal your handle."

Buchanan chuckled. "No problem. I'm getting a little tired of Romeo anyway. Later, boss."

Logan frowned at his phone as he disconnected. Why was Buchanan getting tired of his nickname? He'd always been proud of it and what it implied. There was only one reason Logan could think of, and he didn't like it. This business needed to be finished so he could get home, hopefully with Dani at his side, and keep an eye on his sister.

"For me?" Dani asked, picking up a glass.

Logan nodded, and glanced at his watch, surprised forty-five minutes had passed since she'd left to take care of Regan. "Got her all tucked in for the night?"

"Hopefully." She leaned over the table and studied the photos. "What's that?"

The long, narrow building she pointed to had what looked like small ten-by-ten fenced-in sections abutting it. "I believe that's a kennel and those are dog runs. See this little dot here inside the second fence? I'm guessing it's either a German shepherd or a Doberman."

Picking up his magnifying glass, she held it over the brown dot. "I suppose it could be. There's a dozen of these little fenced-in areas, so I guess that means there are twelve dogs?"

"Unless they aren't all full, or of more importance, they keep more than one in a kennel."

"Oh." Her gaze swept over the photos. "Are you planning to go in there?"

He hoped to God not, because it would mean they'd got to her and he would be mounting a rescue mission. The look on her face was the same as whenever she saw Evan off. Was her fear this time for him?

Lifting her chin with his finger, he turned her face to his. "I'm not planning on it, but you always, always prepare for all contingencies. I don't like not knowing something, and right now, what I don't know is whether Eli's acting on his own or if he's just someone's puppet. So I'm just covering my bases."

"I understand. What's your gut feeling?"

That there was a 99.9 percent chance Ballard was pulling Eli's strings. "Like I said, I don't know. I'm hoping it's nothing more complicated than Eli's always known about his twin, found out Evan died, and for some strange reason, fixated on you as a link to his brother."

"Then his contention that I'm his wife would make sense in a warped sort of way."

A growl rose, and Logan cut it off. He might be starting to feel sorry for Evan's twin, he might not want to see him hurt if what he suspected was true, but she was not and would never be Eli's wife.

He closed his computer, stacked up the satellite photos, and put them aside. "I want you to listen very carefully, Dani. Things are about to come to a head. I want—"

"How do you know?"

"I don't know how, I just do. Maybe it's a skill that began when I had to second-guess what Lovey Dovey and her johns were up to. For whatever reason, it's always been that way for me, so don't blow me off about this. They're going to try something and it's going to be soon."

"I thought you said this was just poor Eli and his mixed up—"

Furious, he cut her off. "I've never once said *poor* Eli. Get rid of those soft feelings you're starting to have about him and do it now. He's out to do you harm whether he realizes it or not. Maybe he doesn't, but I don't give a damn. All that matters right now is this: You don't go anywhere without me, you don't answer the phone and talk to him anymore, and you don't do anything I don't tell you to do. You don't step one foot out your door, even to go to the mailbox, if I'm not at your side. You got that?"

Her eyes narrowed as she stood and backed away. "Who died and put you in charge?"

Red tinged Logan's vision. Unable to hold on to his more rational thoughts, he reared off the sofa, getting in her face. "Evan. Evan died and left me in charge. The last thing he asked me was to take care of you and his child. So that's what I plan to do with or without your permission."

Her face paled, and she sank onto the chair behind her. "The only reason you're here is because of your promise?"

"I'm here because I fucking love you!" The words had tumbled out of his mind, across his tongue, and past his lips before he could stop them. They bounced around the room as he and Dani stared at each other in shock.

What the hell was wrong with him? Stupid, he was stupid. That's not how you go about telling a woman you're in love with her. The hope he'd been clinging to that she would come to love him faded with the vigorous shaking of her head.

"You don't really mean that."

Yes, he did. He was afraid he would only make it worse if he said anything one way or the other, and was so far out of his element that he turned to leave.

"Don't you dare walk out, Logan. I swear to God, don't you dare. You can't make an announcement like that and then go hide away in your room because I didn't react the way you wanted."

He stilled, his back to her, his hands clenched into fists. "You're right, I didn't mean it."

"I think you did," she said softly.

Turning, he looked at her sitting in the chair, her hands clasped in her lap. Her hair tumbled around her shoulders, still damp from the shower, and all he could think of was how beautiful she was. He ached to pick her up, hold her in his lap, and promise her anything in the world, or not in the world. The moon, the stars, fucking Pluto if she wanted it, but the wary look in her eyes held him in place.

How long was this pain in his heart going to last? Forever probably, something he would just have to learn to live with.

"Forget it, Dani. I was just angry and said something I shouldn't have. It's my problem to deal with, not yours."

Dani wished he hadn't said anything either. Three simple words, four if she counted the f-bomb, and he'd changed everything between them. Not one of the three males before him had informed her of his feelings so forcibly and with so much rage.

No, her high school boyfriend, college boyfriend, and Evan had gazed into her eyes with stars shining in theirs and said the words with a sweet huskiness in their voices. Part of her wanted to laugh, the other, cry.

"Do you know what I hated the most when Evan was getting ready to deploy?"

Logan shook his head.

God, she hated the hurt shimmering in his eyes, but she had to make him understand why she refused to consider a future with him. "Would you please sit. You make me feel like you're going to bolt any minute, and there are some things I need to say."

He let out a weary sigh, but did as she asked and sat on the edge of the sofa, though he still looked as if he were prepared to flee. "I'm listening."

"When he stopped shaving and let his hair grow. I hated it because it was a visual reminder every day that he would be leaving again. He always started a month before it was time to go. For four damned weeks, I had to watch him turn himself into someone who would fit in better with the Afghan people in the hope that it would make him just a little bit safer. But he was never safe, none of you were, and I always knew that. I can't do it again, Logan. I can't sit by the phone and wait for it to ring, or for Jake or Jamie to show up at my door telling me you're dead. I won't do it."

His eyes were hard and cold, no hint of sweet shining stars. "In case it's escaped your notice, I'm no longer in the Navy and don't foresee any reason why I would ever return to Afghanistan. But that's neither here nor there because you don't love me and have no intention of trying. I get it."

The last thing she wanted to do was hurt him, but she had. He used that ice-cold demeanor to hide the pain of the boy whose own mother didn't love him, so how could he expect anyone else to? She moved to the sofa and clasped his hand. He held still, refusing to curl his fingers around hers. She might as well be kicking a lost puppy.

"I care about you, Logan. More than I want to, and I don't think it would take trying very hard to love you. But I won't let it happen unless you can promise me you'll never go on another dangerous mission."

"You are asking me to give up who I am, and I don't know how to be anything else." He pulled his hand away and stood. "And just suppose for a minute that I did and it turned out to be for nothing? Then where am I?"

He walked out of the room, his bearing straight and proud. Hot tears coursed down her cheeks. The ache in her heart was so intense, she feared she was already halfway to loving him.

CHAPTER TWENTY

Dani watched the passing scenery as Logan drove her and Regan to the pediatrician. She snuck a peek at him. His gaze was straight ahead, his face devoid of any expression. He'd only said one word to her so far this morning. "Ready?" he'd asked when she walked into the living room with Regan.

Sighing, she turned back to the window. She missed the way he had looked at her as if she were a treat he couldn't wait to devour. He hadn't touched her once that day and she missed that, too.

The night before, she'd decided she was wrong not to give their relationship a chance. Like he said, even if he did stop going on missions, he could still walk out the door any time and get hit by a bus. There were no guarantees in life, and she was coming to believe that letting him go would be the biggest mistake of her life.

The realization had hit her around three in the morning when she asked herself one question. Would she still have married Evan if she'd known he would die? She didn't even have to think about it. Yes. A hundred times, yes. Although their time together had been sadly short, she wouldn't give it up for the world. She wanted the chance to explore the possibilities with Logan.

Just as she turned to tell him she had changed her mind, he pulled up to Dr. Gordon's office. It would be better to wait until they were home, so she remained silent. Carrying Regan toward the door, Dani waited for Logan to put his hand on her lower back, the way he always did when he walked behind her. He didn't.

There was no one else in the waiting room when she signed in. Taking a seat next to Logan, she said, "I always take his first appointment, so we won't have a long wait."

"Good," he said, and picked up a magazine.

Well, wasn't that something? He'd just doubled his word count for the day. "I really like Dr. Gordon, and little stinker here loves him." As if she sensed the tension, Regan had been unusually quiet that morning. "I suppose I could go to one of those fancy, big places where they have fifty doctors, but I always feel like I'm just a number."

He grunted and turned the page of his magazine. All right, she could take a hint. It aggravated her that he was acting like this, but then, who could blame him? Men didn't handle rejection well, something she'd learned from her first boyfriend.

"Regan Prescott," Dr. Gordon's assistant called.

Dani stood. "Do you want to come with us?"

"I'll wait for you here," he said, flipping a page, his eyes never leaving the magazine.

"Suit yourself." If he really were that engrossed in *Parenting*, she would do three somersaults across the waiting room.

She followed Amanda down the hall. "How's that puppy doing?" Dani asked. "What's his name again?"

The girl grinned. "Trouble, and he's all that and more."

Amanda showed Dani into the room, weighed Regan, and then left, saying, "Dr. Gordon will be right in."

Cradling her daughter in her arm, Dani turned to the aquarium and pointed to a fish. "Can you say 'fish'?"

"Ish," Regan said.

The hand that covered her mouth in a crushing hold was unyielding. "Don't try to scream, Danielle, unless you don't care who gets hurt."

She knew that voice, the one that was and wasn't Evan's. "Eli?" she said, pushing the name through his fingers.

His arm snaked around her waist, and he pulled her against him. "I knew it," he breathed into her ear. "You've been waiting for me."

Regan's lips trembled, and her little arms wrapped around Dani's neck as she buried herself into Dani. "Mama, wont Gan." Dani had the absurd thought her daughter had somehow learned how to sense danger and knew who could save her.

"Please," Dani begged, "I'll do anything you want, just don't hurt her."

The body pressed against her back turned hard, anger radiating from him. "We would never hurt you or our child, Danielle. I am he and he is me. You belong to us."

Oh God, he really was crazy.

Logan glanced at his watch. He should have gone in with them, but it was killing him to be anywhere near Dani. The entire night, he'd tossed and turned, unable to come to a decision. He could have her, *maybe*, or he could keep everything he'd worked his ass off to build.

It was the *maybe* that stopped him from signing K2 over to Maria. If he could be certain it was a sure thing, he wouldn't think twice. Dani was worth any sacrifice. But if he gave it all up and then lost her, he would have nothing. Would be nothing. Again.

The sound of Regan's crying reached his ears. Had the doctor given her a shot? He tilted his head and listened for her to stop. Then he heard it.

"Gan, wont Gan!"

Something was wrong. His heart in his throat, he threw the magazine aside and pulled his gun out of his boot. He ran down the hall, pushing past the doctor and receptionist blocking the door to one of the rooms. His blood turned cold, his heart turning to ice when he took in the scene facing him. He raced to the back door, almost tearing it off its hinges as he burst through it, searching the parking lot. Nothing. No car racing away, no Dani.

"Gan!" Regan cried out, and reached for him when he returned to the room.

She was sprawled over a young girl's chest. The doctor glanced up from cutting the plastic ties from the girl's wrists and legs. "What's going on here?"

Ignoring the question, Logan gathered Evan's baby into his arms and pulled the doctor's assistant up. "Tell me exactly what happened," he said, willing her to stay calm enough to talk.

She took a deep breath and then another. "I forgot to bring her file in," she said with a glance at Regan. "When I came back, there was a man in here and he pointed a gun at me." Her eyes veered wildly around the room as if to be certain the stranger was gone.

"After he tied me up, he dragged Mrs. Prescott past me. At the last minute, before he pulled her out the door, she tossed Regan onto me. He got really angry when she did that and turned like he was going to grab the baby, but Regan cried out and he pushed Mrs. Prescott out the door."

She shuddered as she gave Logan a beseeching look. "That's everything. Please, you have to find her."

"What did he look like?" he asked, though he already knew the answer.

"Tall, shaved head . . . I'm sorry, I was so scared, I can't remember anymore."

Logan tried to find his breath. This was his fault. It had been his fucking pride that kept him from Dani's side. He willed the Iceman to return. He'd never needed the coldhearted bastard more.

Grabbing his cell out of his pocket, fumbling it as his shaking fingers dialed, he barked orders at Buchanan. His next call was to Jared and Scott. Jared answered and Logan told him to go to Dani's house, where he would meet him immediately, hanging up before any questions could be asked.

He grabbed a pen from the counter and wrote the license number of the Taurus on a prescription pad. "Call Detective Langley at the Asheville Police and report this. Give him this plate number," he said over his shoulder as he strode out, Regan held tightly against his chest.

At Dani's, he gave Jared a brief explanation and left Regan in the man's care. Knowing it was useless to try and catch up with Eli, Logan drove to the airport and boarded the Lear that Buchanan had waiting for him. He had to believe Eli was taking her to Arkansas; otherwise he'd screwed up so bad he would never be able to forgive himself. He had a little over an hour to berate himself before the jet landed.

When the wheels touched down, Logan picked up his duffel bag and computer case, impatiently standing at the exit door when the Lear came to a stop. Knowing he had to stay focused, he put aside his guilt to be dealt with later. There was no room for more mistakes.

Turner waited at the bottom of the steps, took one look at Logan, and blew out a breath. "Hello, Iceman," he said.

"When do Buchanan and the team land?"

"That's them coming in now."

Logan turned and watched the incoming jet. "You get us a conference room we can use?"

"Yeah. The greedy airport manager charged me two hundred, but it's ours for as long as we need it."

It could have been two thousand for all he cared. Worry about Dani's whereabouts and fear for her safety kept trying to creep into his mind, but he shut the thoughts down. The only way to save her was to stay focused.

As soon as the others deplaned and got their gear stowed in the two rental vans, they all followed Turner into the small airport's lobby. Logan caught the double take the girl behind the counter gave them. Probably not every day ten oversized men and one Barbie-doll lookalike—all wearing camouflage—filed by. The envious look she gave Barbie would have been funny if Logan had been in a mood to laugh.

He pulled Buchanan aside before they entered the room. "Are Jacobs and Boyer on their way to Asheville?"

"Should be landing any minute. Between Dani's friends and our guys, Regan's safe." The look Buchanan turned on him was full of accusation. "How the hell did you let this happen, boss?"

"I fucked up," Logan said, and then entered the room.

Barbie took a seat next to him and opened her laptop. She would man their base of operations, keeping track of each of them and coordinating the mission.

He looked around the table at the two teams, meeting the eyes of each one, letting them see his rage. Each one acknowledged him without a blink. The best of the best sat in this room ready to obey his every command. These men would put their lives on the line to save her. His fear for Dani eased, but only a little.

Buchanan would head up Bravo team; Turner, Delta team; and he trusted both with his life. But it was Dani's life in jeopardy, and as badly as he wanted to rush into the compound and rescue her singlehandedly, he was going to have to put his faith in these men and Barbie.

"I'm going to tell you upfront," he said, getting everyone's attention. "This situation is personal for me, meaning I can't guarantee my actions in the heat of the moment because I don't give a flying fuck about anything but rescuing Dani Prescott. That's a worst-case scenario for any mission because it increases the danger to you. If anyone has reservations about my leadership going forward, now's the time to speak." Holding his breath, he waited.

"Prescott was our brother," Buchanan said.

And that said it all.

Logan took a few seconds to clear his throat. Damned thing felt like it was closing up on him. "We're making an educated guess that Evan's twin is bringing Dani back to the compound. Not only will he feel safe there, I'd stake Buchanan's mother that Herbert Ballard is pulling Eli's strings."

"And he swears he loves my mother," Buchanan muttered.

Logan nodded. "Never doubt it." Barbie handed him the satellite photos and he passed them around. "If Eli drives straight though, he should be here in about twelve hours. Fortunately, there's five miles between the turnoff from the highway and the compound gates. We're going to intercept him somewhere along that road, get Dani, and be gone before anyone knows we're here."

"If we meet any resistance?" Crawford from Delta team asked.

Logan let them see the determination in his eyes. "Then we do what we do best." Whatever repercussions resulted, he would deal with them. "If it eases your mind, I've called my contact at the FBI. I have no intention of hiding what we're up to from the feds."

"What about local cops?" Barbie asked.

"Probably in Ballard's pockets, and if one should poke his head up, tie him to a tree and gag him." His phone buzzed. "Kincaid."

He listened to Detective Langley. Shit and fucking hell. When he hung up, he stared at the phone for a moment and then looked up. "Like we always say, the only easy day was yesterday. Cops found Eli's car at a private airport. Dani Prescott left Asheville in a plane with three men about an hour ago. The only good thing about this news is that they filed a flight plan for Arkansas, so we now know for certain they're coming here." Never had Logan felt so helpless. He didn't appreciate it one bit.

"New plan, boss?" Buchanan asked.

"New plan," Logan answered.

Dani refused to look at or speak to any of the three men in the small plane. Keeping her gaze glued to the window, she tried to guess what state they were flying over, but everything appeared the same from this height. They were headed west, and she thought it a pretty sure bet they were going to Arkansas. Well, she'd never been to the Ozarks, so something new.

"Everything will be all right, Danielle, you'll see," Eli said, and put his hand on her knee.

With great effort, she didn't shudder. Any sympathy she'd felt toward him had vanished the minute he'd dragged her at gunpoint out of Dr. Gordon's office. Was Regan safe? Logan would see to it. That she knew as sure as she knew the sun would rise in the morning. He would take her daughter to Jared and Scott, and then he would come for her. Believing in him was the only thing that kept her from falling apart.

Eli scared her mainly because of his misguided belief that somehow he and Evan were one and that she belonged to them. The man obviously needed a good head doc. But it was the two in the front seats of the Cessna that had her quaking in her boots. The one flying the plane had the meanest eyes she'd ever seen, and the other one kept glancing over his shoulder at her and smirking as if he knew something she didn't, maybe even something Eli didn't know. She pretended not to notice the attention he paid her.

Nor did the gun resting on his leg do anything to settle her nerves.

Both of them had looked her up and down when Eli had pulled her out of the car and pushed her to the plane. "Blessed Son's not gonna be disappointed," Mean Eyes had drawled.

"Kinda wish I was him right now," Smirk Face said.

What did that mean? The hand Eli pressed to her back tensed. She'd wanted to ask who Blessed Son was and why he wouldn't be disappointed, but wouldn't give them the satisfaction—nor was she sure she wanted to know.

"Get in the plane and shut up," Eli growled.

"Watch who you tell to shut up, boy." This from Mean Eyes.

Just one big, happy family. How sweet. A sinking feeling almost brought her to her knees. She'd tried to jump out of the car, but Eli had grabbed her arm and not let go until they arrived at the little airport. She feared a broken leg would have been easy peasy compared to what awaited her.

Dani glanced at her watch. How long did it take to fly to the Ozarks? They'd been in the air for a little over an hour, and as far as she was concerned, they could stay up in the fluffy clouds for eternity. She had no wish to land.

But they did. An older man stood at the end of the grass-strip runway, six men flanking him. "Blessed Son," Smirk Face said with reverence in his voice to the gray-haired man when the four of them piled out of the Cessna and stood in front of him.

Blessed Son? No introduction was needed to know this was Herbert Ballard, the man who'd separated Evan's family. Dani hated him on sight.

Bugs crawled under her skin when his gaze raked over her. Her stomach churned when he reached out and took her hand. His fingernails were longer than any man's should be, his palm damp. His face and the skin on his arms and hands were so pasty, she wondered if he ever allowed sunlight to touch him. Eerily pale blue eyes tried to hold hers captive, but she focused on his chest.

She had landed in hell. *Logan, where are you?*

"Welcome, dearest one."

"I want to go home," she said before she could zip her lips.

"You are home, little one," he replied, the sound of his voice almost hypnotizing.

Was this how he had stolen Ruth, with that soft, gentle sound that implied he understood everything about her? She wouldn't listen to him, wouldn't hear a word he said. Lowering her gaze to her feet, she repeated herself. "I want to go home. This isn't it."

"You do not wish it, you only think so, little dove. You are meant for great things and only I can show you. You have been chosen by God to stand at my side."

Dani threw up on his shoes.

Eli moved in front of her when Blessed Son raised his hand. She was sure BS meant to hit her.

"The plane ride upset her stomach, Papa Herbert. She didn't mean to do it and she's sorry."

No, she wasn't, but she kept that thought to herself. The world around her swayed, colors fading to gray. She leaned toward the one she trusted the most—though that wasn't saying much—and crumbled against him.

A cool cloth brushed over her forehead. "Logan?" She reached for him. He would keep her safe.

Silence.

Dani opened her eyes to see Eli sitting in a chair, staring at her with a hurt expression. Where was Logan? She wanted him. Her gaze darted around the room, the bars on the one window confirming she wasn't safe at home. She lay on a small bed, a thin blanket over her. When she was little, if she got scared, she would pull her covers over her head. The urge to do so now was strong.

"What happened? Why am I here?"

"You fainted."

Something else she'd never done before, but between her nerves and BS creeping her out, it didn't come as a big surprise. Oh God, had she really barfed on BS? Grabbing the edge of the blanket, she held it tight under her chin.

"Please," she begged her husband's twin. "Please take me home. Evan wouldn't want you to do this."

"He didn't like you calling out another man's name."

Not only was it weird he spoke of Evan as if he were alive, but there was no good answer to his declaration. It was highly doubtful Eli would take it well if she told him the truth. There was no one more than Logan that Evan would have chosen for her if something ever happened to him. He would be happy to know she loved his closest friend and SEAL brother.

Whoa, *love?* Crap. Now the realization hits? Why couldn't she have had this insight the night before instead of just thinking she should give them a chance? She didn't give a damn what Logan did for a living. Today had proven that even she, a stay-at-home mom and writer, had no guarantees all was safe in her little world. She desperately wanted to live through this so she could tell him how stupid she'd been.

Time to find out what was going on. "What do you people want from me?"

The hurt look returned. "I thought you would be pleased, Danielle. Didn't you miss him at all? Aren't you happy to be back with him, or has the soldier corrupted you?"

Soldier? He had to mean Logan. Probably not a good idea to talk about him. "Evan died. I wish to God he hadn't, but he did. He's not here, Eli. That is who you are, right?"

Exploding from the chair, he strode to the end of the bed and then came back, standing over her. "Evan's a part of me," he said, pounding on his chest. "Papa Herbert said so, and he knows things like that."

Definitely time to pull the covers over her head. But it wouldn't make all this go away. Feeling vulnerable flat on her back, she pushed the blanket aside and stood on the opposite side from Eli. Until Logan came for her, she was alone and had no one to depend on but herself.

She needed to get Eli to talk, maybe get his sympathy. "Of course he's a part of you. He's your brother, shares a birthday with you, shared a womb with you."

"And when he died, his spirit came to live inside of me. Now he is me and I am him and you are ours."

All righty then, she'd fallen into the rabbit hole, and a damned scary one at that. There was something odd, though. It sounded as if he were repeating a mantra, words he'd been told. She was a writer and good with words herself, so using the only weapon at her disposal, she set about befriending him. She had a strong, uneasy feeling that she might need him to stand between her and BS.

"I wish Evan had known about you, Eli. He would've loved knowing he had a twin brother, but his father never told him. Somewhere deep inside him, I think the memory was there. Sometimes he dreamed about another little boy. The dreams were always the same. He and the boy were playing with a brown dog, a boxer, he thought."

"Thumper," Eli said through a rush of breath.

Hell if she knew. Evan had never said the dog had a name. "Yes, Thumper. He didn't know about you, Eli. If he had, he would have searched for you."

"Didn't he see my face in the dreams? Didn't he see I looked just like him?"

Lord, between Logan and Eli, she really should have majored in psychology. The man who had Evan's face had his eyes trained on her, his expression heartbreakingly and boyishly hopeful. Although she knew nothing about him, she thought it possible someone had done a superb job of stunting his mental growth. If she had to point an accusing finger, she would aim it right at Mr. BS.

Steeling herself, calling up her courage, she walked to him and put her hand on his arm. "I'm sorry, but when he woke up, he could never remember what the other boy looked like. Maybe it was a safeguard kind of thing, maybe he couldn't comprehend he had a twin brother and someone had been cruel enough to separate you."

"But I always remembered him."

"Are you sure? Was it more like you were told about him?"

"Papa Herbert used to tell me about the good little boy that got left behind. When I was bad, he would wish he'd picked Evan instead. I tried really hard not to be bad. Mother said I didn't have it in me to be good, but Papa Herbert said she was wrong, that I only had to try harder."

Man, she was so far out of her depth she might as well be having a conversation with a kangaroo. "Eli—"

The door opened and BS walked in, dressed in a flowing white robe, his only adornment a heavy gold chain with a cross hanging from it. She caught a glimpse of Mean Eyes and Smirk Face standing outside like sentries.

Had they been there all along, and more troubling, had they heard the conversation between her and Eli and guessed what she was up to? BS gave her a benevolent smile, one that said she was a misbehaving child and he the understanding parent.

"Danielle, it is my honor to welcome you to The Temple of God's Divine Children," he purred in his soft, musical voice. "I am Blessed Son of Supreme Lightness, but you don't have to tangle your tongue with all that. Blessed Son will do, or just Blessed if you prefer. Are you comfortable, my dear? You are my guest, soon to be my . . . well, we'll get to that later. Is there anything you need?"

Was he implying that he was the Son of God? Dani backed away, putting the bed between them. If he thought she was stupid enough to fall for his bullshit, he was in for a big surprise. But that didn't mean he didn't scare the daylights out of her. He was like a cobra, swaying prettily in front of her, trying to draw her in until she forgot he was a deadly son of a bitch.

"There's only one thing I need and that's for you to let me go home."

The bastard tsked. "You are home, Danielle. I know you don't understand anything yet, but very soon now, you'll thank me."

Seriously, he thought she would thank him? Why hadn't anyone told her pigs had finally sprouted wings? "You can't just jerk me out of my life. My daughter needs me." She hated how desperate she sounded.

"Ah, sweet Regan. Such a delightful child. Put your fears to rest, Danielle. She's being well cared for as long as you behave like the good girl I know you are."

Dani's knees gave out and she sank to the floor. *Oh God, I beg you, please don't let it be true.* He was lying, he had to be. Logan would have gotten to Regan before anyone else could have, and he wouldn't let anyone steal her away. He wouldn't. Her daughter was safe, she knew it in her heart because she didn't doubt she could depend on Logan. The knowledge calmed her.

As she knelt with her head near her legs, she forced her breathing to return to normal and considered how to go on. BS was counting on her cooperation by using Regan as leverage. Only, he was lying, lying, lying. What would Logan tell her to do? His voice, almost as if he were standing next to her, whispered into her ear. *Buy time, Dani. I'm coming for you.*

Pushing herself up, she squared her shoulders and looked at the creep. He had fish eyes, bulging and weirdly incandescent. Crazy eyes. She would not cower before this self-important blowfish.

"Well then, that relieves my mind. Now I'd like you to leave. I'm tired from all the excitement and would love a nap."

BS gave himself away when his eyes widened in surprise.

Didn't expect that, did you, you freaking asshole?

"Have her bathed and ready to join me for dinner," BS said, his gaze hard on her. "Her wedding dress is in the closet." He turned and strode out of the room.

Dani turned to Eli. Her wedding dress?

CHAPTER TWENTY-ONE

Logan stood on a hill under the branches of a giant pine tree and surveyed the perimeter of the compound through high-powered binoculars. Inside the fence, women garbed in old-fashioned dresses covering them from neck to shoes worked in a large vegetable garden. Men roamed around, seemingly not doing much of anything.

Off to the left was a grass landing strip, an older-model Cessna 182 sitting out in the open. It didn't look well maintained. It would be best not to think about Dani flying in that piece of junk.

Where the hell was she? He swept the binoculars across the camp, stopping when he saw a man dressed in all white enter a small building. An introduction wasn't needed to know he was looking at Herbert Ballard. Two men stood guard outside the door.

Logan took in the details of the building, noting there was one window with bars on the side he could see. That had to be where they were holding her. He kept his sight trained on the door, waiting for Ballard to come out.

Closing his mind to the sounds around him, he tried to sense Dani. If only he could somehow let her know he was there. The air around him grew heavy, his breathing slowed, and something strange happened. For a moment in time, Evan stood next to him and they were with Dani. "Buy time and stay safe," Logan whispered.

"What?"

What the hell had just happened? He lowered the binoculars and blinked at Buchanan. "I didn't say anything."

"Did, too."

Had he? It had seemed so real that maybe he had. "Are the dogs going to be a problem?"

"Decourdeau says not to worry."

"What's his plan, do you know?"

"He's got a tranquilizer gun. Said there's just four Dobermans and they're only half-ass trained, so no big deal. He's been creeping up to the fence at night, cooing to them in Doberish. Man's wonky, if you ask me. Rubs raw meat all over his clothes and then goes a'visiting his doggies."

Logan raised a brow. "And they don't bark?"

"Surprised me, too. Now if you or me tried to sneak up on them, different story altogether. Swear to God, dude's got some kind of voodoo shit going on."

"Whatever works," Logan said. "Stupid of these idiots not to have anyone doing night patrol with the dogs. Not that I'm complaining."

"Yeah, there's only the guard at the gate on duty at night."

Ballard came out and Logan brought the binoculars back up. The man said a few words to the guards and then walked off. Logan tracked him, noting he entered the only building that looked like a house. Besides the house, there were several structures that appeared to be dormitories, along with the kennels and the small building where they were keeping Dani. The big question was, would she still be there at 0300? He unrolled his site map and circled Dani's location and the house.

"Call Turner and tell him to send one of his men here. I want him watching that building from now until we drop in on them. If they move Dani, I want to be notified immediately."

"Hey, boss, look."

Through the binoculars, he saw Evan's twin up close for the first time. Except for the shaved head, Logan would've sworn he was seeing his friend. Eli said something to one of the guards, the man walked away, and then Eli went back inside with Dani. Rage turned Logan's gut sour. He stepped forward, intending to tear the place apart with his bare hands to get to her.

Buchanan grabbed his arm. "Easy, Iceman."

The name grounded him, and Logan stilled, letting the Iceman cool his blood. He'd already made one mistake too many—another was unacceptable. The Iceman didn't screw up. Logan did, and so he was banished until Dani was safe in his arms.

"Meeting at eighteen hundred. I want everyone there except the man assigned to this post. He's not to move an inch until I say otherwise."

Deep in the woods, Logan sat next to Barbie and spread out the satellite photo in the middle of the circle of men. She'd participated in one previous mission on American soil, acting as their operations coordinator. Her goal was to join one of the teams, but she had no combat experience and would have to prove herself to the men. So far, she was doing an excellent job of winning their respect.

He went over the plan, and then went over it again. They didn't have the luxury of their warehouse, where they could build a facsimile of the compound and train for a week or two, but each soul on the mission knew what was at stake and they would do or die. Logan had been on many missions with some of these men, some he hadn't, but they were all ex-SEALs and the most skilled in the world at what they did.

The plan was the best they could come up with under the circumstances, the one least likely to get anyone killed on either side.

If the Iceman had to, however, he would metamorphose into Superman and take a hundred bullets, because nothing and no one would stop him from rescuing Dani.

After reviewing the upcoming night a third time, it was time for a pep talk. "Andre's bewitched the dogs, so you don't have to worry about Doberman teeth sinking into your ass." Logan looked at Decourdeau and shuddered. "You're a scary man, but I can live with that as long as you don't ever turn your voodoo shit my way."

"No problem, *mon ami*, long as you don't go and piss me off."

As Logan had intended, the men laughed quietly. "And you, Romeo, no flirting with the ladies."

Buchanan grinned. "That I can't promise, even if they are wearing more clothes than a nun at Sunday services."

More low chuckles. Logan put his arm around Barbie's shoulders and kissed her cheek. "And you, doll baby, when we get Dani out, throw her in the van and don't look back. Turner," he said, "your only job is to sit outside the gate, engine running. When our girls scramble inside, you don't stop until you get to Asheville. Anyone suspicious comes near you, you shoot to kill. Got that?"

Turner nodded.

"Anything else?" When they all remained silent, he spoke the first words of the SEAL pledge.

"To find us—"

"You must be good," the rest chimed in.

"To catch us,

"You must be quick . . .

"To defeat us,

"You must be . . .

"JOKING!"

Curled fists piled one on top of the other. "God be with us," he said.

"God be with us," the others echoed.

Dani looked for a lock on the bathroom door, but there wasn't one. The room was small, the shower, sink, and toilet crowded so close, she could barely turn around. She turned the shower on, hoping that Eli thought she was doing as told. There was no way on God's earth she was taking her clothes off if she couldn't lock herself in. Who in their right mind would get all smelly-good for BS, anyway?

She stared at the white dress hanging on the back of the door. It seemed ominous, like if she put it on, bad things would start happening. Did Eli really think she would willingly marry him? If so, he was as cracked as BS.

They'd taken her purse and cell phone, so there wasn't any way to contact Logan. The only window in the cabin was barred, giving her no means of escape unless she could barrel past Eli, the two men standing guard outside, and who knew how many others. The odds of success were probably on level with winning the lottery.

She turned on the sink faucet and splashed cool water on her face. *Think, Dani. You have to think your way out of this. Buy time, stay calm.*

The first place Logan would look for her would be the cult's compound. Until he arrived, she would somehow have to manage on her own. She turned the faucet and shower off and left the dress hanging on the door. Eli stood at the window, staring out. He turned, his gaze sliding over her.

"You have to get ready, Danielle."

"What did he mean by 'wedding dress'?"

"Papa Herbert will explain everything at dinner. Please, you don't want to anger him; you have to wear the dress."

Dani sensed he spoke from experience, but she didn't feel particularly obedient at the moment. "I'll take my chances."

Fear flashed in his eyes. "He'll blame me."

Why Eli didn't scare her the way BS did, she wasn't sure. He seemed more like an oversized boy eager to please the adults in his life. And he looked like Evan. Her husband might have been lethal in battle, but where she was concerned, there hadn't been a mean bone in his body. It was impossible to look at his twin and believe he was evil. Misguided and ill used, yes. A bad man, no.

"Eli, you can't just go and steal someone out of their life. Please, take me home."

"Don't you want to be with me and Evan? I thought you would be happy here with us."

The door opened and Smirk Face entered, saving her from having to respond. He handed Eli a brown bag and a bottle of water.

"Blessed Son said seven sharp." He walked out whistling the wedding march.

Dani didn't much like the sound of that, and how they could call the man Blessed Son and keep a straight face was beyond her.

Eli thrust the bag and water into her hand. "I thought you might be hungry since you missed lunch."

She looked in the bag. She was hungry, but it was entirely possible they'd drugged the sandwich. "Thanks, but I'm not, actually." It would be best not to eat anything they gave her. She could last until Logan came. Holding the bottle up to see it was unopened, she twisted the cap off and drank.

"I'm going to leave you alone so you'll have privacy to dress."

Suddenly she didn't want him to leave. What if one or both of the guards decided to have a little fun with her? "No, please stay."

This seemed to please him and he sat down in the chair. "I'll wait here. You can change in the bathroom."

They were going to have to hold her down and put that dress on her if they were that determined she wear it. "I have a better idea," she said, and sat on the edge of the bed. "Suppose I tell you about Evan?"

He glanced away, his desire to learn about his brother obviously at war with his orders from BS. Dani remained quiet, letting him battle it out. Evan would win out, she was certain. If she played this right, maybe, just maybe, she could turn Eli against BS.

His gaze finally settled back on her. "Did he look like me?"

Victorious, she grinned. "Exactly like you, with only one exception. He had hair."

He swept a hand over his head. "Yeah?"

"Yeah. Between deployments, he kept it short, but when it neared time to ship out, he let it grow." Within ten minutes, he had moved to the edge of the chair and seemed to be hanging on to her every word as she told him stories of his brother. All she could think was, poor Eli, and how sad Evan never knew about him. Sad for Eli, too, because Evan would have moved heaven and earth to save his twin if he'd only known.

"He was your brother, Eli, your twin, and in his dreams he knew you, loved you. He loved me, too, and it would hurt him to know someone meant me harm and that you were a part of it. Please believe that, because I would never lie to you. He would only ask one thing of you," she said when she noticed the sun setting, a reminder it was almost time to enter the viper's nest.

"What would he ask?" They were the first words Eli had uttered since she'd started talking.

"That you protect me. He would want you to keep me safe. You're not my husband, Eli, nor will you be. But you are Evan's twin and his family. I do love you, but it's the love one would have for a brother."

"But he's me, so how can you say you can't love me like you loved him?"

It was like talking to a child and trying to answer his endless whys. Even the expression on his face was that of a boy trying to understand the world around him. Instinctively, she tempered her words to ones a child would understand.

"Whoever told you that lied." Damn you, BS. "You're you. You can't be Evan, because you're Eli. Somewhere in this vast world is a woman meant only for you. It isn't me. Love me like a sister and you'll always be a part of my life. Try to force me into something I don't want and I'll hate you for it."

"I don't want you to hate me," he said, his voice plaintive.

This whole situation was bizarre, surreal. Kneeling in front of him, Dani curled her fingers over his hands. "I could never hate Evan's brother, my brother. Please, you have to stop this insanity."

The door banged open. "Ain't this a cozy scene?"

Dani glanced over Eli's shoulder to see Mean Eyes staring at them, his lips curved in a leer. Letting go of Eli, she backed up until she hit the wall. Had her words gotten through? Would he stand between her and danger?

"Don't look to me like she's ready for him," Mean Eyes said. "What's going on here, boy?"

"She's turning out to be a stubborn one," Eli said, his back to the guard. He winked at her before he turned. "I'm having doubts she's gonna be an obedient wife."

"You still think he brought her here for you?" The man laughed, the ugly sound of it filling the small room. "You're stupider than I thought, Eli."

Dani's still-unsettled stomach roiled at the implication of Mean Eyes's words. Pressing her back against the wall, she slid down it and pressed her face against her knees. *BS* meant to marry her? Bile rose in her throat at the thought of those lily-white hands touching her again.

"Get out," Eli said.

She lifted her head, hope blossoming that Eli understood what Mean Eyes implied and not liking it. He towered over the other man by at least a head. If it came to a fight, Dani had no choice but to put her money on her new brother. At least, she prayed he was starting to look on her as a sister he had to protect.

Mean Eyes slid cold eyes her way. "It's almost time. Get the woman ready."

"Get the hell out," Eli said, taking a step toward Mean Eyes.

"Blessed Son's not gonna like your language."

Eli narrowed the distance. "And I'm sure you'll tell him, so I'll say it again slowly just so you don't get it wrong. Get. The. Hell. Out."

Dani bit down hard on her bottom lip to keep from cheering. Mean Eyes slammed the door behind him. She looked at Eli and hoped he saw her gratitude. "Thank you."

He stared back at her for a long moment, and then one corner of his lips twitched. "I'm beginning to think you're too much trouble to marry."

She could live with that, for sure. "There was more than once when Evan would have agreed with you." Raising her hand, she tugged on her hair. "It's the Irish in me. He said my red hair should have been a warning."

"When I listen to you talk about my brother, it hurts that I'll never know him. Are you going to put on that dress, Irish?"

"No."

"Then fair warning, Papa Herbert's not going to be happy. I'll try to direct his anger at me."

That was unfortunate, but there was no way she was putting on the dress. She ran a hand over her jeans, glad she'd worn them today instead of shorts. "I think all this was his idea, am I right?"

He walked to the window and looked out, keeping his back to her as he began to talk. "I know I'm not Evan, but Papa Herbert said we were one and the same. I wanted to believe him. If Evan was in me, then maybe I could be good because he was. I can't explain it, but Papa Herbert can make you believe anything he wants. He said because Evan was a part of me now, that you were our wife, and when I brought you back, we would have a ceremony to make it legal."

He turned and faced her. "Thing is, the longer I was in Asheville and away from him, the more confused I got. Was I really Evan? Were you my wife? Now you're telling me it's all a lie, and I think maybe you're right. Papa Herbert tricked me, didn't he? He really wants you for himself."

From what she'd read of cult leaders, they were masters of mind control and deception, fear and intimidation their weapons. Considering how many years Eli had spent under the influence of BS, Dani thought it amazing he could still think for himself. Whether he realized it or not, he had a strong will and a mind apart from Herbert Ballard. He was more like Evan than he realized.

"Eli, you remind me so much of Evan my heart aches from missing him, but you're not him. Yes, you've been tricked, but I don't understand the motive. What does BS want from me?" There had to be more to this than just BS deciding he wanted a woman he'd never met.

"Who?"

"Papa Herbert." Damned if she would call him Blessed Son.

An uncomfortable expression crossed his face. "It's in the Bible. Wives, be subject to your own husbands, for the husband is the head of the wife. Papa Herbert says that means your worldly possessions will belong to me when we marry, but I guess he really meant they would belong to him."

Whoa. Would that include her trust fund? "Is it my money you want?"

He gave a vigorous shake of his head. "Not me. All I wanted was you, Irish."

"So Papa Herbert wants my money? How does he even know how much I have?"

"He knows everything. He says God tells him, but he spends a lot of time on his computer, so maybe that's how he learns things. I don't know anything anymore."

He walked past her. At the door, he turned. "I've said more than I should have. I'll be back in an hour. It really would be best if you put that dress on."

Alone, Dani sank onto the bed. So, the greedy bastard wanted her money. Did BS think she would just agreeably sign over everything she owned to him? What an idiot. A scary one, but still an idiot.

CHAPTER TWENTY-TWO

Dani jerked awake and sat up, confused. Where was she? Eli stood just inside the door contemplating her as if she were some kind of puzzle he didn't know how to solve. Right, it all came back. She was in hell. She scrambled off the bed. How in the world she had managed to fall asleep was beyond her.

"Eli?" she asked when he continued to stare at her, making her uneasy.

"We have to go."

Dani's feet grew roots into the floor and refused to move. She shook her head. "I can't."

"Do you trust me, Irish?"

Whether it was because he no longer called her Danielle, or the boyishly hopeful look in his eyes, she nodded.

"Then you have to come with me now. We don't have long before they start looking for us."

Relief poured through her, so profound she swayed and grabbed hold of the chair. "Do you mean it?"

He nodded and that was all it took for her feet to let go of the floor and rush to his side. Grabbing her hand, he pulled her out of the cabin and around the back.

Mean Eyes and Smirk Face were nowhere in sight. "Where are the guards?"

"Dinner. I told them I was taking you to Papa Herbert and they'd been released to go eat. If we can make it across this field without being seen, then I think we'll be home free. Until they miss us anyway."

"Just tell me what to do." She eyed the stand of trees they seemed to be heading for. They looked to be a hundred miles away.

"Well, our chances of not being seen might be better if we crawled, but that would take forever, and they'll know we're gone long before we reach the woods. It's dinnertime, so everyone will be in the common room except for Papa Herbert. How fast can you run, Irish?"

She squeezed his hand. "Just try and keep up, brother mine."

When she started to take off, he pulled her back. "Will you still be my sister when all this is over?"

More than anything, she wanted to put distance between her and BS, but sensed Eli needed reassurance he was doing the right thing. She met his gaze. "Yes, Eli, it's what your brother would have asked of me if he'd known about you. Even so, aside from Evan, it's what I want. Now, let's haul ass."

"If I'd ever said 'ass,' I would've had my mouth washed out with soap and then been sent to the detention cabin." He grinned down at her. "All right, Irish, let's haul ass."

Every second of the five minutes or so it took them to reach the woods, Dani expected to hear a warning shout, or worse, the sound of a gun firing. When they scrambled behind the first tree, she bent over and gasped for breath. Eli hadn't once let go of her hand, pulling her along, helping her to keep up with him.

"Thanks," she wheezed.

"We're not safe yet. Maybe you should save that thanks until we get you home, or at least get you back to your soldier."

Well, that was irritating. He wasn't even breathing hard. "My soldier?" she gasped. "Do you mean Logan?" To be safely home with Logan and Regan seemed almost too good to be true.

He pulled her deeper into the trees. "Yeah, him. Do you love him?"

"Yes, I do. You should also know Evan loved him. He was your brother's closest friend."

"Do you think he'll like me, too?"

The man was such a child at times. "He'll like you if I ask him to."

That seemed to satisfy him. He picked up the pace, and she jogged along beside him. Did he have a plan, or was he just winging it? She didn't want to slow them down by talking, so she kept her questions to herself for now. All that mattered was getting out of this place.

The woods grew thicker, tall weeds and bushes slapping at her legs. For whatever reason, she'd decided to wear jeans and tennis shoes that morning, and she could only be thankful. Eli slowed and put a hand on her arm, stopping her.

"My dogs are just ahead. Don't be afraid, they won't hurt you as long as you're with me."

Huh? "What kind of dogs?"

"Dobermans. They're guard dogs, but they belong to me and they'll obey me. If I'd left them behind, all Papa Herbert would've had to do was let them go and they would've led everyone right to us."

"That wouldn't be good." She peered through the branches and saw four black dogs sitting on their haunches, staring back at them. "So, they're not going to attack me, right?"

He grinned. "Not unless I tell them to."

Right. Stay on Eli's good side. "They're just sitting there."

"Because I told them to. They won't move until I give them the okay."

Taking her hand, he led her to the Dobermans. "Irish, meet Matthew, Mark, Luke, and John."

"Nice to meet you all," Dani said, absurdly, biting back a giggle. This day had been so nerve wracking and strange, why not talk to four killer dogs named after Jesus's disciples?

"Friend," he said, and held her hand out to them. Each one sniffed her and then looked expectantly at Eli. He slashed his hand through the air.

"Why'd you do that?"

"I just told them not to bark. We'd best be going. They're going to miss us any minute. Surprised they haven't yet."

"I'm all for that. Lead on."

"Heel," Eli said, and they took off again, four Dobermans trotting along beside them.

In another few minutes, they came to a locked gate. Eli twirled the combination lock and opened it. After they were through, he closed the lock and spun the dial. Imagination or not, the air on this side of the fence seemed fresher, more welcoming. They turned to go and a loud horn blared.

Eli lifted his head and looked back the way they'd come. "That took longer than I thought. Let's haul ass, Irish."

Logan's cell buzzed. "Kincaid."

"Hey, boss, our bad guy just took off across the back of the compound with Mrs. Prescott," Reynolds, the lookout, said.

"Going where?" Logan demanded.

"Not sure. They disappeared into the woods on the north side of the compound, running like a pair of agitated rabbits. Looked like the evil twin was dragging her along."

"Keep watching and report anything you think I need to know."

Logan slammed his finger onto the END icon and grabbed the satellite photo out of Barbie's hands. There was nothing on the north side but woods. "Who's the closest to here?" he asked, jabbing his finger at the area where Eli and Dani had disappeared.

With only a quick glance at where he pointed, she tapped a key on her computer. "Decourdeau. It's where he asked to be, why?"

The man really was beyond spooky the way he seemed to sense the perfect spot. No wonder his teammates had nicknamed him The Seer. "Looks like Eli's gone rogue. Question is, is that good or bad? Cancel the plane. We won't be parachuting in. Get Buchanan back here to take command. I want this compound surrounded, and under no circumstances is Dani to be taken back inside. Tell him I'll keep in touch."

She handed him two fully charged satellite phones. He put one in his pants pocket, the other in a backpack along with several bottles of water and some protein bars.

"May God be with you, boss."

Logan nodded, his mind already on finding Dani, and find her he would. There was no other option. He set off to search for Decourdeau. It took two hours. He'd had to evade men from the compound with the same goal as his. They wanted her back, but not nearly as much as he did. He'd kill every one of them if need be. No one but him was ever again putting his hands on her.

"Andre," Logan hissed.

"Heard ya coming a mile away, *mon ami*. What took so long?"

Logan emerged from behind a pile of rocks. "Fuck you. Where is she?"

Decourdeau lifted his chin. Logan looked up at the mountain. She was up there, but where? And what was Eli up to? The sun was setting fast, but fortunately, the night was clear and the half-moon would give them some decent light. "Let's rock while we still have some daylight."

The heavy wheezing of men sounded behind them. Andre did his disappearing act, and Logan followed suit. Three men—hunting rifles slung over their shoulders—stopped and began arguing only feet away from where Logan had burrowed next to Andre under leaves and dead branches. Every minute their argument lasted was time away from finding Dani. If they didn't settle it soon, Logan was going to do it for them.

"I ain't gonna get ate by no mountain lion or get bit by a rattlesnake I can't see in the dark. I say we go back down and hole up 'til morning."

"Blessed Son said we're not to come back without the lady."

"Then you go tramping around in the dark, Joe, acting like mountain lion bait. We don't even know if they came this way. As for me, I don't care what Blessed Son says. 'Sides, he don't gotta know. Come to think about it, if he wants the woman so bad, why ain't he out here looking for her? What 'bout you, Richard, you gonna go with him?"

Logan narrowed his eyes at Richard. Make up your mind, man. Decourdeau nudged him, and Logan gave a slight shake of his head, holding up three fingers. He'd give the assholes three minutes before he and Andre settled the discussion for them.

"Yeah, I'm with Joe," Richard finally said, although Logan thought he sounded reluctant.

Too bad. It would've been better if the three had called off the search until morning. Now, with the two idiots stumbling around in the dark, he and Decourdeau would have to do something about it. At least one of them had eliminated himself from the game.

The unnamed man shrugged and turned to go.

"I'm going to have to report you to Blessed Son when I see him," Joe said.

The man turned around. "Know what, Joe? I don't rightly care 'cause I'm tired of this crazy place anyhow. I'm thinking I'm gonna walk myself down this mountain and just keep a'going. Wish I could say it's been fun."

Smart man. Logan listened to him blundering his way down,

half-tripping over rocks and bushes, until the sound of his mutterings ceased.

"Ignorant heathen," Joe said. "He was never a true believer anyway, so no loss."

Richard remained quiet. Logan had the impression he envied the heathen and longed to join him. The clock was ticking. The remaining two had less than a minute before they got the surprise of their life. Next to him, Andre shifted like a cat gathering his leg muscles under him, getting ready to spring.

Joe and Richard received a reprieve when they walked off. "Damn, *mon ami*, why you be wanting to spoil all my fun?"

Logan chuckled. "You'll get your fun. I'd just rather sneak up on them. Safer that way." He sat up, pulled the satellite phone out of his pocket, and called Buchanan.

"There's a man headed back down," he said, and gave a description when Jake answered. "Claims he's leaving the cult. Pull him in and if he's serious, get him out of the area. Then send word to the teams to start rounding up any of these clowns they come across. They're stumbling around here like a bunch of idiots. Find a place to keep them until we're done."

"Got it, boss. You be careful out there."

"No need to worry, I'm with Decourdeau."

"Ah, you're with the demon. In that case, you rule the night."

"Let's go put those two out of their misery," Logan said after hanging up the phone.

He and Andre tracked the cultists for about a half mile. Finally, Richard collapsed onto a rock.

"Hold up, Joe. I need to rest a minute."

Joe came back and sat next to Richard. He took a canteen off his shoulder, opened it, and drank deep, then handed it to Richard.

"You think Eli came this way?"

"Who knows with that boy," Richard said, handing the canteen back.

Logan walked his fingers in the air, telling Andre to circle behind them, and then watched the Cajun fade away into the dark. Careful where he put his feet, Logan slipped close to the men, taking a position behind the trunk of a tree. When he heard the hoot of an owl, he lifted his gun and screwed a silencer to the end.

"If either one of you moves so much as a finger, you're a dead man," he said quietly.

The fools jumped up from the rock, grabbing for their rifles. Logan took aim and shot the barrel of Joe's rifle, the silencer keeping the noise to a minimum. Both men froze. "Going on the assumption you're both hard of hearing, I'll say it one more time. You move, you die."

"Who's there?" Joe said, his voice trembling.

"Me, I'm the good guy. It's the devil behind you that you need to worry about."

Their heads swiveled. Logan sighed loud enough for them to hear. "Are you boys just stupid or what? My gun's aimed right between the eyes of one of you. The question is, which of you is going to die first?" That had the desired effect. "Now, here's how we're going to do this. While you stand there all nice and quiet, my friend's going to step up behind you. All you have to do is remember the rule. You move, you die."

Decourdeau slid behind them like a thief in the night. Both men startled when he put a hand on each of their shoulders and gave them a demonic laugh. Richard peed in his pants. Andre confiscated the rifles and put them on the ground, then pulled plastic ties out of his pocket.

Once Joe and Richard were bound, gagged, and tied to separate trees, Logan called Buchanan, gave him the GPS coordinates, and told him to send two men to retrieve the dumbasses. Taking the rifles with them, he and Andre started up the mountain. When they were a short distance away from the prisoners, Logan pushed the busted rifle underneath a fallen tree.

"That was too easy, *mon ami*. You gotta let me have a little playtime before we're done."

"The night's not over yet, my friend. Where do you think Eli's headed?"

"Got no idea where the boy and your woman are. It's the dogs I'm tracking."

"I don't follow."

"The kid took his Dobies with him. Smart thinking on his part. If he'd left 'em behind, they would've led everyone right to Eli and your woman."

What was Eli up to? He'd stolen Dani, and Logan wanted to hate him for it, but he was Evan's twin, raised in a warped environment. Until he found out whether he had been brainwashed, he'd give Eli the benefit of a doubt. God help him if he so much as put a scratch on her.

"How do you track the dogs?" Logan ignored Decourdeau's rolling eyes. It was a good question. He saw nothing that indicated the passing of any canines.

"I can smell 'em."

"You're shitting me."

"I shit you not, and you take one more step, *mon ami*, you're gonna smell 'em, too."

Logan looked down at where his foot hovered. Right, dog shit. He stepped carefully around the pile. "Consider me a convert. Lead on, spooky man."

Andre grunted and took point.

Dani tripped over a dead branch. "Sorry," she said when Eli caught her arm, keeping her from falling on her face. She searched behind them, but all she saw was the outline of trees.

Eli had said the dogs were agitated, which meant someone was probably following them. She'd considered leaving a trail, breaking off branches, dragging her feet whenever they were on dirt, anything to make it easier for Logan to find her. That would also lead the men from the compound right to them, so she'd discarded the idea.

"I think it's okay to rest for a minute," Eli said.

Thank God. She started to lean back on a boulder, but he stopped her.

"Wait. Let me check for snakes." He pulled a small flashlight out of his back pocket and holding his hand around the light, he squatted and surveyed the crevices of the rock.

Right. Snakes. Just one more thing she hadn't thought to worry about. *Note to self. No leaning against rocks, no sitting on rocks, no turning one over to see what crawls out.*

Eli finished his inspection and turned the light off. "It's safe."

Ha. Those suckers were good hiders. He could've missed seeing one. "No thanks. I'll just stand here." The Dobermans sat in a circle surrounding them. If anything long and sneaky crawled out, the dogs would surely warn her.

He shrugged, then started unbuttoning his shirt. Okay. Time out. Why was he stripping? Granted it was summer, but once the sun had set, it had turned a little chilly. "What are you doing, Eli?"

His fingers paused on a button. "I've got something for you." He pushed his hand into his shirt and pulled out a cell.

Squinting, she leaned forward to see better. Hers? Dani grabbed it. Hot damn, it was. "Awesome." Logan better have his phone on him. She flipped it open and the disappointment of seeing no bars was almost too much to bear. "No service. Maybe if we go higher?"

"I don't know, maybe. I'm sorry I got you into this mess, Irish. Somehow I'll make it up to you."

"Just get me back home, that's all I want."

"I'm gonna do my best." He reached into his shirt again and brought out her wallet. "Papa Herbert would've noticed if your purse was gone, so I took out the phone and wallet. I didn't think you'd want them having your credit cards or personal information."

That was an understatement. "Thanks, I really appreciate it."

Back his hand went, this time pulling out a bottle of water. "Don't drink it all, it's the only one we have."

"Jeez, you're like a magician. You going to pull out a rabbit next?"

That got a grin. "That's it, nothing else. Wish I'd thought to grab some cookies or something." He held up her wallet. "You want me to hang on to this for now?"

"Sure, but I'm keeping the phone. Do you have a particular place in mind, or are we just going to keep moving all night?"

"I've got a place. It's not much farther. Hold on to the back of my belt and I'll pull you the rest of the way up."

"Did you know you'd make a wonderful tour guide, Eli?" She grabbed ahold of him. "Let's get to it, then." Curious about his change of mind, she said, "You surprised me when you agreed to take me out of that place. Why? I mean, one minute you're going to take me to that evil man you call a stepfather and the next we're running for our lives."

Not slowing his uphill jog, he glanced over his shoulder at her. "Did you know I'd never watched TV until I went to Asheville to find you?"

"There's no way I could have known that, Eli, but what does that have to do with now?"

He stopped, grabbed her hand, and pulled her alongside him. "Hard to talk when I'm running, so we'll walk the rest of the way. I'm not sure you'll understand, but when you grow up the way I did, closed off from everything, I had no reason to doubt Papa Herbert. Then all of a sudden, I'm out in the world for the first time and things aren't the way he said. At first, I didn't know what to think. Was the whole world a lie and Papa Herbert the truth, or was it the other way around?"

Dani couldn't imagine how it must have been for him. "Are you saying you learned the truth from watching TV?"

"Papa Herbert says TV is the devil's instrument, so at first I didn't turn on the one in my motel room."

"And then you did?"

The same grin she'd seen on her husband's face so often appeared on Eli's. "And then I did. Have you ever been to Disney World, Irish?"

"Yeah, it's a fun place."

"I watched a show about it one night. I want to go there sometime."

Although he'd veered off track from what she wanted to know, Dani couldn't help feeling sorry for him. "You get me back to Asheville, and I'll take you there."

"Promise?"

"You have my word. I still don't understand, though, how TV made you see the truth."

"I guess things Papa Herbert said just started not adding up. Have you ever watched Dr. Phil?"

Dani stumbled over a root and he steadied her. "Thanks, didn't see that. I have. Why?"

"One day, he had this girl on who had been raised in a cult. She was confused and sad, and I saw myself. Some things Dr. Phil said got me to thinking. There were other shows, too, that made me wonder if Papa Herbert had been lying all these years. Aside from all that, it was what you said about Evan, that he'd want me to protect you. I thought Papa Herbert meant for me to marry you, but he lied about that, didn't he?"

"Yes, Eli, that was just another one of his lies."

He stopped, and troubled eyes turned to her. "I don't want you to hate me, Irish. Even if Papa Herbert's a liar, I still believe in God and heaven. That means my brother's looking down on me, needing me to do right by you." His eyes watered. "I'm sorry I made such a mess of everything."

If the men in her life didn't stop breaking her heart, Dani thought she just might join a nunnery. "Oh, Eli," she said, and wrapped her arms around his waist. "When we get out of this, you and I are booking a flight to Disney."

"Without your soldier? He won't like that."

Dani laughed. "I daresay he'll insist on coming with us. Come on, brother, let's haul ass."

Dani held the flashlight Eli had left her and scanned the small cave for snakes and bats. Leaving two of the dogs behind to guard her, he'd gone out with the other two, telling her he wanted to scout around and make sure no one had followed them. Keeping up hadn't been easy as they'd climbed the mountain. Even in tennis shoes, her feet were screaming in protest at the trek he'd forced on them.

Once her vermin search was satisfied, she checked her phone for the sixth time. Still no signal. With nothing else to do, she curled into a corner and waited for Eli to return. The dogs, Luke and John, she thought, came and sat in front of her, their eyes focused expectantly on the entrance to the cave. She'd seen Eli give them a hand signal. He must have told them to guard her, and she had no complaints with that.

She was dozing off when low feral growls from both dogs had her pushing up against the rock wall. She shone the flashlight on them, saw the razor-sharp hair on their backs, and raised the flashlight to illuminate the entrance.

Mean Eyes slowly grinned. "Well, well, what have we here?"

Smirk Face poked his head around his companion's shoulder and smirked. "Hello, little girl. Blessed Son's not very happy with you right now."

The dogs stood and bared their teeth. Mean Eyes pulled the rifle off his shoulder and lifted it, aiming the gun at Luke, or was it John? It didn't matter, she refused to give him the chance to hurt either one. Dani scrambled forward and grabbed their collars, pulling them in front of her. "You shoot one of them, you risk shooting me. What's BS going to say about that?"

Mean Eyes slipped farther inside the cave, Smirk Face following closely behind. "Let them go, and I won't hurt them," Mean Eyes said.

Liar. "No."

A smile so evil it sent shivers through her formed on his face. "I was hoping that's what you'd say."

It was only by sheer will that she didn't allow her gaze to flicker to Eli creeping up behind them.

"You touch her or the dogs, and he dies," Eli said.

Mean Eyes turned and lifted his rifle. Eli held Smirk Face close, his arm pressing on the man's throat and a pistol pushed tight against his head. "Go ahead, Eli. Shoot him. Because as soon as you do, I'll shoot you, and then where does that leave the woman? Blessed Son wants her, and he'll get her no matter what you do."

Eli's gaze flicked to her, uncertainty in his eyes. Oh God, he didn't know what to do. She glanced at the Dobermans. They stared at Eli, their skin rippling as they waited for instructions. Mean Eyes had his back to them and would never see them coming. She caught Eli's gaze, then looked pointedly at the dogs and gave a slight nod. Would he understand?

It appeared he did. Keeping his pistol pressed against Smirk Face's head, he lowered his other hand to his side and made a motion with his fingers. Luke and John were on Mean Eyes before Dani could blink her astonishment. Flying past Eli, the other two dogs went at the man from the front.

Mean Eyes's rifle went off, and both Smirk Face and Eli crumbled to the ground.

CHAPTER TWENTY-THREE

The sound of a gunshot echoed across the mountain, followed by a scream so primal the hair on Logan's arms stood on end. He took off, his attention fixated with single-minded focus on the direction from which he'd heard Dani's cry. Another shot sounded, then another.

"Slow down," Decourdeau said, coming up next to him. "We have to assess the situation before we go blundering in."

Reason returned—somewhat. "Right." He slowed and took a deep, calming breath. "I estimate they're about a half mile away." He started up the hill. "They better pray they've not hurt her."

Five minutes later, the Iceman stood at the entrance to a cave and surveyed the scene. One man lay on his back, obviously dead. Eli, crying and covered in blood, slumped against the rock wall, one Doberman sprawled over his lap, the other three surrounding him and baring their teeth at Logan and Decourdeau.

"Tell them to stand down, little brother, so we can help you," Andre said softly.

Eli lifted a cloudy gaze to Logan. "I tried to bring her back to you. He said he'd kill her if I didn't call the boys off. I did, but he shot Matthew anyway. Then he shot me. Why'd he do that?" He looked at the dogs. "They got him pretty good, though, so he's hurt and bleeding. You can follow his trail, can't you, and get Irish back?" He coughed and blood trickled down his chin.

Logan was transported back to another time and place when he'd held a dying man in his arms who looked just like this one. "Don't you dare die, Evan," he whispered.

"Easy, *mon ami*," Andre said, giving Logan's shoulder a firm grip. "Eli, listen to me. We're here to help you, but you have to tell your boys to stand down. Do it now."

Eli made a hand signal. "Friends," he said, and then closed his eyes. "It hurts."

Andre eased toward Eli, and Logan followed, careful not to startle the dogs. Logan picked up the flashlight from the floor next to Eli and shone it on his GPS. While Andre saw to Eli's wound, Logan called Buchanan, gave him the coordinates, and told him to get a medic and several men up to the cave.

Finishing his call, he squatted down. "It doesn't look good," he said quietly.

Andre nodded. "No, not so good."

Eli jerked his head up. "I'm sorry. I thought . . . I was confused. I'm sorry."

"Where's Dani?" Logan asked.

"Samuel has her, but he's hurt. His legs, the boys got his legs. Go. I'll be okay. Just go get her."

Logan exchanged a look with Decourdeau. Eli wasn't okay and they both knew it. "You stay with him until help arrives."

Logan left the cave and started down the mountain. He'd been a step behind since they'd taken Dani. When he got her back, he was going to install a tracking device on her, not that she was going to need it because he was never letting her out of his sight again.

"Ow. You're hurting my arm."

Logan stilled at hearing Dani's voice.

"I told you to shut up, Miss Danielle. One more word and I'll gag you."

Logan eased forward, careful of where he stepped. There, at the edge of the tree line. His men would stop them before she could be taken back into the compound, but he didn't know the man, Samuel. Would he keep his cool? He'd already killed his partner and had seriously wounded Eli. Logan darted left, and using the trees for cover, made his way to Dani.

Just as Logan started to show himself, Ballard stepped out from behind a large rock. "I see you found my wayward bride, Samuel." He looked around. "Where are Eli and Peter?"

"Eli shot Peter, and then he turned on me so I had to shoot him."

"That's a lie," Dani said.

Logan clenched his jaws to keep from yelling at her to shut up.

Samuel shot her a glare before clasping his hands in front of him and bowing his head. "She's upset, Blessed Son, and doesn't know what she's saying."

Logan studied the man who claimed to be the Son of God. He had no weapon unless he was hiding one under his white robe, but this was the kind of man who let others do his dirty work. Logan turned his attention back to Dani. She'd slipped a few feet away from the men. Good girl.

"I'm upset, all right, but you two can argue it out, 'cause I'm outta here." She turned to leave. Samuel reached for her, but she danced away. "Sorry, guys, just not my idea of a good place to vacation. No offense." She backed up.

"Such a delight you are, my dear," the cult leader said, a tolerant smile on his face that Logan longed to wipe off. "Now, Samuel, retrieve Miss Danielle. She has a wedding to attend."

Over his dead body. Logan stepped forward, his SIG held by his side in one hand and a knife in the other. "Touch her, Samuel, and you die."

"Logan! I knew you'd come for me."

"Always," he said, not taking his eyes off the men. "Come here, Dani."

Samuel pointed his gun at Logan. "Who the hell are you?"

"Samuel, your language," Ballard said. "I believe Miss Danielle called him Logan, so that means he's Logan Kincaid. This does not concern you, Mr. Kincaid. Why you are here, I can't imagine, but you should go on about your business elsewhere before you get hurt. My people will protect me at the cost of their lives. I should think you have enough blood on your hands as it is."

A hypnotist had once been a part of a USO show he'd attended in Afghanistan. Ballard's soft, intimate voice reminded him of the entertainer's. An owl hooted three times in the woods at the same time his phone vibrated.

"I have a phone call coming in and I'm guessing it will be information you'll find of interest." He slowly removed his phone, listened to Buchanan, and then flipped it closed. "You have a few problems, Herbert. One, your man here killed his partner and wounded Eli. Two, the FBI are at your gate with a search warrant. I believe they mean to arrest you on kidnapping charges. After Eli gives a statement, I'm certain they'll add accessory to murder to the charges against you."

While he talked, Logan kept an eye on Samuel. The man's eyes were darting from him to Dani, who was inching her way to him. Logan gave Dani a look, glad when she interpreted it correctly and froze.

"I didn't kill Peter, Eli did," Samuel said.

"Eli has lately become very unstable, Mr. Kincaid," Ballard said. "We've been trying to help him, but then he disappeared, and when he returned, he had this young lady with him. When I told him we must return her to her home, he took off with her. I've been very worried about her safety, and of course, attempted to find them before he did something rash. I fear we were too late for poor Peter, but at least Miss Danielle is safe."

Dani opened her mouth, and Logan knew she was going to dispute Ballard's story. "Well, we'll just let the FBI sort all that out, then," Logan said, cutting her off.

"The woman's going to try and blame me," Samuel said. His finger on the trigger, he swung his rifle toward Dani.

"Down!" Logan barked, and then threw his knife into Samuel's throat. *Stupid fool, you should've gone for me first, your biggest threat.* The gun went off, but Dani was safely facedown on the ground.

Ballard turned and started to leave. "Oh, I forgot to mention, Ballard," Logan said. "You're surrounded, so you're not going anywhere."

Three men from Delta team stepped out, along with Bobby Moore, his friend from the FBI. Moore walked up to Ballard. "Herbert Ballard, you're under arrest for kidnapping and accessory to murder. You have the right to remain silent."

Logan tuned out everything but Dani. He started to go to her but before he could, she pushed up, flew into his arms, and wrapped her legs around his waist. Logan buried his face against her neck, his heart drumming a ferocious tattoo in his chest.

"Christ, you're going to be the death of me yet," he said as laughter overtook him.

She pushed away and looked at him. "What's so funny? I don't think anything about this is funny."

He kissed her soundly, shutting her up. He had no idea where the laughter came from, couldn't explain it. Leaving Ballard to Moore and his men, he carried her down the mountain. It might be days before he let her walk on her own.

"You did really good, Dani. I was afraid you wouldn't know I was talking to you when I said 'down.'"

"Hey, ninja man, you said when you gave an order I was to obey without question. I was confident you weren't telling Samuel to get down."

"What's with this ninja-man business?"

"It's what Detective Langley calls you. I kinda like it."

"Do you? I liked when you called me 'babe.'" He glanced up at the moon and estimated it was around three in the morning. The temperature had dropped to the high sixties. "Are you cold?"

She lowered her mouth to his. "Actually, I'm feeling a little hot," she said against his lips. "Must be all that testosterone you're emitting, *babe*."

"No doubt," he said before he backed her against a tree and kissed her senseless. When he came up for air, he rested his forehead on hers. "I've never been so afraid in my life."

"That makes two of us, but I knew you'd come for me." She put her hands on his cheeks and pushed his face up, looking into his eyes. "I love you, Logan Kincaid."

Words escaped him, and he was sure his answering grin was a silly-looking one. "Tell me again."

"I love you, Logan. I love you. Will you marry me? Will you be a father to Evan's daughter?"

Logan braced his knees to keep them from buckling. "Yes" was all he managed to get past his throat.

She punched him on the arm. "That's all you have to say? What about 'I love you, too, Dani'?"

He swallowed hard and nodded. "I do. God, I do."

Her eyes narrowed. "You do, but you can't say it?"

"Give me a sec." She had no idea what her words meant to him. The sound of his men escorting Ballard away came to him. Not wanting her to have to see the man ever again, he pulled her against his chest and left the shelter of the trees.

Logan put his mouth to her ear. "I love you, Dani Prescott, but if you ever put me through something like this again, I'm going to lock you away for the rest of our lives."

Her laughter was the sweetest sound in the world. "Good luck with that, ninja boy."

The ambulance sped away, its lights flashing and the siren blaring. Dani stood next to Barbie as it disappeared into the night. "Do you think he's going to be okay?"

Eli had been unconscious when they'd loaded him into the back. She'd wanted to go with him, but Logan wasn't letting her out of his sight. She had argued a little, but since she didn't want to leave his side either, she hadn't put up much of a fuss.

Barbie wrapped her arm around Dani. "I don't know, honey. The boss will take you to the hospital as soon as he finishes up."

Hopefully it would be soon. This place gave her the creeps, and the sooner she was away from it, the happier she'd be. Ballard's men sat on the ground, guarded by Logan's guys. Nearby, a group of women huddled together, all their gazes on Herbert Ballard. Did they expect him to talk his way out of this?

Although handcuffed and surrounded by the FBI, the man somehow managed to give the impression his arrest was all just a silly mistake. For a few minutes, she listened to him try and blame Eli and Samuel for everything. Disgusted, Dani turned and walked a few feet away. The sun was peeking up over the trees, and she stopped, took a deep breath of the pine-scented air, wishing it was her mountain air she was breathing. Or the salty breeze of Logan's ocean. Anywhere but where she was.

Logan finally came to her. She slipped her hand into his. "Can we go to the hospital now? I'm really worried about Eli."

"The FBI wants a statement from you, but Moore will meet up with us later. He'll need to anyway because we're taking his car."

"I've always wanted to steal a car. Is grand theft auto worse when it's an FBI car?"

"My woman's nothing but trouble," he cheerfully grumbled.

Logan held her hand all the way to the hospital, as if he couldn't bear to let go of her. She closed her eyes, thinking to catch a catnap, but the image of Eli bleeding from his chest was there, as if it had been painted on the back of her eyelids. Had Logan lived with that image of Evan? How did he stand it?

"I keep seeing Eli getting shot. Does it ever go away?"

He squeezed her hand, but stayed silent so long, she didn't think he was going to answer.

"I wish I could tell you yes, but it's still there for me," he finally said. "I know this sounds like a cliché, but it does get better with time. I just try to think of Evan as being in a much better place. Sometimes it helps, sometimes it doesn't."

"And I wish Evan had known about his brother." She swiped at the tears streaming down her face. "In the end, Eli tried to do the right thing."

"I don't blame him, Dani. Ballard had him from the age of two, and he never had a chance for a normal life."

No, he hadn't, but she was going to do everything in her power to see that he had a better life going forward.

When they arrived, Eli was still in the emergency room. The hospital was small, with no trauma center, and only one doctor on duty, Eli the only patient.

"I'm having trouble stabilizing him," Dr. Brooks said after introducing himself. "We're moving him to Little Rock. Helicopter should be here any time."

"Can we see him? I'm his sister-in-law," Dani said.

"Are you Irish?"

"Yes, it's what he likes to call me."

"He's been asking for you. Come with me."

Logan put his arm around her waist, and she leaned into him as they walked up to Eli's bed. He appeared to be sleeping. She took his hand, and his eyes fluttered open.

"Irish, I was worried about you," he said, and then his gaze moved to Logan. "I'm sorry. I never wanted to hurt her." He coughed and gasped for breath.

"Hush, Eli," Dani said. "As you can see, I'm perfectly fine. As soon as you're well, you're coming to live with me and Logan." She caught the brow Logan raised and ignored it.

Eli tightened his grip on her hand. "No, there are things I have to say. Will you take care of my dogs?"

"They're with my friend, Andre Decourdeau, right now," Logan said. "As soon as you're well, he'll get them back to you."

"Not getting well." Eli looked past them and smiled. "He's waiting for me. My brother's here and he doesn't hate me."

Dani looked over her shoulder, half-expecting to see Evan. It might be the ramblings of a medicated man, but just in case, she leaned down and whispered in Eli's ear. "Tell him I love him, and that his daughter's beautiful."

"He knows, Irish. He wants you and his friend to be happy." His eyes closed and his breaths faded to nothing.

Dani buried her face in Logan's chest and wept for the boy who'd only wanted to be good like his brother.

CHAPTER TWENTY-FOUR

The October day promised to be perfect. Logan stood on the deck outside his bedroom and watched the sun come up over the gulf. At his feet, Luke yawned mightily.

"No one said you had to get up," he told the Doberman. Luke's answer was another yawn.

The baby monitor crackled to life. "Wont Uke."

The dog scrambled to get his feet under him and took off. Logan chuckled. It was a toss-up which of the two was more besotted. Regan considered Luke hers, while Luke thought the baby belonged to him. Sadly, they hadn't been able to save Matthew, but John and Mark were deliriously happy hunting alligators with Decourdeau. Logan thought Luke had gotten the better deal.

He turned back to the sun, rising bright yellow over the water. Yellow was a happy color, and he hoped her toenails were painted that glittery color that day, their wedding day. He looked out over the gulf and thought of his friend. "I'm marrying her, Evan. I hope you're okay with that."

A group of pelicans flew past. One broke from the flock, veered toward him, and left his calling card on the railing in front of him. Logan jumped back. "Son of a bitch, Evan, always with the jokes." Logan stared down at the gray and white wet pile and grinned.

His heart might not survive the day. Everyone was there but his soon-to-be wife and her mother. His sister sat on the sand next to Buchanan, Regan on her lap and Luke leaning on the baby. His new daughter gave the Doberman a smack on his head. "Uke," she said. Logan would swear the dog's eyes blissfully crossed.

Jared and Scott, smiling at Regan's antics, sat next to Mrs. Jankowski. He'd flown the two men in the day before as a surprise for Dani. Dani's father stood near the stairs waiting to escort his daughter to Logan.

They had dinner the night before on the beach with all their family and friends around a roaring fire, sharing in their joy. The numerous toasts had been embarrassing in their insinuations, and he couldn't wait for them to come true.

Dani had, for reasons he still didn't understand, put a hold on sex of any kind until they were married. "So you'll be really horny on our wedding night," she'd said. He snorted. As if he didn't always have a hard-on any time he was in her general vicinity.

Spread out on blankets, Barbie, Ken, Turner, and the rest of his employees chatted while they waited for the ceremony to begin.

Logan stood ankle deep in the gulf and waited for his bride. Movement at the top of the stairs leading down to the beach caught his eye. Lifting his gaze, he let out a sigh. She hadn't run away. Why that had worried him, he wasn't sure, but until she appeared, he hadn't been able to believe he could be this blessed.

With her father on one side and her mother on the other, Dani held his gaze as she approached, a beautiful smile on her face. Logan's heart did a merry dance. In a matter of minutes, she would be his.

On seeing her mother, Regan pushed away from Maria and crawled toward Dani. Dani's father picked her up and brought mother and child to Logan.

"I believe these two belong to you," he said.

Logan glanced down at Dani's toes and smiled. "Yes, they do."

He married the woman of his heart with Evan's daughter in his arms and Eli's dog pressed against his leg.

The three-quarter moon was high in the sky, the fall night warmer than normal. Logan walked up behind Dani and pressed himself against her back. He put his arms around her and lowered his mouth to her ear. "I love you, Mrs. Kincaid."

She turned and in her hand was a yellow rose. "Ditto, Mr. Kincaid. Friends forever?"

"I prefer friends and lovers forever." He took the flower and traced the swell of his wife's breasts with the petals. *His wife.* He'd never believed he would have one. Yet, there she was, his ring on her finger, and looking up at him with soft, warm eyes.

Well, hell, what a lucky bastard he'd turned out to be.

Since one of the benefits of having a wife was that he could kiss her any time he wanted, and God above, he wanted, he lowered his mouth to hers. He tasted the spicy berries of the wine she'd been drinking, felt the warm wet of her tongue on his, and heard her soft sigh.

He lifted his hand and slid his fingers through her hair. The fragrance of her shampoo drifted to his nose, and he breathed deep, drawing in her scent. Trailing kisses across her cheek to her neck, he nipped her earlobe.

"Apple pie. You do know I'm going to have to lick you from here," he said, tapping the rose against her forehead, "all the way down to your yellow toes?"

"Technically, it's not my toes that are yellow."

"Technically, I don't give a damn." He broke off a large part of the rose's stem, dug the thorns off with his thumb, and then slid it into her hair, over her ear. Leaning back, he admired his handiwork. "Perfect," he said before lifting her to sit on the railing.

"Whoa." She grabbed ahold of his shoulders and looked down.

He wrapped his arms around her waist and pushed between her legs. "I won't let you fall. Ever. I have something I want to tell you, wife, so listen. Last night, I told Buchanan I wouldn't be going on any more operations. I'll still train with the men, help plan their missions, and run the business, but when we were in Arkansas, I realized something."

"I never—"

He put his finger on her lips. "Let me finish. We both know there are no guarantees in life. Something unforeseen could happen to either one of us tomorrow, but missions are dangerous, high-risk business. You've lost one man you loved, and I love you too much to put you through that again."

Her eyes searched his. "I'm not sure you can possibly know how much that means to me, but I came to terms with what you do and would never ask it of you."

Her tears and trembling smile went straight to his gut. He'd just given her a gift she would never ask for, but wanted more than anything. "I know. I've been thinking about it for a few weeks. When they took you, I couldn't think straight, and that made me a danger to you and my teams. That's never happened to me before, but I've come to the conclusion that if I did participate in an operation, all that'd be on my mind would be getting home safely to you."

"That wouldn't be good for your men, would it?"

Logan pulled her close and pressed his lips to her forehead. "My wife is a smart woman." It still amazed him he could call her *wife.*

He silently promised she would never be sorry she married a man such as him.

She slipped her hands under his shirt, down the back of his loose trousers, spreading her fingers over his ass. "Are you going to talk all night, or are you going to make love to your bride on her wedding night?"

He hissed when her fingers found his balls. "The second thing you said."

"Jeez, husband, you're so easy."

"You've no idea." Logan scooped up Mrs. Kincaid and carried her to their bed, where she had spread yellow rose petals over the sheets. He planned to keep her there until it was time to leave for their first Christmas in Asheville.

His last thought as he slid deep inside her was that he was one lucky son of a bitch. Then, he stopped thinking.

Acknowledgments

A writer spends long hours alone . . . well, that's not really true. There are people talking to us, whispering their stories in our ears so we can make them come alive on a page. As for living, breathing people—at different stages in our work, we reach out to friends, critique partners (who end up being some of our best friends), other authors on social media, wherever we can find the support we so desperately need.

Above all, I want to thank those who read my books, and the ones who take the time to send an email because they want me to know how much they loved my story, or my hero or heroine. To the ones who make the extra effort to write a review, you have my deepest gratitude.

There is always someone different to thank with each book, but some stay the same. As ever (and I hope always) the first two people I must thank for keeping me on track, for sometimes being brutally honest, and for giving me endless encouragement, Jenny Holiday and Erika Olbricht, I thank you. You two are amazing and I love you.

Then there's the edits, almost as important as the writing of the story. My agent, Courtney Miller-Callihan of Sanford J. Greenburger Associates, is, thank God, an editing agent and her suggestions on how I could improve my manuscript were spot on. My Montlake Romance editor, Melody Guy, was the best. She put a shovel in my hands and told me to dig deep, showing me where I needed to flesh out a scene or delve deeper into the head of Logan or Dani. Thank you both for making the process as painless as possible.

Finally, I wish I could list all the names of those who have touched me or this book in some way from the day the idea was just a bubble in my head. My Golden Heart sisters, the Lucky 13s, y'all are just so much fun, and your cheerleading keeps me going. There are friends I've never met, but have shared late night chats with, arguing or sighing over books and heroes. Those conversations recharged me, made me want to give you a book you would label a keeper, a hero worthy of your sighs. Thank you all. I am truly blessed.

About the Author

JCP 2013

A native of Florida, Sandra Owens once managed a Harley-Davidson dealership, before switching from a bike to an RV for roaming the open road (though she's also chased thrills from sky-diving to upside-down stunt-plane flying). In addition to *Crazy For Her*—a 2013 Golden Heart Finalist for Romantic Suspense—her works include the Regency Romance novels *The Letter* and *The Training of a Marquess*, winner of the Golden Claddagh Award. A member of Romance Writers of America, and potential cat owner, she lives with her husband in Asheville, North Carolina.